"Are you a mind reader?"

"You've mentioned your concerns about a true crime book before, and I saw the doubt in your eyes. But I swear, I just want to help. I know you have questions the police and doctors haven't answered, and if I can help settle your mind or find answers that will speed the investigation, then why not let me use my skills?"

She lifted a shoulder, glanced out the side window at the haze-shrouded mountains in the distance. "Am I making too big of a deal out of a little thing like a buckled floorboard?"

He skewed his mouth to the side. "I guess we'll see once we take a closer look. What do you say? Want my assistance?"

She studied his chiseled profile, the square cut of his stubble-dusted jaw. Spending more time with Matt would only fuel this maddening attraction she had for him. Why feed that fire if she knew nothing could come of it? Yet the thought of missing an opportunity to get to know Matt better poked her with fingers of disappointment. So she nodded. "Okay. I accept. Thanks."

Dear Reader,

Several years ago, friends of ours recommended a small cabin rental getaway located near Maggie Valley, North Carolina, called Boyd Mountain Log Cabins. We stayed there once and were hooked for life! We have made several pilgrimages back to Boyd Mountain Log Cabins over the years to savor the beautiful scenery and quiet retreat offered by the Boyd family. How could I not set a book series based on this idyllic place? That said...Cameron Glen is a fictional place, and while based on Boyd Mountain Log Cabins, the people and events in the series and town of Valley Haven are purely from my imagination.

First up from the Cameron family is Cait, the middle daughter and property manager at Cameron Glen Retreat. When a dead woman is found in one of the cabins, Cait teams up with retreat guest Matt Harkney to uncover the truth behind the woman's death and subsequent break-ins. Cait and Matt find more trouble than they bargained for—and abiding love along the way.

I'm so excited to introduce you to the Cameron family and Cameron Glen Retreat! This series is truly from my heart and an ode to a place I love!

Happy reading,

Beth Cornelison

MOUNTAIN RETREAT MURDER

Beth Cornelison

HARLEQUIN
ROMANTIC SUSPENSE

HARLEQUIN®
ROMANTIC SUSPENSE™

Recycling programs
for this product may
not exist in your area.

ISBN-13: 978-1-335-75968-9

Mountain Retreat Murder

Copyright © 2022 by Beth Cornelison

This edition published by arrangement with Harlequin Books S.A.

For questions and comments about the quality of this book,
please contact us at CustomerService@Harlequin.com.

Harlequin Enterprises ULC
22 Adelaide St. West, 41st Floor
Toronto, Ontario M5H 4E3, Canada
www.Harlequin.com

Printed in U.S.A.

Beth Cornelison began working in public relations before pursuing her love of writing romance. She has won numerous honors for her work, including a nomination for the RWA RITA® Award for *The Christmas Stranger*. She enjoys featuring her cats (or friends' pets) in her stories and always has another book in the pipeline! She currently lives in Louisiana with her husband, one son and three spoiled cats. Contact her via her website, bethcornelison.com.

Books by Beth Cornelison

Harlequin Romantic Suspense

Cameron Glen

Mountain Retreat Murder

Colton 911: Chicago

Colton 911: Secret Alibi

The McCall Adventure Ranch

Rancher's Deadly Reunion
Rancher's High-Stakes Rescue
Rancher's Covert Christmas
Rancher's Hostage Rescue
In the Rancher's Protection

Visit the Author Profile page at Harlequin.com for more titles.

For my dad. You are missed every day.

Prologue

Something was wrong with her. She couldn't say just what, but she hadn't felt well all morning. Maybe she should have stayed home. No one would thank her for spreading germs—assuming she had something contagious and not just general age-related fatigue and aches. But Mary needed the income she received from cleaning the cabins at Cameron Glen Retreat, so she'd dragged her sixty-two-year-old bones to work that morning, despite feeling like she'd been hit by a Mack truck.

She finished tidying up the kitchen of the Hemlock cabin and headed in to start the first floor bathroom, dreading the backbreaking task of scrubbing out the tub. She was tempted to shortcut the job, to just wipe the walls of the shower with rags and call it a day. But the Cameron family insisted on first-rate work. Irma Jean was let go when they grew unhappy with her shoddy work.

Not that Mary could blame them. Irma Jean was a lousy housekeeper. Anyone in town who'd ever hired her services knew that. The woman should get a clue. If you do a crappy job of cleaning, you won't get invited back.

Right. So don't cut corners, or you could end up cooling your heels with Irma Jean at the employment office.

Stretching her back, Mary mustered her motivation and nudged the air conditioning a couple degrees cooler as she marched back to take on the master bathroom. She blinked when she read the current setting of sixty-eight, four degrees cooler than the lowest setting the Camerons wanted the thermostat on. Yet she was sweating from head to toe. How could it be sixty-eight in here and she was sweating?

She stumbled a little as she dragged her weary self to the bathroom and got to work cleaning the mirror, wiping the counter and sink with sanitizing wipes, scrubbing the toilet. Finally she faced the bathtub and, knowing she couldn't stall any longer, applied a heavy spritzing of cleaning spray. The directions said to let the spray sit for a couple minutes before rinsing.

She chuckled to herself. "No problem there. And while you sit, so will I."

Turning to go back into the front bedroom, she swayed on her feet, her head spinning with a bout of vertigo. She grabbed for the bedroom dresser and knocked off the wood carving of a bear that decorated the chest. She didn't dare bend over to pick it up now. She'd probably fall over. *Let the dizziness pass.*

She staggered to the bed she'd made earlier with fresh sheets and collapsed with a sigh. She couldn't remember ever feeling so tired, so weak and dizzy. And what was with the crazy sweating? She cut a side glance to the comfy pillows and with a groan, she flopped over and raised her feet to the bed. She'd have to remake it likely, but so what? Right now she needed to rest. Maybe even a nap. The next guests for this cabin weren't scheduled to arrive until after the three o'clock check-in time.

Mary closed her eyes and tried to catch her breath. Her chest tight, she struggled to fill her lungs. Good grief. She really should go see her doctor when she left. She'd started to doze off, when she heard a noise at the front of the cabin. In the main room, maybe the kitchen. Male voices. Thumping.

Gracious! Had she fallen asleep and let the guests arrive with her still here and the cabin half-cleaned? She sat up wearily and checked the bedside clock. One-thirty p.m. So no. Not the new guests.

"Yeah, well, you better find it!" one of the men said, his voice raised in anger. The shout was followed by a low mumble and the scraping of chairs being dragged across the kitchen floor.

Curious, and a bit concerned—no one was supposed to be in the cabin but her until the guests arrived—Mary rose from the bed to see what was happening. Her head felt thick, unfocused, as if coated in cobwebs then submerged in water. Her vision blurred, but she shuffled forward slowly. Reaching the doorway to the main room of the cabin, she peered into the kitchen. Two men knelt on the floor under the oak breakfast table. One man held a flashlight while the other worked with a flat-edged tool, prying at the wood planks of the hardwood floor.

Dismay rippled through Mary. "What in tarnation do you fellas think you're doing? You'll ruin the floor!"

Both men jerked their heads up and angled their bodies to face her. "Who are you? What are you doing here?"

She staggered farther into the room, her chest squeezing tighter. "I…could ask…the same…of you." Damn, she was short of breath.

"Never you mind what we're doing. You ain't seen nothing. Hear me?" one of the men growled.

The second man, glared at his companion. "Are you crazy? She's seen plenty! Too much. Our faces, what we're doing…" He swiped a hand down his face, then reached behind him to pull a gun from under his shirt.

Mary gasped when she saw the weapon, and spots danced before her eyes.

"We can't have her shooting off her mouth, givin' us up!"

The man aimed his gun at her, and panic rose in Mary's gut. Her chest squeezed so hard, she'd have thought an elephant had stepped on her.

Elephant… That was how Hank Winfred from church had described…

Mary clutched her breast. The pain shooting from her chest down her left arm left no doubt. Heart attack! Again she reached for something to steady herself and knocked the decorative lamp to the floor. Colored glass shattered and littered the floor.

"Help…me!" she rasped as she crumpled. When she gasped for another breath, her vision dimmed.

Chapter 1

"This place sucks."

Matt Harkney sent his sixteen-year-old son a withering glance. "And your judgment is based on driving onto the property and not even getting out of the car yet?" Matt snorted and shook his head. "Give it a chance, Eric. I'm sure it'll be great."

Eric returned a grunt that Matt interpreted as general teenage disdain and turned to stare out the passenger-side window of their Jeep Wrangler.

Spying the smaller cabin with the sign that read "Office," Matt parked and cut the engine. "Wanna come in?"

"Why should I? You can't check us in by yourself?"

Matt squeezed the steering wheel and shoved down his frustration with his son's bad attitude. "I can, but we're a little early. We may have to wait a while for our cabin to be ready. Thought you might want to stretch your legs or—"

"Fine. Whatever." Eric shoved open his door and tumbled out of the vehicle before Matt could even get out of his seat belt. By the time Matt made it out of the car and up the walkway, Eric was already standing by the office door, waiting impatiently for him.

Matt gave his son a stern look. "Can you at least try to have a good time?"

Eric lifted one shoulder in a negligent shrug. "Doubt it. If you'd wanted me to have fun this summer, you should've let me stay with Mom. Or at least in Charlotte with my friends."

"Your *friends*—" he paused a beat to let the sarcasm in his tone sink in "—are the reason I brought you here. I'm trying to keep you out of trouble. Save your neck before you end up a junkie or in jail or—"

"Save the lecture. I've heard it before."

Matt bit the inside of his cheek to hold back the angry retort that would only alienate him further from his son. Building a meaningful bond was hard enough when he only saw Eric every other weekend and a couple months in the summer. But that was how custody had been decided years ago. Matt had learned through hard experience that it was better to play the hand you were dealt and make the most of it rather than wallow in regrets and could've beens.

A small bell tinkled over the door frame as they entered. Both the brunette woman behind the crowded desk and the teenaged girl sitting slouched on a loveseat across the small room with her nose in her phone looked up. Matt gave the girl a nod and a warm smile, but she spared him only the merest of smiles before her attention shifted to Eric. Of course. What teenage girl wouldn't notice his six-foot-two son with the swarthy skin tone and chiseled bone structure he'd inherited from his mother? Eric's raven bangs hung in his eyes, but he flipped them back with a toss of his head. He gave the girl a casual glance, obviously trying to play it cool.

"Hi there. Welcome to Cameron Glen," the brunette behind the desk said. "Can I help you?"

And now it was Matt's turn to try to act cool, because the brunette flashed a knock-'em-dead smile. Her dark brown hair curled softly around a striking oval face with pale blue eyes that radiated the same warmth as her smile.

"Yeah, I'm Matt Harkney, and this is my son, Eric. I reserved a two-bedroom cabin for the next couple months."

If possible, the brunette's face brightened further, and Matt's internal radar scrambled as if there were incoming fighter jets.

"Of course. I'm Cait Cameron, the property manager, and this is my niece, Fenn." She offered her hand, and Matt stepped forward to shake it. Her hand was small, but her grip was firm, and Matt liked the way she maintained eye contact. It spoke of confidence and good people skills. A good thing, if she was the face of Cameron Glen Retreat.

"Your cabin should be ready and waiting. The door will be unlocked and keys on the kitchen table." She consulted the screen of the desktop computer she sat behind and scrolled through a document. "Ah, here it is. You're in the Hemlock cabin. It's number five, just up this drive and to the left when you pass the fishing pond."

"Great. Thanks." Matt gave her a grin and with his

elbow, nudged Eric, who was only half-discreetly eyeing the girl and vice versa.

"Enjoy your stay, and let us know if there's anything we can do to make your visit more comfortable."

Matt shuffled out of the office and down the walkway to his Wrangler, taking a deep breath of pine-and-floral-scented air, letting the peace and beauty of his surroundings wash over him.

Eric trailed behind him silently, sullenly, and climbed back in the passenger seat.

"Great scenery, huh?" Matt asked as he started the engine.

Eric sent him a flat look. "If you're talking about the girl in there, then step off."

"I meant this awesome scenery," Matt said, motioning with his hand to the pines and leafy hardwoods casting their shade over the neatly landscaped grounds, flush with blooming flowers, split rail fences, a babbling creek and a large, centrally located pond with decks for fishing. He arched an eyebrow at his son. "But the girl was kinda cute, huh? I saw you checking her out."

Eric rolled his eyes. "Was not."

Matt made a teasing noise of disagreement as he put the Jeep in reverse.

His son grunted. "Like you weren't checking out the old lady."

Matt whipped his head toward Eric, barking a laugh of surprise. "Old lady? She was no more than thirty, thirty-five tops. That's hardly old."

"Is to me."

"Uh-huh, we'll see how old it seems to you when you're thirty. But since you mentioned it, yes. I noticed how attractive she is, same as I noticed how nice these grounds are. I have an eye for detail. Comes with the territory in my profession." Putting the Wrangler in Drive, Matt drove slowly up the road, grinning as they passed a speed limit sign that read, "Slow! 12 mph."

"Twelve," he muttered with a chuckle. "How precise."

"Which profession would that be? Army cop, fiction writer or hard-ass father?"

Matt let the hard-ass moniker slide. He knew Eric disliked the rigid stance Matt had taken in recent months, but so be it. "All of the above, actually. My military deployment required vigilance and an eye for subtleties, and as a writer, I like to notice details about people, smells, scenery. It helps create a more vivid picture when I'm describing scenes, getting into character psyches—"

"Riding your kid's back about his every move," Eric grumbled.

Matt sighed. "Yes. Until said kid starts showing more responsibility and trustworthiness, my job as your parent is to keep you safe and out of trouble."

"*Your* definition of trouble. We weren't hurting anyone."

"Well, it happens that my definition of trouble and the law's definition are pretty similar. So we'll go with my definition for now."

Eric heaved a dramatic sigh. "So much bullshit."

Matt clenched his teeth and tightened his grip on the steering wheel. "Let's start by cleaning up your language. Okay?" As he parked beside cabin number five, a quaint log building with a front porch and rocking chairs, Eric shot him a look of disbelief.

"Now you're the word police, too? I thought you believed in the First Amendment, Mr. I'm-a-Writer-Now. Or wasn't that why you went to Afghanistan and got your leg blown up? To defend American freedom? Or just the freedoms you choose that I can have?"

Matt twisted on the seat to face his son, his jaw so tight he thought he might crack a tooth. "Yes, Eric, I went to defend freedoms. Yours and a whole lot of other people's, both here and other places around the world. But as a parent, I prefer you not abuse your right to free speech by allowing your speech to wallow in the gutter or disrespect me. *Capisce?*"

Eric's only reply was another glower and eye roll. Good Lord, give him the patience and strength this summer not to kill his son. No point keeping Eric from turning into a petty criminal if it made Matt a murderer in the process.

Matt bent to pop the latch on the tailgate. "Grab your bag and let's get unpacked. We can order a pizza for dinner or head into town and see what we find that looks good."

Eric met him at the back of the Jeep and took the duffel bag Matt slid out to him. "By 'town,' I guess you mean the rinky-dink hillbilly hole we just drove through and not Asheville?"

"We'll hit Asheville later. There are plenty of interesting things to explore there, I understand. But by town, I meant the small, folksy and welcoming town we just drove through. Yes. I saw a number of restaurants that looked good. Ma's Mountain Kitchen advertised all-day breakfast, and today's hot plate special was smothered pork chops or chicken and dumplings. You like chicken and dumplings, right?"

Eric shrugged and took a second bag in his other hand. "Whatever."

In a few long strides, Eric made his way up the short

walking path to the porch and mounted the steps. Matt caught up, needing a few extra steps to cover the distance. His days of quick, long strides were a thing of the past thanks to the roadside bomb near Kandahar. Eric set the duffel bag on the porch long enough to yank open the front door of their cabin and bustle inside. Matt almost plowed into his son's back when Eric pulled up short and muttered another of those gutter words he'd just been warned about. But when Matt's eyes adjusted to the dim interior lighting, he wanted to use the same word.

A woman lay on the floor in the middle of the front room amid the debris of a broken lamp.

Matt dropped the bags he was carrying and rushed over to the woman. Lowering himself to the floor, he felt for a pulse on her neck. Her skin was cold, her eyes hazy.

"Should I call an ambulance?" Eric asked, the fear in his tone making him sound much more like the six-year-old boy Matt remembered than the sullen teen he'd become.

Matt's gut turned, and he raised a troubled gaze to Eric. "Go back to the office and tell them what we've found. Tell them to call the police. And the coroner. She's dead."

"Dead?" Cait stared at the teenaged boy who'd just checked in and tried to mentally process what he was telling her. A dead woman. In their cabin. Good God, this couldn't be happening!

"Dad's waiting up there. He said to call the police."

"Wh-who is it?" Fenn asked, uncurling from the ball she'd been in on the loveseat while buried in her phone. Her face was pale and worried, much as Cait could guess her own was.

"How should I know?" the boy—Eric, was it?—returned. "Some old lady."

An old lady? Mary? Cait's heart squeezed when another possibility occurred to her. Or could the dead woman be her mother or Nanna? She forced herself to take a breath. *Don't make any assumptions.*

Fenn started for the door, and Cait called, "Stop right there, young lady. You don't need to get in the way or see anything gruesome."

Cait's niece turned to Eric, wrinkling her nose, a mix of horror and intrigue filling her young countenance. "Is it gruesome? How'd she die?"

Eric shrugged. "I don't know. I didn't stick around to look closer after Dad checked her pulse."

"Fair enough," Cait said, fumbling for the phone with a trembling hand. She punched in 911 as she divided a look between the teenagers. "Fenn, go back to your house and stay there. Eric, please tell your father I'll be moving you to—" While she consulted the reservations list on her desktop screen, the emergency operator came on the line. "Yes, I need the police at Cameron Glen Retreat. We've had a death and possible break-in at one of the cabins." She glanced back at Eric. "Cabin seven is available. Fenn, on your way home, will you show the Harkneys to the Fraser cabin?" Then, to the operator, "Yes, I'm still here. The address is 213 Cameron Road. Yes, I'll hold."

The teenagers stood staring at each other with stricken expressions. Cait could relate. She was rather numb and horrified by this turn of events.

She made a shooing motion with her hand, but when her niece shuffled stiffly toward the office door Cait called to her. "Fenn? Wait." Carrying the landline receiver with her, Cait circled her desk and hurried over to Fenn, pulling her into a hug. "Everything's going to be okay, honey."

Fenn returned the hug, her body trembling. "You don't know that."

"I do know it. Because Camerons are strong. Resilient. We've weathered storms in the past, and we'll get through this, too…whatever it is." She felt Fenn nod, gave her a final squeeze and a smile as she released her. Then, because Eric looked as if he could use a hug as well, she stepped over to the boy and embraced him, also. "I'm so sorry your visit has started in such a terrible manner. We'll do everything we can to make it up to you."

Eric looped his arms loosely around her. "Um, sure. Whatever."

Breaking the hug, she met the teen's dark eyes. His father's eyes, she noted, remembering Matt Harkney's espresso-brown eyes. Eyes that had caused her breath to stick in her lungs when he'd flashed his charming smile.

Cait cleared her throat and shoved the alluring images from her mind. She had serious, tragic business to deal with. This was no time to be swooning over their newest guest, a man with a teenaged son and, therefore, presumably a wife.

"Please send my apologies to your parents for this terrible start to your stay." Cait's pulse wobbled. Bad enough that someone had died on their property, but if word of this tragedy got out, their business would surely suffer.

"It's just my dad. My folks are divorced," Eric said as he backed toward the door.

"Oh, well, your father then." Cait nodded, telling herself she hadn't been fishing for information. She really hadn't, but… "Yes, I'm here," she said, as the operator came back on the line.

Fenn and Eric headed out, and Cait shifted her full attention to the crisis at hand. A death at Cameron Glen. The police. Her hand tightened on the phone when a more frightening notion occurred to her, now that the initial shock had faded. Could the dead woman, whoever she was, have been murdered?

Chapter 2

Cait watched numbly as the coroner's wagon crept down the gravel drive, carrying Mary's body away. A small crowd had gathered to witness the unfolding drama. Her siblings, Emma's children, her parents and some of the other retreat guests who were drawn by the sirens and commotion. Across the lawn of cabin five, Matt Harkney stood under the shade of a hickory tree, giving his statement to a plainclothes detective. Matt cast a concerned glance toward his son, who was being interviewed by a uniformed officer nearer one of the squad cars. Her stomach turned, knowing how worried she'd be for Fenn or Daryl if they'd witnessed such a shocking scene.

How was she ever going to make it up to the Harkneys? Their first impression of Cameron Glen was a dead body. How could that not have disturbed them? She would be surprised if they didn't repack their car and leave as soon as the police released them from questioning.

"No obvious physical evidence of anything amiss besides the broken lamp and a wooden bear on the floor in the bedroom," another uniformed policeman said to her mother and father, and Cait turned her full attention to the officer.

"No evidence?" Cait's mother, Grace Cameron, countered. "Mary is dead! That's amiss!"

"What I mean is, there were no gunshot, stab or blunt force trauma wounds, no bruising at the throat to indicate strangulation. The medical examiner could always find something suspicious during his exam, but at this point we have no way to know, for certain, how she died."

"Thank you, Officer," Cait said.

The officer cast a glance around the cabin yard. "Do you have security cameras or surveillance equipment anywhere on the property that might have recorded any unauthorized person on the grounds?"

Cait shook her head.

"We hadn't felt it was necessary," her father said. "This area is so safe. Wildlife is a bigger concern to us than human thieves or killers." Neil Cameron scowled. "But I guess we were wrong."

The policeman flipped his notepad closed. "Well, I think we have everything we need at the moment."

"Oh, Mary," Grace said on a choked sigh. "This is so awful."

Her father pulled her mother into an embrace, and Cait also laid a comforting hand on her mother's shoulder.

"I'm sorry for your loss," a male voice said behind her.

Cait spun around to face Matt, who met her gaze with genuine sadness in his dark eyes. "Oh… Mr. Harkney. I— Thank you," she sputtered.

"I'm sure she must have been a friend?"

Cait nodded. "Of my mother's. Well, all of us really, but Mom had known her since high school." She hitched her head a bit to one side, silently asking Matt to step aside with her. He followed as she moved toward a less-trafficked spot. "I don't even know how to start making amends to you for this horrible—"

"Did you kill her?" he asked, interrupting her awkward apology.

She blinked. Frowned. "No! Of course not. Why would you—"

"Then stop apologizing. You don't owe me anything. You've already given us a larger cabin, which was very generous. You couldn't have known about Mary."

She squared her shoulders. "Of course I could have known. I should have checked the cabin before I sent you up there. I should have—"

"Is that standard practice? Checking the cabins after the cleaning crew leaves?"

"Well…no. Mary's very dependable and thorough." She paused. "Was dependable… I—" Feeling a bubble of grief swell in her throat, Cait stopped to gather her composure.

"So why would you have done anything differently today? You couldn't have known anything would happen to Mary or anything was out of the ordinary at the cabin."

"I guess, but…"

"You have plenty on your plate without worrying about me. So please don't."

She released a small sigh. "And your son?" She turned to look for Eric and found him now talking to Fenn, his hands shoved deep in his pockets. "Should I worry about him?"

Matt grunted. "You tell me. I can't figure him out most

days. One of the reasons we came up here this summer was because I was hoping to reconnect with him. Keep him out of trouble."

Cait gave a humorless laugh. "Instead, trouble found you. Or us. Well, Mary mostly. Ugh…" She waved a hand. "Ignore me. I'm just…rattled by all this."

He touched her arm, his expression warm, gentle. "Let me know if I can do anything to help."

She tipped her head to one side and gave him a wry smile. "Isn't that supposed to be my line?"

"Well, let me snag Eric and get out of your way. You know where to find me if you need me." He gave her a wink as he walked away, and a small tingle, like she used to experience when Greg Allen would notice her in high school, drifted through her veins. She shook her head, dismissing the schoolgirl reaction to Matt. Even if Eric had confirmed that his father was divorced, what business did she have thinking of Matt Harkney in any terms other than as a guest of Cameron Glen?

Cait had just noticed Matt had a slightly uneven gait when her younger sister, Isla, moved up next to her and wrapped an arm around her shoulder. "You okay?"

She leaned her head against Isla's and released a sigh. "I guess. It's kinda surreal, ya know? Bad enough that Mary died, but for it to happen while at work in one of our cabins—" She angled her head just a bit to glance at Isla.

"I know. Cameron Glen is supposed to be a safe haven. A refuge for people looking to relax and escape all the bad stuff."

Cait nodded. "Of course we think so. It's our home. But it's not like we have a magic dome protecting us from outside influences."

Isla squeezed her tighter, then nodded toward Matt.

"Speaking of outside influences, who was that you were just talking to? A detective?"

"No. His name's Matt Harkney. He's the guest that found Mary."

Isla pulled back so she could face Cait more fully. "A guest found her? *Crivvens*," her sister said, using one of their Scottish grandmother's favorite expressions. "I hadn't heard that." Isla studied Matt more closely. "He's the writer? The guy staying all summer?"

"Yeah."

A humming sound rolled from Isla's throat. "Yummy."

"Isla!"

"Well, don't you think he's good-looking? That wavy black hair and square jaw. Mmm. And that bod! I thought writers were pale and scrawny from too many hours inside at their computer. He looks like he works out."

Cait chuckled mildly. "And I thought you knew better than to stereotype. Besides, he's a guest. So wipe that drool off your chin and behave yourself."

Across the lawn, Matt motioned to Eric, and the teen fell into step behind his father.

Cait saw the small dent of confusion that pocked Isla's face. "Yes, that is Matt's sixteen-year-old son."

Isla nodded. "A family man. Okay, I get it." She raised both hands in surrender. "This is me backing up." She made a beeping noise like a construction vehicle as she walked slowly backward. "I have things to do. I'll see you at the house."

Guilt plucked at Cait as Isla walked away. It wasn't so much that Matt was a family man—he was divorced after all—or that he was a guest—no rule against fraternizing with customers. From the moment Matt Harkney had walked into the office that afternoon, she hadn't been able to stop thinking about him. And not because he'd been the one to find Mary. She couldn't shake thoughts of his dark good looks, his charming smile, the certain *something* that had been in his eyes when he looked at her. Maybe she was wrong. Maybe she was imagining things she wished were true because she'd found their guest—well, yummy, as Isla put it.

What was she doing? She wasn't ready to get into another relationship yet. Not after spending so many months on one that had left her with nothing to show for it except disappointment and broken dreams. Not when anything she might start up with Matt would clearly be temporary. A summer fling. No, she wanted a relationship she could build her future on. She wanted to start a family. She wanted to be someone's priority and not just a companion with whom to pass the time.

A plainclothes police officer approached Cait, and she pushed thoughts of Matt Harkney aside. She had a tragedy on her hands, and as the property manager, she needed to handle it. What's more, Mary's family deserved to hear the news from her, someone they cared about and trusted, instead of the cops.

"Are you Ms. Cameron?"

"Yes. My family owns the property, and I'm the manager."

"While we won't know anything for sure until the medical examiner finishes his autopsy—"

Autopsy. Cait's stomach churned at what the term implied. *Oh, Mary...*

"—please leave the yellow tape up and make sure no one enters the cabin or tramples on the area around the windows and doors. Until we can rule out foul play with confidence, we need to be able to re-examine the scene for further forensic evidence."

Cait nodded her understanding, and he handed her a business card. "You can reach me here if you have questions or concerns." He touched the brim of his hat as he excused himself and walked away.

"All right." Cait stared at the police tape barricade around the porch and crisscrossed over the front door. *Foul play? Forensic evidence? A death at Cameron Glen?* There was nothing *all right* about any of it. None of it was right at all.

Matt ushered Eric up the steps of the Fraser cabin, located on the opposite side of the Cameron Glen property, and cast a glance across the fishing pond. A small crowd stood in the street against the backdrop of strobing police lights. He'd wanted to stay to observe, ask questions and take notes, but had deemed it inappropriate. The Cameron family had lost a friend, the police needed room to work and he was an outsider. No matter his interest as a crime writer, his presence wouldn't have been welcome.

"Dad?"

He turned back to Eric, who rattled the doorknob, demonstrating he was waiting for Matt to unlock it. "Right." He fished in his pocket for the key Cait had given them to their new accommodations, a bigger cabin that had been one of only two available. Cabin seven, the Fraser cabin, had been locked since it wasn't expected to be used. Unlike five, which the cleaner was supposed to have left open.

Matt frowned as he considered that point. Hemlock cabin had been unlocked, awaiting the cleaning crew and later his and Eric's arrival, leaving it a target for unforced entry. Anyone familiar with this practice could have entered the cabin earlier today and killed Mary. He unlocked the door and strolled into the stuffy front room, still lost in thought.

Had Mary died of natural causes? Despite the items knocked to the floor, the police had indicated she showed no wounds or bruising to indicate she'd been murdered. But that didn't mean someone hadn't—

"Geez, Dad. I know that look. You're wanting to write about this, aren't you?"

He blinked Eric into focus and dropped the key on the kitchen table. "What?"

"You finding that murdered lady is like Christmas to you. A gift."

Matt huffed angrily. "Don't be crass. A woman died. There's nothing good about that."

Eric dropped onto the couch and propped his feet on the coffee table. "But you were thinking about it just then, weren't you? I saw the look in your eyes that said your mind was back at the crime scene."

Matt adjusted the thermostat to cool down the cabin, then walked into the living room and pushed his son's feet back to the floor. "Treat this place like it's your own home, please. No shoes on the furniture." He sank into a stuffed chair and plowed his fingers through his hair. "And it's not exactly a crime scene. No crime has been established yet."

"What do you mean? A lady was killed!"

"A woman was found dead, but there's no evidence she was murdered. And no, I'm not planning to write about it. I have other contracted projects to finish this summer." He paused, lifted a shoulder. "But you're right.

I was thinking about it. Hard not to. Not every day you find a dead woman in your lodgings."

Eric grunted his agreement. Or that was how Matt chose to interpret the nonverbal response. Maybe it meant "Get lost. I resent you for your parenting strategy," as had all the eye rolls and pouts and sighs he'd gotten driving up from Charlotte today.

Matt rubbed a hand on his chin. "So…finding that lady was pretty messed up, huh? You okay? Want to talk about anything?"

Eric gave him a blank look, then said, "Yeah. What's for dinner? I'm starving."

"Dinner? Really?"

"Really."

"Didn't you eat a whole bag of Doritos like two hours ago?" Good Lord, his teenager was a bottomless pit. "All right, we'll have dinner soon. But if you want to talk about anything later—"

"I'm fine," Eric cut him off, flashing an exasperated look at Matt. "Just hungry. Can we order that pizza *now*?"

"Pizza delivery!" Cait said with a chipper grin when Matt answered the door.

He gave her a smile and a curious look. "You're working for Jimmy's Pizza now?"

She chuckled. "No. They brought it to the office, asking where your cabin was, so I used it as an excuse to check on y'all. Everything okay here? Do you need towels or soap or—" She shrugged, and her nose wrinkled in an adorable way. "I don't know. Another apology?"

Matt took the warm boxes from her. "We're fine. Really." He turned to hand off the pizzas to Eric, who tossed Cait a quick "thanks" before he rushed off with his booty.

Pulling out his wallet, Matt asked, "How much do we owe you? I'm assuming you paid the guy if he left the food with you?"

She raised both hands. "Forget it. Buying your dinner is the least I can do…considering."

He thought about arguing the point with her but had a better idea. "In that case, there is something you can do for me."

She stood a bit straighter as if encouraged. "Oh? Name it."

He opened the door wider and hitched his head toward the living room. "Stay. Eat with us. We have plenty, as you see, and we'd enjoy the company." Her brow furrowed, and she was shaking her head even before he'd finished speaking, so he added, "You did say to name the favor."

She ducked her chin, grinning sheepishly. "I did. Are you sure? It does smell good, and I skipped lunch."

"Then it's settled. You must." He stepped back to let her inside and caught a whiff of something sweet and floral as she passed him. Forget pizza. *She* smelled good to him, and it fed a different sort of hunger in his core.

"Eric, get another plate—" He frowned when he spotted his son eating straight from the box on his lap while slouched on the sofa. "Correction, get yourself a plate and sit at the table, please. Cait is joining us, and I'd prefer she not think I'm raising a Neanderthal."

To his credit, Eric complied without snark, possibly for the first time since they'd left Charlotte that morning. If Cait was the trick to getting Eric to be more cooperative, he might have to have her move in for the summer. He watched the gentle sway of her hips as she sidled past him and pulled out a ladder-back chair from the pine table.

"Pick your poison—pepperoni, veggie or sausage and extra cheese." Matt caught her curious glance as he maneuvered into his chair, but she smoothly shifted her attention to Eric.

"Something tells me you had nothing to do with the veggie choice," she said to his son.

"You'd be right. He thinks he's going to trick me into eating something healthy, but I prefer a diet rich in fats, sugar and preservatives." Eric took a large bite of pepperoni pizza and wiped his mouth with the back of his hand.

Matt rocked his chair back far enough to reach the roll of paper towels on the counter. He ripped one off and slapped it beside Eric's plate.

"Well, I wouldn't want to deny a growing boy his fat and preservatives, so I'll have a slice of the veggie, thank you." Cait sent Eric a conspiratorial grin, and his son lifted the lid on the veggie pizza and scooted it closer to her.

After Cait chose a slice, Matt took two and closed the lid to keep the pie warm. "We're open to recommendations of other good places to eat while we're here. We'll cook a bit, but between us our repertoire of cooking skills includes about four meals."

Cait gave him a sympathetic cringe.

"More if you count all the different combinations of bread and lunch meat separately," Eric said with his mouth full.

Matt resisted the urge to correct him again in front of Cait. *Pick your battles.* They had all summer and bigger challenges than table manners ahead of them.

After Cait listed a number of local restaurants, several of which she cautioned not to judge on appearances, she changed the subject, asking, "So you're a writer? What do you write?"

"I'm currently working on a military suspense, but after leaving the Army six years ago, I wrote about crime for a news journal. Subscriptions fell off, like for a lot of print newspapers, and I got laid off a couple years back. Switched to true crime books for a little while before I queried my publisher about doing a fiction thing that's been rattling around in my head for years."

Cait set her pizza down, her eyes widening. "True crime? Like what?"

"I wrote about an unsolved murder in Maine for my first book, then a cold kidnapping case in Ohio and, most recently, a series of murders in a small town in Georgia where the guy they arrested proved to be innocent. My research for the book led the police to reopen the case, and DNA tests proved the real killer was someone they'd picked up years later for another killing."

"And they released the man wrongfully charged?" she asked, leaning toward him, her expression bright with intrigue.

Matt bobbed a nod. "They did."

A smile blossomed on her face. "You're a hero!"

The term slashed through him like a jagged blade. He'd seen real heroism in Afghanistan, but not from him. How could he possibly compare to the men and women who'd saved so many lives under the worst of circumstances? Like that last dark day in Kandahar...

Chapter 3

While Matt looked for a tactful way to deny Cait's "hero" assertion, Eric said, "He hates that word. They tried to give him a medal when he got back from his tour in Afghanistan, and he refused to even go to the ceremony to collect it. They had to mail it to him. I think he threw the medal away."

"Eric." Matt glared at his son, hoping to silence him before he overshared any more of his private life.

Cait, whose eyes said she clearly wanted to ask about the medals, took a moment to school her face then turned her attention toward his teenager. "And what about you, Eric? What are your interests and hobbies? Do you do any writing like your dad?"

Eric froze with his pizza halfway to his mouth, curling his lip in disdain. "God, no. Not if I can help it." He took a huge bite of pizza, then, talking with his mouth full, said, "I like normal stuff. Video games. EDM."

"EDM?"

"Electric dance music," Matt clarified.

Eric grunted. "*Electronic* dance music." He shot Matt a look that said he thought his dad was beyond stupid.

"Oh, right! Like Deadmau5?"

Eric shrugged. "Well, yeah. He's old-school, though. I'm more about ATLAST, Avicii, Marshmello."

"Old-school, huh?" She glanced at Matt and pulled a face. "So much for sounding cool. I won't even mention the singers I grew up with. That'd really date me."

"Too late," Eric said.

Matt glared at his son. "Eric! For God's sake, where are your manners?"

"I don't know. Maybe back home in Charlotte?" Eric returned, his tone dripping sarcasm. "Did you pack them when you loaded the car with all the fishing gear? That's where I put them."

Without missing a beat, Cait asked, "Charlotte, huh? We head down there every now and then to catch a concert or see the Panthers play. I'm not sure I'd like living in a city that big. Traffic, you know. Do you like living in Charlotte, Eric?"

Another shrug. "Whatever. You gotta live somewhere. It's all right."

Cait glanced to Matt, her smile still in place despite Eric's gruffness, and he mouthed, "Sorry."

She gave him a dismissive head shake. "Well, I'm glad you packed your fishing poles, because our ponds are stocked and waiting for you. And I can introduce you to my youngest brother, Daryl. He lives with my parents, up the hill that way—" she turned toward the bay window behind the table and pointed past the small lake

"—in the house with dark green shutters. Daryl loves video games, too."

"Cool," Eric said, his eyes brightening.

"Um…" Matt arched an eyebrow and directed a firm look toward his son. "Eric is taking a holiday from electronics and video games this summer."

Eric's jaw tightened, and with a growl of disgust, he glared at Matt.

"All electronics? All summer?" Cait blinked her surprise.

"He gets an hour with his cell phone in the evening to text his mom and check his social media."

Eric's eye roll said what he thought of the small concession.

Cait divided a look between them and kept any commentary on the situation to herself. "Well, we've got lots to offer. Fenn, my niece that you met earlier, and Daryl can show you around." She detailed the activities available at Cameron Glen and in the small town down the highway.

Thankfully, Eric refrained from dissing the suggestions the way he had when Matt enumerated them in the car on the drive over today.

"I'm done." Eric shoved his plate away and scooted his chair back. "Can I go to my room?" Without waiting for the permission he'd requested, Eric rose and shuffled out of the room.

"Nice to meet you, Eric," Cait called after him, and the teen gave a small wave as he departed.

Matt exhaled a tense breath. At least Eric hadn't shown his butt as badly as he had other times recently. Apparently his son reserved the worst of his acting out for private moments with his father. "Can you move in with us this summer?"

Cait arched a delicate eyebrow in confusion. "Pardon?"

Chuckling, he waved her off. "Nothing. Bad joke."

She flashed a polite smile and moved her napkin from her lap to her plate. "I should get out of your way, let you settle in."

They reached for her empty plate at the same time, and their fingers bumped. "Let me get that for you."

She didn't withdraw her hand right away, as if surprised he'd offer to clean up, and he used the moment to notice she wore no ring, wedding or engagement. Of course, that didn't mean she wasn't dating someone…

As if her relationship status mattered. He wasn't at Cameron Glen shopping for a new girlfriend. This summer was about straightening out the wrong turns Eric had taken lately. And getting some writing under his belt. But mostly about Eric. His son was his priority, and he didn't need distractions from healing that relationship. Ergo the quiet and bucolic Cameron Glen.

Matt tossed the clean lids from the empty pizza boxes in the recycle bin, left the plates in the sink and escorted Cait to the Fraser cabin's front porch. The summer heat had cooled to a pleasantly warm evening, and in the deep golden light of gloaming, the scent of pine and fresh-cut grass perfumed the air. Chipmunks scampered up and down the driveway to the cabin and across the roadway and near a large fir tree, a rabbit nibbled his dinner. Birdsong filled the air as cardinals and sparrows gathered for the night in the branches of the pink rhododendron at the edge of the yard.

Matt took a deep breath of the fresh air and shook his head in wonder. "This place is like something out of a Disney movie. I don't think it could be more idyllic if you tried."

Cait laughed. "Well, thank you. We work hard to make it as peaceful and pretty as we can." She smirked playfully. "Mickey will be by your cabin for a photo op at nine tomorrow morning. Have your mouse-ears hat ready."

He winked at her. "Will do."

Matt's flirting stirred a happy tickle in Cait's belly. When was the last time she'd enjoyed a teasing repartee with a handsome man? If she couldn't remember, it had been too long. Certainly things with Peter had gotten flat and dull before she left him. Was that what her attraction to Matt was about? The thrill of something new and intriguing? Would she feel this way about any man who smiled and kidded with her?

Glancing awkwardly at her feet as the conversation stalled, she nudged the gravel on the walking path with her toe.

"How are you getting home?"

"Um…" She raised her head, caught a bit off guard by his question. She met his dark eyes and felt the jolt of attraction all over again. Nope, it was definitely him. Handsome, charming Matt Harkney. Pressing a hand to her stomach as it quivered with fresh flutters of desire, she said, "Same way I got here. I'll walk. I live with my sister in the white house on the hill to your left as you enter the grounds."

He furrowed his brow, and his brown eyes got a faraway look as if he were trying to recall what she was describing. "With a barn beside it? And a really flourishing garden?"

She chuckled. "That's the one."

His gaze narrowed on her, and even in the encroaching darkness, his eyes reflected…something. A light from within, an intensity that burrowed inside her. The shimmer of sweet sensation that had coiled in her belly now rippled throughout her, and she rubbed her arms as giddy goose bumps rose on her skin. She took a few steps backward and lifted a hand. "Well, good night."

Matt jammed the dirty part of the pizza boxes in the outside trash can, resecured the bear-proof latch, then walked toward her, his stride a bit uneven. "Let me walk you home."

The shimmer sparked brighter, and she couldn't hide the smile that bloomed on her lips. "No need. It's not that far."

"Maybe so." He closed the distance between them and cupped her elbow. A simple enough gesture, but fireworks shot through her veins. "But we don't know what happened to your friend Mary yet, and I'd feel better knowing you got home safely."

"I am home. This place, these grounds are my home. You really don't need—"

His grip on her arm tightened slightly. "Humor me. Just until we know more about what happened at the Hemlock cabin today."

His reminder of Mary's death and the disturbing circumstances sent a chill down her back. She hated to think that anything, *anyone* vile had caused Mary's death. That some kind of evil had breached her safe haven. "All right. I'd enjoy the company."

She wanted to ask him about his limp, if he was really up to the distance, but she supposed he wouldn't have offered if he weren't capable of walking that far. After he stuck his head in the front door and called to Eric, letting him know he'd be back in a few minutes, Matt returned to her side and matched her pace. His gaze cast about the grounds as they set out, and she tried to see it through his eyes. What did a newcomer see that she'd grown accustomed to? Matt had compared the property to a Disney movie set. Did she take the beauty of the property for granted?

Fireflies had come out, hovering near the ground and bushes as they began their evening light show. The yellow blinking of the lightning bugs wrapped in and around the fir trees like strands of Christmas lights. Every season at Cameron Glen had a beauty and wonder all its own, and Cait reminded herself how blessed she was to live in such an idyllic place.

"Thank you," he said, drawing her out of her musing, "not just for dinner, but for your company. Eric was much more pleasant tonight because you were there."

"He's not usually pleasant?"

Matt grunted. "He's in full resentment mode lately and doesn't hesitate to let me know I'm the worst father ever."

She scoffed. "I doubt that." Then seeing his look of surprise, she clarified, "That you're the worst father ever. Not that he's resentful. I think, based on my observations of my teenaged niece and youngest brother, a certain amount of rebellion and grumpiness is just part of the whole teenager shtick."

"Maybe. But I feel like Eric has elevated it to a new level."

"Don't you imagine all parents feel that way at some point?" She glanced up at him as they moved through a pool of light when a security lamp flickered on. The bluish white glow from above cast the chiseled features of his face in stark relief, and her pulse quickened. "I mean, I'm not a mother, but my sister talks to me about Fenn. I know raising a girl is different, but—" *Shut up!* said a voice in her head. *Let him talk!* "I'm sorry. I'm blathering on when what I should have said was something like, why do you feel like Eric resents you?"

He sent her a crooked smile that shot warm honey to her core. "You're not blathering. And I shouldn't unload my troubles on you."

"Nonsense. We all need a listening ear now and then. It's not healthy to keep stress bottled up. Tell me about Eric."

Matt's gaze moved away, and he took a deep breath. Exhaled slowly. "He fell in with a bad crowd this past school year. My ex-wife did her best to keep him on the straight and narrow, but he's a strong-willed kid."

She made a quiet humming noise of encouragement to say she was listening without interrupting.

"Jessica, my ex, thinks she smelled pot on him a time or two. And he came home drunk one night about a month ago. He'd been driving."

"Oh no!"

He cast a side glance to her and grunted. "Yeah. Not good. Not at all good. The proverbial straw that broke the camel's back for me." He turned his gaze back to the dim driveway and jammed his hands in his pockets. "His hostility and resistance to her attempts to reel him back in seem only to push him farther away. The weekends when I have him aren't any better. His nose is always in his phone, or he's got headphones on, playing video games, and he's carrying a chip the size of an iceberg on his shoulder."

She wanted to say that, to a degree, that was the case with all the teenagers she knew, but held her tongue.

"I brought him here this summer for a couple reasons. I wanted a quiet place where I could get a lot of writing done. But more than that, I wanted to get Eric away from the bad influence of the kids he'd been hanging out with. I wanted to immerse him in an environment with fewer technological distractions. I took away his phone, except for that one hour a night after dinner that we mentioned, and left his video games at his mom's."

Cait raised a startled look to him. "Wow. I'm guessing that didn't go over well."

"To put it mildly. But I want him to…you know, read books. Go fishing. Take hikes in the woods." He motioned to the volleyball net set up in the grassy field they strolled past. "Play volleyball. Healthy things." His sigh was sad, frustrated. "And I hoped, probably in vain considering the restrictions I put on him this summer, that without all the other stuff pulling him away, that he and I could reconnect. We were close when he was younger, before—"

When he didn't finish his sentence, she angled her head to study the frown he wore. "Before?"

"Before my deployment. Before the divorce. I don't know, Cait. Something's going on with him. I just don't know how to reach him. How to help him. Most of the time I want to strangle him, and I know yelling at him does nothing to help. Pushes him farther away. But I—"

He fell silent and jerked his gaze to her. "Geez, listen to me. Now I'm…what did you call it? Blathering?"

"You're letting off steam. Which I am perfectly content to listen to. Sounds to me like it was overdue." She tipped her head back to look at the stars just becoming visible against a navy blue sky. The moon hung low over the mountains, and the fireflies floated like fairies in the branches of the trees. "I hope that Cameron Glen will do the trick for you. That you'll be able to relax and get some writing done, and that you and Eric will enjoy the activities we have to offer. Together. I'd think a little friendly cornhole competition or fishing would be good for father-son bonding."

He graced her with another smile. "I'm looking forward to it. I haven't gotten a fishing line wet in too many years."

She waved a hand to her right where the night sky reflected off the surface of the stocked pond. "Well, our little lake awaits. We restock it every spring with trout and crappie. We only ask that, if you plan to catch and release, then please use barbless hooks."

He ducked his chin in a nod. "Roger that." He slid a hand out of his pocket and motioned to her. "So now you know all about me—divorced, surly teen, former Army. Tell me about Cait."

"Not much to tell. Homebody. I've lived with my sister here on the grounds since February. Property manager. No kids."

He cast a lingering side glance. "Since February? That's a rather specific detail. What happened in February that changed your living arrangement?"

She met his dark eyes and chuckled awkwardly. "Wow. Perceptive of you. I didn't even realize how telling that comment was."

"Former military police. The devil is in the details."

"Right." She'd have to keep that in mind when she was around Matt. Not that she had deep, dark secrets, but what might she reveal to him unwittingly? "Um, so I had a heart-to-heart with my boyfriend of three years on Valentine's Day. I'd been living with him but had been getting more and more restless, wanting evidence from him that he was as committed to the relationship as I was. But our conversation that day made it clear he was not. Nothing like feeling you're just a way for someone to kill time until something better comes along, huh?"

"Did he say that? He thought he'd find someone better than you?" Matt asked, his tone rife with shock and affront, God bless him.

"Not in so many words. But marriage was nowhere in his plans. And it was all too obvious his feelings toward me had cooled. I broke it off rather than let things linger and die a slow, painful death."

"I'm sorry."

"Thanks, but I'm not. As Nanna, my grandmother, puts it, I'm well rid of him. Now I can be ready for the life I was meant to have."

"And what life is that? How is it different from your current life?"

She blinked at him and laughed wryly. "Such weighty questions! I'm not sure my brain can think that hard while in a pizza coma."

"Didn't mean to tax you. Just wondering…what do you want from life? Marriage, kids? Travel? First woman president?"

"Oh," she scowled and shook her head. "Hard no to that last one. I don't have the stomach for politics. But the others? Yes, yes and yes. Family means the world to me. I want my own kids, and I hear that clock ticking." She raised a hand, adding, "Not that I'll settle for just anyone in order to have kids. My parents adopted Daryl, and it got me thinking. I could adopt if the right man doesn't come along first."

"And what makes a man the right one for you?" He sent her another quick side glance.

"You are full of questions tonight!"

His lopsided grin was unapologetic. "I'm a writer as well as former Military Police—ergo, a student of people and what makes them tick. And an observer. I'm fascinated by human nature and the nature of humans." He sighed heavily. "Ironic, huh, seeing as I can't make heads or tails of my own son?"

"Evidence that teenagers are not human." Her comment drew a bark of laughter from Matt. "My sister Emma has suspected as much since Fenn turned thirteen."

"Interesting theory," he said and casually draped his arm around her shoulders.

A rush of heady sensation spun through her. The gesture should feel too familiar, but it didn't. It felt...right.

"An idea worth exploring," he said. "If not human... what are they instead?"

They passed cabin five, its dark windows all the more bleak because of the discovery made within its walls today, and a chill slithered down Cait's spine.

As if he sensed the change in her mood, Matt slid his wide palm to the base of her back. "You all right?"

The warmth of his touch dispersed the gloom that had assailed her. "Yeah. It was nothing."

Matt gave the cabin a long look as they walked past, then returned his attention to her. "You said that, other than a broken lamp and a decoration on the floor, the police found no evidence of foul play? Nothing missing from the cabin to indicate... I don't know, maybe a robbery that she interrupted?"

"That's right. Nothing's missing, so they don't suspect a robbery."

"Did Mary have any enemies? Mention anything, even a disagreement or jealousy?"

"You sound like the cop who questioned me this afternoon. And no. No enemies. I can't think of anyone who might harbor ill will toward her. Mary was like family. She'd worked for us for years. She was a friend of my mom's from way back and the sweetest person you'd ever meet. Hardworking. Thoughtful. I can't imagine why anyone would want to hurt her."

"And it's likely no one did, based on the lack of obvious injury. Her death could have been from natural causes. I was just…curious." He frowned and sent her an apologetic grin. "I'm sorry. My questions are morbid and inappropriate so soon after your loss. Forgive me."

She slowed her pace, prickles of suspicion poking her like brambles. "Wait a minute. You said at dinner that you used to write about crime for that newspaper. You're not asking because you plan to write about Mary's death, are you?"

"Eric accused me of the same thing." He shrugged. "I don't know. The incident has me intrigued though. Not every day you find a dead body. I guess my writer's imagination has just spun this into something bigger, something worth digging into." When she grunted her disapproval and frowned at him, he raised both hands in surrender. "But I have no plans to do so. I have a fiction book to finish in the next couple months first, and another project in the works before I can write any true crime."

His response wasn't exactly the decided *no* she'd hoped for, but she let it pass. For now. But it disturbed her to think of Matt writing about Mary's death, drawing any negative attention to Cameron Glen that could hurt the retreat's reputation. She set the notion aside for the time being. As Nanna said, no point borrowing trouble. Instead, she changed the track of the conversation.

"I meant what I said earlier about my younger brother being a companion for Eric this summer. He's a little younger than Eric, but maybe…"

He nodded. "That'd be great. Perhaps I could bring Eric by one day to break the ice?"

"Definitely. In fact, why don't you come for lunch on Wednesday?"

He slowed his pace. "Oh, I wasn't hinting at an invitation."

"I know, but you're more than welcome. We do a big family meal at lunch on Wednesdays and supper on Sundays." She chuckled. "As if we didn't see enough of each other every day—this being a family business and everyone living so close to each other. It's mostly for Nanna's sake. She doesn't get out much anymore, and her family is everything to her."

His expression reflected reluctance, so to appease his conscience, she added, "If it would make you feel better about coming, you could bring the salad."

He smiled, and nodded. "All right."

Pointing across the meadow where the volleyball court was set up, past the fishing pond and up the wooded hill to her parent's house, she said, "That's Mom and Dad's place way over there. Nanna and Daryl live with them. You can just see the porch light on. Say noon?"

"Roger that." He rubbed the thigh of his left leg before they set out again. "How big is your family? Where do the others live?"

"Well, as I mentioned, the house I share with my younger sister, Isla, is at the front of the property near the entrance. My older sister, Emma, and her husband, Jake, live that way—" she pointed to the right of her parents' house "—up that hill. You can't see the house from here because of the trees. They're Fenn's parents. They have another daughter, Lexi, who's four. Brody, my brother, lives in town, but he owns the landscaping company we use to maintain the grounds, so he's here a good bit. The Christmas trees are his pet project."

He shot her a puzzled side glance. "Christmas trees?"

"We raise Douglas and Fraser fir trees and sell them at Christmas. People come to pick and cut their own trees around Thanksgiving and the first week of December. You may have seen some of them behind cabin five before—" She let the rest of the thought drop.

"This area grows a lot of the trees for the country, doesn't it?"

"It does. Can't beat the Smokies for its cool, moist mountain climate and slopes for fir trees."

His brow dented in thought. "And the large vegetable garden by your place. Who's the gardener?"

"That'd be Mom and Isla. Though Emma helps with it sometimes. I love it. Fresh vegetables all summer. We also have two apple trees on the grounds, a scuppernong vine and blackberry bushes that Mom tends." She hoped she didn't sound like she was bragging, but she was so proud of the little haven her family had created.

"Wow. A little bit of everything. That's awesome."

They'd reached the end of her driveway, and she paused there, facing him. "It didn't all happen overnight. My great-grandfather had a plan in mind when he bought the property years ago. My family has nurtured and improved and landscaped and planted this property for almost one hundred and twenty-five years."

"Talk about roots," he said with a chuckle. "What a fantastic legacy."

"It is. It really is." She smiled, reflecting on her good

fortune, then aimed a thumb over her shoulder. "Well, this is me." She fell silent as he started up her gravel drive.

"Is your sister home? The house looks dark."

She caught up to him. "She might be reading in her room. It's off the back hall."

Clearly he intended to see her all the way to her door. Or was he angling for an invitation in? Something more? The notion of having Matt come inside for a drink—or more—was tantalizing. But was that what she wanted? She'd largely recovered from the wounds left by her failed relationship with Peter. Why would she risk the potential heartache that a fling with a summer guest might mean? As she'd just told Matt, she was looking for something real. Something long-term. Someone with whom she could start a family. Someone—

He caught her arm, stopping her as she headed up the sidewalk. "Hold on," he whispered, a wary stare focused on the side yard.

"What?" A prickle chased up her spine.

"I think I saw someone over there."

Chapter 4

"Someone's in my yard?" Cait asked in a hushed, frightened whisper.

"Maybe. I saw…something. Some movement."

She froze for a moment, until she realized what he must have seen. The tension uncoiled as she followed his gaze to the goat pen. "I think you saw Pickles and Petunia."

He cut a glance to her. "Who are Pickles and Petunia?"

"Isla's goats." Even in the dark, she saw the surprise register on his face, and she laughed.

"Goats?"

"Mmm-hmm. Want to meet them?"

"Um…"

She climbed the last few steps, opened the front door and flipped the switch just inside to turn on the flood lights that illuminated the goats' pen. "Come on. They'd love to say hello. Petunia's pregnant, and we're expecting the birth any day."

"Uh…congratulations?" He stepped over to the fence gate with her and studied the two brown-and-white goats with a slightly bewildered look.

"Meeeeh," Pickles bleated as they approached, propping his front hooves on the fence to beg for snacks.

She patted Pickles's head and neck. "Sorry, pal. No treats tonight."

"Goats," Matt said, amusement lacing his tone as he reached for Pickles's long brown ear. "Why goats?"

Cait laughed. "Oh, so many ways to answer that. Let's see… I could say, 'Have you met my sister Isla?' But clearly you don't know her so… Or I could say, 'We're lucky it's just goats at the moment.' She's talked about alpacas, chickens, sheep and, last year, she nearly adopted the peacock from a zoo that was closing."

"Wow. You could start a petting zoo with that kind of menagerie."

"You tease, but I think that was in her plan. Pickles here was found wandering down a rural highway in Alabama and no one claimed him. Isla drove down to get him and brought him back in the front seat of her Prius. She thought he would be lonely, so she found a farmer who sold her Petunia three weeks later. She started talking about a petting zoo here at Cameron Glen after that."

"So they're just pets?"

"Well, she does get milk from Petunia that she sells to a local artisan or two for soap, cheese— " she waved a hand "—whatever else you do with goat's milk. I don't ask. Oh, and of course, the yoga thing is popular."

"Goat milk yogurt?"

Cait smiled as she faced Matt. "Not yogurt. *Yo-ga*. Goat yoga. Isla leads three sessions a week, and they're always sold out."

His confusion and disbelief were clear in his frown. "Yoga for goats? What are you—"

"Yoga for people. The goats just wander through the class and provide additional stress relief with their antics. They climb on people's backs while they cow pose and wander beneath the arch of their downward-facing dog. People love the interaction with the goats."

Matt stared at her as if she had grown an extra head. "Goat yoga."

Cait patted his shoulder. "Google it. It's a thing."

An amused grin tugged his lips. "I'll take your word for it."

"Better yet. Why don't you come join us for a session? Yoga is a great stress reducer."

He waved off her suggestion. "Yoga's not my thing."

"It could be. Try it once and see what you think."

He gave her a steady look. "I'm just not sure how it would work, what with…" He patted his left thigh.

She got lost staring into his dark eyes, mesmerized by the fringe of black eyelashes and the way his pupils reflected the moonlight. He must have taken her silence as confusion, because he arched one raven eyebrow and reached down to inch up the leg of his jeans.

She angled a curious glance down, expecting to see a scarred calf or knee brace. Instead, a pale rod connected a prosthetic foot inside his tennis shoe to his knee. A startled gasp slipped out.

A soft grunt rumbled from his chest. "Yeah."

"I'm sorry," she fumbled, "I didn't… I mean, I saw your limp…well, not a limp exactly, but… I didn't realize."

A warm grin spread across his face. "It's okay. You had no way to know, really."

"What, um…how…?" She caught herself and shook her head. "Sorry. I shouldn't—"

"Roadside bomb while I was deployed in Afghanistan six years ago."

She pressed a hand to her mouth. The pizza in her stomach churned. "Oh, Matt. Good God. I'm so sorry. I—" She fell silent, processing this new information about her handsome escort. That explained the uneven gait she'd noticed…

"That's three *sorrys* in one minute." He let the leg of his jeans drop back over his prosthetic leg. "And you have nothing to apologize for."

"I'm sorry. It just—"

"Four."

A nervous laugh escaped before she could catch it. "Okay, then, why don't I just say good-night? And thank you for the escort. And for sharing your pizza. And… I'll see you tomorrow."

He reached for her cheek, brushing a wisp of her hair back and canted closer. His touch sent a sizzle of anticipation through her. He tipped her chin up, leaned toward her…

When the porch door squeaked, Matt yanked his hand back as if caught with it in the proverbial cookie jar. Disappointment speared Cait. The zing of anticipation faded to an unfulfilled ache that settled in her core. But hadn't she just told herself she didn't want a fling that could go nowhere? Her head understood that, but the tingle in her veins disagreed.

Isla stepped out on the porch. "I thought I heard voices. Everything okay?"

"Yeah. Just saying good-night after Matt walked me back from his cabin." She hitched her head toward the door. "My younger sister, Isla. Isla, our new guest in the Fraser cabin, Matt Harkney."

He lifted a hand in greeting. "The goat yoga yogini."

Isla chuckled. "Among other things, yes. Nice to meet you, Matt."

"Likewise." He backed up another step, nodding to them both. "Well, good night, then, ladies."

Cait opened her mouth, wanting to call him back, feeling something was left unsaid, but an odd reluctance stopped her. She settled for a simple, "Good night," then stayed on the front steps until Matt disappeared around the turn in the road and was hidden by the massive rhododendron bush that was older than she was.

"Since when do you need someone to walk you home from the Fraser cabin?" Isla asked from the porch.

Cait strolled up the steps, swatting a mosquito out of her face. "He offered, and I took the opportunity to talk with him alone, without his son listening."

"Oh, that's right. He's got a kid, the teenager from this afternoon. Did you find out if he's married?"

"Divorced."

"Ohh," Isla said with speculation rife in her tone. "Divorced *and* pretty."

"I'm not sure *pretty* is the right word for a six-foot-plus, former Army guy like him." She brushed past her sister to walk inside.

Isla followed. "Okay, what word would you use?"

"Off-limits for starters. He's our guest." Cait turned to flip off the porch light and turn the locks on the door.

"Why does that make him off-limits?" Isla asked with a smirk, then frowned as she pointed at the door. "If he's divorced, he's fair game in my book. And why are you locking everything? You think he's dangerous?"

"Not him, just…" She twisted her mouth in thought. "I guess what happened earlier has me a little spooked. What if there's more to Mary's death than meets the eye?"

"What? Like…*murder*?" Isla's disbelief filled her voice and put a crease between her aqua eyes. "What makes you think that?"

Cait shrugged. "Never mind. It's probably nothing." She gave her sister's arm a squeeze. "I'm headed to bed. Too much excitement today for this girl."

As Cait went through her evening ablutions, she tried to pin down the uneasiness that rattled through her. What was it exactly that had her off balance? Certainly, Mary's death was upsetting. The strain between Matt and Eric was heartbreaking to observe. And the missed opportunity to kiss Matt good-night left her feeling hollow and disappointed.

But her brain kept circling around again to the scene at the Hemlock cabin that afternoon. After Eric had brought the devastating news of their discovery, she'd rushed up to the cabin to see for herself, to wait for the police. The waxy look of Mary's skin was haunting, but that wasn't what bothered her.

She stabbed her fingers into her wavy hair, raking it back from her face as she stared into the mirror and frowned at her reflection. Something beyond Mary's death had been off about the cabin. She was sure of it. And she wouldn't rest well until she figured out what.

Chapter 5

"*There!*" Captain Smithe pointed to the dark-clad figure who appeared in the camera shot sent back from the drone. "That's him. That our target!"

"Are you sure? I need official confirmation." Bellingrath narrowed his eyes on the blurry figure moving across the oversized monitor. "I can't see his face. General Norris?"

"Dammit, that's him! I'm sure of it. He's got the briefcase. Take him out!" Smithe paced closer to the screen.

The drone pilot's voice sounded in his headset. "Corporal, we're locked on."

"Hold your fire!" Bellingrath snarled. "I said I need confirmation before—"

"Can we order a pizza?" Eric asked. "There's nothing to eat in this place."

Matt fisted his hands over the keyboard in frustration

and gritted his back teeth. His train of thought broken, he leaned back in the desk chair and rubbed his eyes. "Pizza? You just had pizza two nights ago. And you ate breakfast an hour ago."

"More like four hours ago. I'm starving."

"It hasn't been four—" Matt blinked at his watch. "Geez, is it one o'clock already?" He'd been in the zone, immersed in his writing and oblivious to the passing minutes.

"Yeah," Eric said. "Pizza o'clock, since there's nothing else to eat around here."

"There's plenty to eat. We just went to the store yesterday."

Eric snorted. "Nothing good."

"Man does not live by pizza alone. Have some fruit." Matt rolled the mouse and clicked the icon to save his work, just in case. He'd had a productive morning and didn't want to lose anything. All it took was one power surge, computer glitch or accidental click, and hours of work could go down the drain. A nightmare for a writer.

"Can I have one of your beers?" Eric asked.

"Are you twenty-one?" Matt backed up his file to a flash drive as well.

An all-too-familiar sigh wafted toward him from the kitchen. "Mom would let me."

"Would she now? That's not what I heard."

A short silence followed. "Look, I know it was a mistake to drive while I was buzzed, but no one got hurt."

Matt turned to face his son. "This time. What about next—" He stopped himself and waved a hand. "No, forget that. Because there's not going to be a next time. Ever. You will not drink until you are legal, and you will never drink and drive again. Understood?"

"For the millionth time, yes!" Eric snapped. "I get it. I screwed up! But I shouldn't have to pay for it for the rest of my life!"

Matt nailed a hard look on his son. "You're lucky you didn't pay for it *with* your life. Or someone else's."

"I'm so tired of this…" Eric muttered as he stormed out the front door.

"Eric!" Matt considered going after him, but since the kid had a head start on him, there was little chance he'd catch up to him.

Later. Let Eric cool off, then…

Matt's shoulders slumped. Would Eric cool off? His son seemed to be in a permanent state of hostility and rebellion. And Matt was in a state of perpetual frustration trying to rein him in while not alienating him further. Was such a thing even possible?

When his own stomach growled, he closed the lid on his laptop and headed into the kitchen for some of the lunch Eric had rejected. Turkey and cracked wheat bread, a peach, maybe some fresh hummus and bell pepper strips.

As he assembled a sandwich for himself, he made two for Eric and wrapped them in wax paper to await his son's return. Through the kitchen window, he spotted Cait, a bag in her hand, strolling along the narrow paved driveway that meandered through the retreat property. Just the sight of her lifted his spirits and helped disperse the tension Eric left in his wake.

Matt set his sandwich aside and headed out to meet her. "Cait?"

She turned when she heard him and waited for him, a sunny smile gracing her face. "I just saw Eric head off toward the lake. Has he tried fishing yet?"

"Doubt it. Not unless he managed to work it in between griping to me about how bored he is and staring into the refrigerator complaining about my grocery choices." He heard himself and quickly shook his head. "I'm sorry. I'm just as bad, letting off steam to you. Let's try again, huh?" He flashed a grin. "Beautiful day, isn't it? Made all the prettier by this setting." He motioned to the woods, the blooming landscaping, the bridge that crossed a gurgling creek where the waterway transected the road.

"Thank you. I'll pass on your compliments to my brother."

"The landscaper," he said recalling what she'd told him about her family.

"That's right. Brody's the chief groundskeeper and landscaper. Of course, he has a crew that helps him, but he'll be happy to know his efforts have been appreciated."

Grounds crew. He hadn't been fishing for information regarding the housekeeper's suspicious death early in the week, but the fact that Cameron Glen had outside help come in for landscape maintenance pinged in his brain. Maybe he should start a list of all the people who had ready access to Cameron Glen and the cabins.

"How well do you know the people on the grounds crew?"

Her eyes widened, clearly startled by the implications of his question. "Um… Brody hired them. But I…" She pointed to the bag she carried. "Let me drop this off at cabin eight, and then we can talk if you want." She took a few backward steps before heading up the gravel drive where a small sign designated it as the Loblolly cabin.

Matt shoved his hands in his back pockets and watched until the guest staying at cabin eight answered Cait's knock and disappeared back inside. He tipped his head back, gazing up at the bright sun shimmering through the branches. The heat had already built to near sweltering, even in the shade. A good day for swimming.

He closed his eyes briefly, remembering the baking heat of the Afghan summer. Sweating buckets under his uniform and flak jacket. The dust. The vehicle exhaust when he worked the guard gate.

"The temp agency's cleaning crew didn't restock the supplies of soap and shampoo, dishwasher detergent, paper towels and so forth." Cait's voice reached him before the crunch of gravel that would have signaled him of her return. "Isla, Emma and I have been doing some of the housekeeping ourselves until we find a permanent replacement. But Isla has class, I have the office duties and Emma has a four-year-old, so that's not a solution for long."

She wiped perspiration from her brow with the back of her hand. "So was there something you needed, a reason you flagged me down?"

Matt hesitated. *Because I've been thinking about you a lot the last two days, and when I saw you, I just wanted to be near you, talk with you, see your smile again.* But he couldn't tell her that without giving her the wrong impression.

Or maybe the right impression. If he were honest with himself, he was captivated by her.

Matt shrugged. "Not…really. I was just taking a break from the writing and thought I'd say hi."

"Oh, is it going well? The writing?"

"Yeah. Not bad. Got a chapter or so written today before Eric came in looking for lunch."

She nodded. Glanced away.

"I'm keeping you from something." He raised a hand in apology. "If you need to go…"

"Why did you ask about the grounds crew?" A deep crease appeared between her eyes when she glanced back at him.

He compressed his lips in thought before answering. "It just occurred to me that there are people with access to the grounds, the cabins and so forth who aren't your family. If the police did find reason to suspect foul play in Mary's death—"

"They didn't," she said, cutting him off. "Sorry. I didn't mean to interrupt."

He waved a dismissive hand. "The autopsy report came back?"

She dipped her head in the affirmative. "She had a heart attack. The police think she knocked over the lamp when she collapsed."

"I see." Matt squared his shoulders. "So no foul play and everyone can move on?"

"Well, yeah." She glanced down the road again, rubbed her hands on her jeans. "They released the Hemlock cabin as a potential crime scene, and we are free to clean it up, rent it out. In fact, I had a call this morning of a couple hoping to squeeze in a last-minute reservation, so…"

Was it his imagination or was she acting nervous? Awkward with him? Unsure she agreed with the police verdict?

"Cait, is everything all right? You seem distracted. Maybe upset about something?"

She blinked and snapped her gaze back to his. "No. I'm fine."

Face it, Matt, ole boy. You were rather forward with

her the other night, trying to kiss her the same day you met her.

She twisted her mouth and exhaled loudly. "Well, maybe I'm distracted." Flashing an apologetic grin, she added, "Sorry. Family stuff. And I need to go ready the Hemlock cabin for the couple arriving tomorrow. It's a tad unsettling to go in so soon after Mary died there." Cait flapped a hand. "Ignore me. I'm being silly." As she began backing away, she aimed a finger at him. "We're still on for lunch tomorrow? Noon at my parents'."

"The house just there on the hill?"

"That's the one." She gave a little wave, and when she turned to go, he stood in the middle of the private road and watched her walk away, his pulse doing a little happy dance.

Oh, yeah. He was definitely feeling something more than just a passing attraction for her. But a voice of prudence whispered that he needed to rein in his feelings for her. She'd been pretty clear when she spoke about her last broken relationship that part-time and temporary relationships were not for her. He didn't want to start something he couldn't finish, didn't want to hurt her, didn't want to give her false promises. He hadn't come to Cameron Glen looking for love. He'd come to focus needed attention on his son and his career. And that was what he meant to do.

Chapter 6

"Why are we here?" Eric grumbled as they waited the next day at exactly noon for their knock on the senior Camerons' door to be answered. "We don't know them."

"Yet. That's the point. To get to know them better."

Eric snorted. "This is so...wrong. Beyond awkward."

"Well, be nice. Who knows? You might actually enjoy yourself, if you try."

The front door opened, and Cait smiled warmly at them. "Right on time. Come in!"

Matt let his son enter first, and he gave Cait a private smile as he handed her the salad. She looked even prettier than he remembered, her light blue sundress setting off her pale blue eyes and chestnut hair. *Stop it, Harkney.*

"This way," she said, hitching her head toward a front room. "Nanna is eager to meet you. I'll just hand this off to Mom and join you in a moment."

Matt couldn't help but notice Cait's long, shapely legs as she left for the kitchen. Whether his son appreciated the opportunity to get to know the Cameron family better or not, he was looking forward to spending more time with Cait.

As they entered the family room, where several members of the family were gathered, Matt's attention went immediately to the older woman in a wheelchair, whose bright smile welcomed them and whose aqua eyes sparkled when she spotted them. "Oh, what joy! You must be Matt and Eric."

Matt nudged his son toward the older woman, encouraging him to greet her politely. "We are."

"I'm Flora Cameron, Caitie's Nanna. Welcome!" The woman's hair was coppery and generously streaked with white, and despite her frailty, her bright expression spoke to a clear, fit mind.

Matt clasped the small hand she offered gently. "Thank you for including us today."

Eric followed suit, then moved to sit on the opposite end of the sofa from Fenn, who flashed him a shy smile.

"Our pleasure! It's always nice to have company visit."

Cait joined them, three more women with her. In addition to Isla, the goat yogini, whom Matt remembered meeting earlier, one of the new women was about Cait's age and the other a generation older. Her mother and another sister, Matt presumed.

"Caitie, dear, you were right! Your new friend and his son are indeed braw lads," Flora said.

Color filled Cait's cheeks, and she sputtered, "Uh—umm…"

"Braw?" Eric said and cast a curious glance to Fenn.

"It means good-looking. Nanna thinks she's still in Scotland."

"*Nae*, Fenn, I *ken* just where I am. But I treasure ma homeland and keep it close, *aye*?"

Fenn sent Eric a smirk and an eye roll, winning a grin from Eric.

Cait's mother stepped forward, offering her hand. "Grace Cameron. And my eldest daughter, Emma. Fenn is hers. And I think Cait said you'd met Isla, my youngest daughter."

Matt greeted them both and introduced Eric, who smiled and nodded.

"Well, Brody is on his way, and Jake called to say he would be late, if he makes it at all—some problem at the office—so I say we start serving before it gets cold." Emma waved a hand toward the next room, and Matt followed the family into the dining room.

An older man with graying auburn hair was already seated at the table, and Matt remembered vaguely meeting him at the Hemlock cabin just after their arrival, while the police were questioning the family about Mary's death. Cait's father.

The man stood, nodding to Matt. "Neil Cameron, nice to meet you."

"Yes, sir. I'm Matt." Matt stretched to reach across the table and shake Neil's hand. "I believe we met earlier in the week?"

Neil frowned. "Oh, yes. You're the one who found Mary." He sat again and rubbed a hand on his chin. "I'm sorry. This week's been a blur. So upsetting."

"Which is why we'll not talk about it at lunch. Right?" Cait's mother said pointedly, then crossed the living room and called down the hall, "Daryl, Lexi, lunch is ready."

A young girl with a light brown ponytail scampered down the hall and raced to the table. When no one else appeared, Grace called again, "Daryl?"

"In a minute. I'm in the middle of a battle!" came the reply.

"Now, young man, or so help me I will turn off the Wi-Fi!"

"Moooom! Geez…just five minutes."

Grace huffed loudly and disappeared down the hall.

"See?" Cait said quietly, sidling up to Matt. "It's not just your teenager." She ruffled the young girl's hair and helped her scoot a chair up to the table. "This rascal is Lexi. Emma's youngest. She's four."

Matt smiled at the girl and mentally tried to keep score of the Cameron family tree.

Everyone took their seats around the table, Eric choosing the one nearest Fenn, and Cait taking the chair beside Matt. Bowls were passed and serving began. A couple minutes later, Grace returned with a sullen African American boy behind her. "Matt, Eric, this is my youngest son, Daryl."

Daryl gave a half-hearted wave as he dropped into a chair next to Cait.

"Whatcha playing?" Eric asked.

"Fortnite." Daryl took the platter of grilled chicken that was passed to him and slid two pieces onto his plate.

"Cool," Eric said, nodding his approval.

Daryl grinned shyly.

Flora offered Eric a bowl saying, "Neeps and tatties, Eric?"

"Huh?"

Matt cleared his throat, and Eric quickly amended, "I mean, ma'am?"

"Neeps," Flora said, spooning out a white vegetable onto his plate, "and tatties." She scooped out a small, red potato.

He pointed to the plate. "Okay, I recognize tatties. That's a potato. But that's…?"

Fenn leaned over. "A turnip. Just be glad we talked her out of trying to feed you haggis."

Eric turned to Fenn with a wrinkled brow. "What's haggis?"

"You don't want to know," Daryl piped in.

Fenn pulled a face as she shuddered.

The adults around the table chuckled, and Cait said, "Nanna's always looking for a chance to introduce Americans to Scottish food, but we talked her down a bit for today. Didn't want to overwhelm you on your first meal with us."

"But we're having sticky toffee pudding for dessert," Fenn told Eric. "Now that's good stuff!"

A back door slammed, and a male voice called, "Emma?"

Cait's sister pushed her chair back. "That's my husband, Jake. Excuse me."

"So what are you looking forward to doing while you're staying with us, Eric?" Neil asked.

Matt held his breath. *Please don't be disrespectful.*

"I'm looking forward to getting my phone back. Dad's got it locked up for all but an hour a day."

Fenn sent him a look of horror. "Seriously?"

Grace patted her granddaughter's hand. "He'll live, baby. We all survived before cell phones."

Neil grinned. "Well, until you get your phone back, we have swimming and fishing, volleyball, horseshoes, hiking trails…"

Eric nodded and offered a mild smile. "I'll probably try some fishing later today."

The sound of the door opening and closing again sounded from the kitchen, and another male voice joined Jake's.

A young man with short-cropped blond hair appeared in the dining room, rubbing his hands together. "Sorry I'm late. Accident on the highway had traffic blocked both ways."

"Oh, dear! Was anyone hurt?" Grace asked.

"Don't know." The newcomer—Brody, Matt surmised—settled next to Daryl and gave the young teen's shoulder a squeeze and pat. "You save me any, D?"

"Nope." Daryl scooted the basket of biscuits out of Brody's reach.

"Don't make me hurt you, bro," Brody said with a grin. "I'm famished." As if only then realizing they had guests, Brody blinked at Matt and glanced to Eric. "Oh, hi."

Another round of introductions began but was interrupted by raised voices from the next room.

"I don't know what happened to it, Emma! That's kinda the point!"

"Well, don't yell at me! I didn't take it!"

"Did I say you did? No."

Matt glanced toward Fenn, whose face had grown dark. She stared down at her plate with a deep furrow in her brow. Poor kid, hearing her parents argue. Considering that her expression seemed angry or hurt rather than startled, Matt guessed it wasn't the first time she'd heard her parents fighting.

"Mom, the chicken is great. Did you use a new marinade?" Cait said a bit too loudly, false cheer in her tone.

"But you asked why I was in a bad mood, and I told you," Jake said in the next room.

Emma said something at a lower volume, and Jake replied, "I can't! I don't have time for long family lunches until I get this mess straightened out."

Grace pasted on a stiff smile. "No. Just a bottle of Italian dressing. Easy-peasy."

"Typical. You never have time for me and the family anymore," Emma said in the next room.

"Well, considering the way you bitch at me whenever I'm home, is it any wonder I don't want to be around you?"

"Fine! You don't want to be around me? Then leave! Just go!"

"Yeah, well, you don't have to ask me twice." The door slammed, and an awkward silence fell around the table.

Touching his arm under the table, Cait sent Matt an apologetic look and mouthed, "I'm sorry."

He covered her hand with his own and returned a subtle, dismissive head shake.

Neil cleared his throat. "So Caitie tells us you're a writer, Matt. What is your book about?"

Matt turned his attention to Cait's father. "It's a military thriller. Spies. Anti-terrorism. That sort of thing."

Fenn shoved her chair back and fled the dining room. Eric's gaze followed her, then landed on Matt, dark with accusation. Didn't take much deciphering to know his son was remembering the spats he'd had with Eric's mother before they divorced.

Grace gave a sad sigh. "Fenn, darling…"

"Let her go, dear," Flora said softly. "I'm sure the lassie just needs a moment to clear her *heid*."

Emma returned from the kitchen, carrying a basket

of biscuits that trembled in her hands. Every eye in the room lifted to her, and she stopped short, her face flushing. "Oh. I…guess you all heard that."

"Hard not to," Brody mumbled, and Isla elbowed him.

"I'm so sorry. And embarrassed. Everything's fine, really. It's just…" Emma fumbled. "Well, Jake had a thing come up at work and—"

"*Dinna fash*, darling. Every *marrit* couple fusses from time to time," Flora said, then patted the table. "Come sit. I'll have one of those biscuits you've brought."

Emma returned to her seat, handing her father the basket of bread for him to send on to Flora.

Matt watched Eric, keeping tabs on his son's reaction to this awkward twist to lunch. Unfortunately, Eric had witnessed too many arguments between his own parents. One of many regrets Matt carried like a loaded rucksack.

"Emma, dear. Has Jake lost something? Can we help?" Flora asked.

Cait's sister sent their grandmother an awkward look, then sighed and shot a quick glance to Matt. "My husband owns Turner Construction and—" she spoke to her father and Flora now "—during a recent audit it became clear that there was money missing." Emma paused and sent her family a frown. "So he's been under a great deal of stress and working long hours trying to figure out where the money went."

Neil set his fork down. "Emma, dear, why didn't you say something earlier?"

"Jake didn't want you all to know. He thinks it reflects badly on him that somehow on his watch something went so terribly awry." She grunted a humorless laugh. "But clearly the cat is out of the bag, thanks to…" She waved a hand back toward the kitchen where she and

Jake had been shouting. She glanced to Fenn's empty chair. "Where's Fenn?"

"She…left the room. Right before you came back in," Cait said, her gentle tone saying she clearly knew the news would upset her sister further and she hated to be the bearer of the news.

Emma muttered a curse word under her breath. Pushing her chair back, she sighed. "Excuse me. I think I should go talk to her."

"Let me go," Eric said, rising from his seat.

His son's offer was so surprising, Matt didn't know what to think for a moment. "Uh… Eric, this isn't any of your bus—"

"No," Emma cut him off. She gave Eric a bewildered look. "Are you sure?"

Eric nodded. "I have experience with parents that fight, and sometimes it's easier to talk to a stranger. Besides, I'm guessing you're the last person she wants to talk to right now."

"Eric!" Matt scolded. *Way to be blunt and cold, son…*

"No," Emma said, lifting a hand. "He's probably right." She nodded to Eric. "If you don't mind? Her room is the last one on the left."

Rubbing his hands on the seat of his jeans, Eric strode out of the dining room with more purpose in the set of his shoulders than Matt had seen in weeks. Months even.

Eric found Fenn's room easily, but she wasn't there. Nor was there anyone in the hall bathroom. Rather than continue poking around in the family's house, he headed outside to look for her.

Sure enough, after only a short walk around the property, he found her sitting on a bench swing under an arch of some kind of flowering vine.

When he stepped on a twig and it broke with a *crack*, she jerked a startled gaze to him. She stiffened and looked away nervously, swiping at her cheeks. "What do you want?"

"Nothing." He shoved his hands in the back pockets of his jeans. "Parents suck sometimes, huh?"

She lifted a shoulder in a deflecting shrug. After another moment of awkward silence, she angled a hostile glance at him. "Do you want something? 'Cause…I'd really rather be alone right now."

"No. I get that. In fact, that's kinda why I'm here. Your mom was about to come looking for you, and I stopped her. Told her I'd check on you."

Fenn's nose crinkled. "Why?"

He raised a casual glance to the web of branches above them, admiring the bright sun that filtered through the dense network of leaves. "'Cause my parents used to fight like that before they divorced. I never wanted them crowding me afterward. Getting up in my grill with their 'talk to me about your feelings' bullshit."

Fenn snorted a laugh, then chuckled a bit more, covering her mouth with one hand. She nodded. "Mood."

"Well…" He took a step backward. "Later."

"Wait," Fenn called as he turned to go. She slid to one side of the two-seater swing. *'Nuff said.*

Eric took the empty seat beside her and, avoiding eye contact, he swept his gaze around the yard, the wooded hillside and the valley below them with the green fishing pond. "Y'all do have a pretty sweet place." He cut her a quick glance. "Don't tell my dad I said that, though. He's convinced that bringing me here this summer is gonna be like some magic pill to fix all the ways he's screwed up in the past." He blew out a frustrated breath. "Like after a few weeks in the woods, we'll suddenly be best friends, and I'll be signing up for a monastery or something."

Fenn laughed quietly again. She met his gaze, and her smile caused a little kick under his ribs. He hadn't really noticed before how cute she was. When she turned her head, he gave her a longer look, careful not to let her see him studying her.

Huh. Kinda hot, actually.

"My parents are clueless." She glanced up at him, caught him looking, but Eric held her gaze until she shifted her focus to her lap again. "It's like they don't know we can hear them fighting—Lexi and me—or they don't care that we can hear. Which sucks, because… I mean, it scares Lexi. She comes and gets in bed with me at night when they argue."

"Hmm," he hummed, not really sure what he was supposed to say. "That…bites."

She raised a horrified look to him, and her face flushed. "God, I'm— You don't care. I shouldn't be… I'm just—"

He saw tears fill her eyes, and his chest tightened. Commiserating was one thing. Dealing with a crying girl—one he'd just met—was a whole 'nother matter. Awkward flutters flapped in his gut, and he searched his brain for a way out of the uneasy moment. Distraction usually worked when he didn't like where his dad's conversational track was going.

A black cat strolled down the hill from the thicket of trees toward the back deck. Any port in a storm. Wasn't that what his dad said?

"That your cat?" As soon as he asked, he cringed. *No shit, Sherlock.*

She glanced where he pointed. "Sorta."

"Sorta?"

"That's Magic. She's feral."

"Huh? What's feral mean?"

"A wild stray. Lives outside and mostly takes care of herself. My grandparents have been feeding her for years, so they call her theirs, but my mom likes to say no one really owns a feral cat. Dad calls her a freeloader." She turned a sad, lopsided grin to him. "He's only teasing. We all like Magic. It's just frustrating that she won't let us close enough to pat her."

Eric studied the sleek black cat again as she flopped on the back deck in a spot of sunshine, her glossy coat reflecting hints of brown. "She looks like a small panther."

Fenn hummed her agreement and looked away.

O-kaaay. Enough about the cat. Next distraction?

"Um, so do you ever play *Fortnite* with Daryl?"

Fenn sniffed and shrugged. "Some. I'm not that good, so I don't play much." She thumbed a tear from her bottom lashes, but as she raised a glance to him, a beam of sunlight caught the remaining moisture and made her eyelashes sparkle as if lined with diamonds. His chest squeezed again.

"So...do you play *Fortnite*?" she asked after a brief silence.

"At home. My dad's banned me from gaming and my phone and stuff. A *technology holiday*, he calls it." He lowered his voice to mimic his dad, then said, "I just call it bullshit and boring as hell."

Fenn chuckled awkwardly again. "Geez. That sucks. But we do have stuff to do around here."

"Oh, yeah..." Eric shifted on the swing. "I didn't mean—"

"I know. But…if you want, I can show you around later. It sounds kinda lame, but horseshoes and cornhole can be kinda fun. Did you bring a swimsuit? We have tubes and can float on the lower part of Lame Goose Creek."

The yard games did sound rather lame to him, but what else was he going to do? Besides, it would give him a chance to hang out with Fenn some more, which was *way* better than staring at the ceiling, bored out of his skull while his dad worked on his book.

"Lame Goose Creek?" Eric snorted.

"What?"

"Oh, nothing. Just…some of the names of places around here."

She grinned. "I know. They go back a whole lot of generations in most cases. In case you missed it, my great-grandma, Nanna, is big on family history and stuff. Preserving our link to the past, she calls it. Which is kinda cool. I actually kinda like hearing her stories about living in Scotland and meeting my great-grandpa during World War II. She was his nurse, and since they were both Scottish, they hit it off. And got married a couple months later. Or *marrit* is how she says it."

Eric wondered if Fenn knew that her face kinda glowed when she talked about her great-grandmother. He felt a little prick in his gut. Jealousy maybe. He'd never known his grandparents, much less his great-grands. Well, his mom's mom was in a nursing home but had Alzheimer's.

"Your Nanna seems pretty cool. All that peepers and tats business was weird…"

Fenn laughed. "Neeps and tatties."

He smiled. "Whatever…"

She sat straighter. "That reminds me. Dessert! You've

got to try the sticky toffee pudding." Fenn's gaze moved toward the house, and she twisted her mouth in thought. "In fact, I don't want to miss it. Maybe we should go back to lunch?"

Eric nodded and rubbed a hand on his stomach. He was pretty hungry still, and the food had been good before he'd bolted to look for Fenn. "Yeah. Let's do it."

"So later today, I'll come by your cabin, and we can do something?"

He heard the question mark at the end of her comment. He nodded and flashed her a lopsided grin. "Sure. Sounds good."

"Collateral damage report?"

Bellingrath squared his shoulders, but shame rode hard on his back. "Twelve children, sir."

"Children? How the hell did that happen?"

"Target was at a school, possibly picking up his own children. It was the first sighting of him we'd had in months and we didn't want to lose the—"

The general slammed his fist down on the table so hard the foam coffee cups toppled. "Children, Bellingrath! Do you know the political nightmare this will create? The black eye to our humanitarian—"

A movement outside the dining room's bay window snagged Matt's attention, and he glanced up from his laptop screen. Blinked. What was—

He rose from his chair, stretching kinks from his back and walked closer to the window to get a better look. Yep. Turkeys. Three wild turkeys were strolling idly across the lawn just outside his window.

He tugged his mouth in a lopsided grin, fascinated, and folded his arms over his chest as he watched the birds strut along without a care in the world. He'd wanted a scenic, remote getaway, and Cameron Glen was delivering in spades.

"Dad!" Eric called as he burst through the front cabin door and slammed it shut behind him.

Matt spun and pressed a finger to his lips. "Quiet. C'mere. Quick!" He pointed out the window. "Look."

Eric hurried over, bringing a stench of manure and teenage sweat with him, and peered outside. "What the— Are those…?"

"Wild turkeys. Cool, huh?"

His son grinned, nodded. "Yeah. Pretty cool." Then turning a face bright with enthusiasm toward Matt, Eric added, "That's not all that's cool. Guess where I've been."

Matt arched an eyebrow. "Wallowing with pigs by the smell of you."

Eric shot a "yeah, whatever" look, then became animated again. "Fenn's aunt has goats and the female just had her babies. I was there! I watched the whole thing. Some of it was kinda gross, but the kids—you know, the baby goats?"

"I know what a kid is, yes," Matt said with a wry grin.

"They're so flippin' cute. And they can already walk. By tomorrow, Isla said they'll be jumping around. You've seen those crazy YouTube videos of baby goats jumping around, right? So funny. Anyway, I got to hold one, and, yeah, it got crap on me, but—" He shrugged. "I don't care."

Matt stared at Eric, stunned by the change in his attitude. That was the most his son had said to him in one speech in months. Maybe years. And he was smiling. Over baby goats. Amazing…

"Wow. That's incredible. Glad you got to experience that."

"Yeah, well… I gotta shower, and then I'm meeting Fenn again to head over to Daryl's for a while to hang out. It's weird to think he's Fenn's uncle. Well, he's adopted, but…whatever. He's just fourteen, so he's actually younger than her, too." He paused to snort his amusement. "But he seems pretty cool."

"Good. Have fun." He returned to the table and his laptop, then before Eric disappeared into the next room, Matt called, "Eric, you do understand that your electronics and gaming ban means not at Fenn and Daryl's house either."

Eric pulled up, his muscles tensing. Turned to glare at Matt, grating, "That is so…"

"Consistent with the restrictions you knew were in place this summer?" Matt cringed internally. He knew he had to be "the bad guy" to give his son some structure and guidance. But he immediately hated the loss of joy and light in his son's eyes, the evidence that the happy little boy he'd known still resided somewhere inside Eric. Dear God, he hoped in his attempt to be a firm, responsible parent he wasn't destroying his relationship with Eric forever.

"As long as you're already grimy, why not go fishing? I can wrap this up and go with you," he offered.

Eric's reply was terse, coarse and clearly a refusal. His son stormed out and within minutes, Matt heard the shower come on.

He stared at the blinking cursor on his laptop screen, but whatever line of thought he'd had for his book was now shattered. He slapped the lid down and sighed.

Just as he turned his attention to finding something

else productive to do—a jog maybe to burn off restless energy—a hesitant tap sounded on the front door. Through the door's glass, he spotted Cait, and his spirits lifted.

"I hope I'm not disturbing you," she said when he pulled open the door.

"Not at all. You're a welcome diversion in fact. I was just deciding what to do with the rest of my day."

Cait extended a plate covered with aluminum foil toward him. "Nanna thought we should send the remaining sticky toffee pudding over for you two. She saw how much Eric enjoyed it, and since my dad is supposed to be watching his sugar intake, we didn't need it tempting him."

Matt took the dish. "Wow. Thanks."

Cait glanced toward the back of the cabin where the shower was running. "I'm guessing those plans you're making don't currently include something with Eric?"

Matt's shoulders wilted. "Not based on the response my last request to go fishing met."

"Oh. That bad, huh?"

"Yeah. Cover your children's ears."

"I thought I saw him with Fenn earlier, out by the goat pen?"

"You did. He had a great time and was enthralled with the birth of the new kids. But then I wasn't there to ruin that for him."

Cait frowned. "I'm sure you don't ruin anything."

He waved her off. "Well, he certainly isn't interested in my company. Not that I can blame him. Seems whenever we're together I can't help reading him the riot act at every turn and spoiling rare moments of camaraderie with parental nagging."

She stood taller and raised her chin. "Well, I enjoy

your company, and I've finished the books for the day and don't have another interview for a housekeeper until tomorrow. So I'm free to go fishing with you, if you want."

"You? Want to go fishing with me?" As soon as he asked, he wanted to reel the words—or at least the stunned tone—back in. Maybe Eric was right. He was so uncool.

Cait laughed. "Which part of that is so hard to believe?"

"I ju—" He buzzed his lips. "Forget I said it. I'd love your company."

"Great! Let me go change into my fishing clothes, and I'll meet you at the pond in ten minutes." The smile that lit Cait's face spun through him and filled his chest with warmth. Her sunny expression pushed aside any thoughts of his surly teen, writer's block or his parenting failures. For a few blissful moments his world narrowed to one beautiful and cheerful woman and the prospect of an afternoon alone with her.

"Well?" The man sitting in the passenger seat of the black pickup truck sent him an impatient glare. "Where's my money?"

He swallowed hard, fighting the nausea rising in his gut. He'd heard stories of what Gene Gibbs did when he ran out of patience with someone.

But he was trapped. Gibbs had cornered him at the Pump-N-Save and forced this confrontation. He locked his knees as he stood by the passenger window, wishing the parking lot would open and swallow him rather than leaving him to face this dangerous man.

After clearing his throat, he said, "I don't have it." When Gibbs's face darkened, he amended quickly, "Yet. But I will have it—all of it—soon. I swear!"

"That's what you said last time. I'm beginnin' to doubt you mean what you say. Why should I believe you? Tell me why I should give you more time when all I've got from you for the last six weeks is excuses. Huh?"

His bowels knotted, and cramps gripped his belly. "I know. I know! I'm sorry. I will get it. Tonight. I swear." With the back of his arm, he swiped the trickle of perspiration that had reached his eyes, then dug in his pocket to pull out the only bills he had. A ten and a five. "Here. Take this. It's not much, I know. But it's a start—"

Gibbs took the two bills and examined them like he'd been handed dog crap. "Are you kiddin' me? Fifteen bucks? What the hell am I supposed to do with fifteen bucks?" Gibbs threw the money back at him, and the bills fluttered to the pavement like dead leaves from a tree.

Without warning, Gibbs's hand lunged from the open window, grabbing the front of his sweat-stained shirt. "This is your last chance, man. I'm tired of your games."

He swallowed hard, nodded.

Gibbs released him and motioned to his driver. The black truck drove away with a puff of gray exhaust, and he choked on the acrid cloud.

Last chance, Gibbs had said. And he believed him.

Chapter 7

Fenn had just closed her book and turned off the light that evening when she heard a tapping sound on her window. She sat up in her bed, staring toward the drawn blinds, while her heart raced. She was familiar with the many strange rustles and clatters from outside. Between foraging animals, noises from guests' cabins and her own family knocking around at night for whatever reason, she'd learned not to worry about the things that went bump in the night. But this was a very specific knock. On her window.

Mustering her courage, she crawled out of bed and scrambled to the edge of the window. Parting the slats of the blinds the teeniest bit, she peeked out. She spotted the dark figure, her heart leaping, at the same moment the person knocked again and said, "Psst, Fenn! It's Eric. Open up."

Relief coursed through her, a balm to her ragged

nerves, but her pulse scampered faster. Eric. Was here. Knocking on her window late at night.

So Romeo and Juliet! She took a moment to squeal into a pillow, then compose herself before she pulled up the blind and opened the window.

"Hey," he whispered, smiling. *OMG! He is so hot!*

"Hey," she said, trying to play it cool. As if having a guy knock on her window at night was everyday.

"Were you asleep?"

"Nah. Why?"

He lifted the tackle box in his hand to show her. "Want to sneak out? Go for a walk?"

"To fish? At this time of night?" As soon as she said the words, she wished she could take them back. *Stupid!*

He chuckled. "Nah. You'll see." He hiked his head toward the woods. "C'mon."

Fenn glanced back toward her bedroom door. The house was quiet. Mom and Dad were asleep. Probably. Could she do it? Could she sneak out and not get caught? Did she want to?

She looked back at Eric, his dark hair and eyes barely visible in the shadows outside, but enough to make her breath catch. Yeah. She wanted to. In fact, the idea of doing something rebellious like leaving the house after bedtime to be with a boy excited her. She'd never done anything crazy before. It was time she lived a little.

She grinned at Eric and nodded. "Let me get my shoes."

Once she'd jammed her feet into her tennis shoes, she shoved the window open wider and turned to crawl out. When he put his hands on her waist, helping her climb down, she thought her heart would jump out of her chest.

Tingly sensations raced through her, made her feel light-headed.

"This way. Come on." As soon as her feet touched the ground, he grabbed her hand and towed her toward the woods. Not toward the fishing pond or his cabin or her family's driveway. Away. Into the black cover of the trees. She knew the woods like the back of her hand, had played there since she could walk. But not at night. The forest was strange and a little spooky at night, especially with the nearly full moon making bushes and limbs cast shadows that looked like gnarled, reaching hands, fairy-tale goblins and wild animals.

Stop it! she scolded herself when her pulse pattered. She couldn't let on to Eric that she was scared. Gripping his hand tighter, she followed him deeper into the trees and darkness, circling the property until they reached the hill behind the Hemlock cabin, where her uncle grew Christmas trees. Here, without the canopy of hardwood branches to block the moonlight, she could see better and felt safer. He led her to a spot in the middle of some of the younger, shorter firs and sat on the ground.

Fenn sat down beside him, curious what he was up to. "What are we doing here?"

She glanced down the hill toward the Hemlock cabin, and a chill chased through her, knowing someone had died in there last week.

"Just hanging out." Eric turned to open the tackle box, but instead of fishing equipment and lures, the case held bottles. Of beer.

Again her pulse stumbled.

He twisted the top off a bottle and handed it to her. "Here. Want one?"

"Where'd you get beer?"

"My dad bought it. Well, for himself. I nabbed it on the way out." He held it out to her again, and she took the cold bottle, not wanting to look lame.

Eric opened a second bottle for himself and took a long drink.

"Won't you get in trouble when he finds out?" she asked, then flinched. She had to stop sounding like such a Goody Two-shoes.

"Maybe. But what's he gonna do? He's already dragged me out to the middle of nowhere and taken all my rights away."

She frowned. "This isn't the middle of nowhere. There's lots of stuff around here to do and places to eat and stuff. And Asheville's like only a half hour away."

He twisted his mouth. "Sorry. Didn't mean to sound harsh. It's just—" He shrugged.

She returned a shrug. "It's okay. I guess I can see why you think we're small time."

"You gonna drink that or what?" he asked, nodding toward her bottle.

"Of course." She took a sip, hoping he'd think she did stuff like this all the time. But the beer was as bitter and gross as it smelled, and she coughed and grimaced after she swallowed.

"I know. Not as good once it gets warm, but…" He leaned back on his elbows and looked up at the sky. "Man, you can see a ton of stars out here. Look at that." He motioned to the heavens with his beer.

She glanced up, smiled. She'd seen it a million times, but she had to agree that the night sky over Cameron Glen was pretty amazing. "Yeah. One of the advantages of being in the middle of nowhere. No city lights to kill your view of the stars."

He chuckled and tapped his beer bottle against hers. "Okay. I'll give you that one."

Eric's smile made her feel a little dizzy. And special. Being out here alone with him in the dark was…*romantic*? No. That word was too old-school. But it was fun. Exciting. Made her feel less like the geek she was at school. Fenn took another sip of beer and stifled the wince when the bitter aftertaste soured on her tongue.

Eric laughed. "Be honest. Have you ever drunk beer before?"

She opened her mouth to lie, to play it cool, but she caught herself. She sighed and lifted a shoulder. "No."

His smile brightened. "I thought so." He chugged a little more of his bottle and smacked his lips. "It's an acquired taste. You don't have to drink yours if you don't want."

"Naw. It's okay." She took another big sip and felt a warm buzz swim through her.

When she glanced at him again, he was staring at her, and a self-conscious prickle crawled up her spine. She wiped her mouth. Smoothed her hair. "What?"

"You're pretty."

Pleasure poured through Fenn like the best of sugar highs. "You really think so?"

He tugged his mouth in a lopsided grin. "Yeah. I do."

Then—*OMG OMG*—he leaned toward her, his eyes focused on her mouth. Fenn's breath snagged in her lungs, and with a buzz of adrenaline in her ears, she angled toward him. The kiss was brief, warm. His lips were soft and tasted like beer. And she thought her heart might beat right out of her chest. When he didn't kiss her again, she opened her eyes, found him watching her.

"You okay?"

Oh no! What had her face revealed? "Sure. Why?"

"Have you ever kissed anyone before?" he asked and batted at a mosquito that flew by his ear.

"Yeah. Of course." *If you count Tommy Jones, who was really just a dare in junior high.*

He scooted closer. "Okay. Just wondering." He reached for her face, touched her cheek softly, then leaned in for another kiss. And another.

Fenn kissed him back, wondering if she was doing it right. More mouth? Closed lips? She didn't want to screw up and give away her lack of experience. She opened her eyes to look at Eric, see what clues his expression might give her, when a movement in her peripheral vision startled her. She jerked back with a gasp.

"Fenn?"

"Shh," she said, covering his mouth with her hand. Squinting, she refocused her gaze on the hillside where she'd seen something big and black moving. Oh God, what if it was a bear?

"What's wrong?" he said in a barely audible whisper.

She pointed to where she'd seen the movement just as a man in dark clothing appeared from the line of mature firs near the top of the rise and crept down the hillside toward the Hemlock cabin.

Eric flattened himself against the ground and tugged her shirt. She hunkered down beside him, fear tickling her belly as she watched the stranger traipse through the rows of Christmas trees.

"Who is that? Your uncle?" Eric whispered in her ear,

his breath a moist caress she might have found pleasant if she weren't distracted by the trespasser.

She shook her head. "No. Brody's a lot skinnier than that guy. I don't know who that is."

Uneasy with the situation, Fenn continued watching as the stranger crept up to the back of Hemlock, tried the doorknob, peeked in a back window.

"Is anyone staying in that cabin now?" Eric whispered.

"Yeah. An older couple. They arrived today but…"

"Could that be the old guy that's staying there? Maybe he went out for a midnight walk?"

Fenn shook her head. "No. I don't think so. He didn't walk fast like that. He had a cane."

They continued watching the man, who returned to the back door and started lifting flowerpots, feeling around the frame and lifting the doormat.

"Looking for a key," Eric said, reaching the same conclusion she had.

"We don't hide keys outside. Too obvious for robbers."

"Case in point, huh?" he muttered.

She snapped a wide-eyed gaze to him, her pulse thundering. "Do you think that's what he's doing? Robbing the place?"

Eric shrugged. "Don't know." He frowned. "Sorry. Didn't mean to upset you. It's probably nothing. A friend of the old folks who forgot the key when he went out for a walk or something."

She refocused on the stranger, who pulled something large from his pocket and set to work near the doorknob. "What's he doing?"

"Picking the lock would be my guess. Or prying open the latch."

Panic swelled in Fenn's chest. She sat up, knocking

over the beer she'd set aside. "We have to do something! Call the police!"

Eric shook his head. "Whoa! Don't overreact. We don't know he's not with the old couple."

"He's not. They came alone. This...doesn't feel right. I mean, that's the cabin where Mary died, and—"

"Hey. Take a breath. Calm down."

She was hyperventilating, she realized. Eric put a steady hand on her shoulder while she took a moment to close her eyes and breathe more slowly. "We have to let someone know, Eric. I have a real bad feeling about this."

His face darkened, and he hung his head. "Fenn, we can't. Think about it. How are you going to explain to your folks what you were doing out here?"

"I—" A fresh jolt of panic swooped through her stomach. If her mom and dad knew she'd snuck out, had been drinking beer, had been hanging out in the middle of the night with a boy...

"I'm already in enough trouble with my dad because of stuff I did back home. If he knew I'd stolen the beer from him and snuck out here..." Eric shook his head. "Please, Fenn. Don't say anything. We can't let anyone know we were out here!"

Now he cared about getting caught? When it mattered that they say something? She wanted to call him out for his hypocrisy, but found herself nodding. The weight of the secret she'd be keeping from her parents sat on her chest like a brick. A whole brick house. The sips of beer she'd drank earlier curdled in her gut. "I...think I'm gonna be sick." She scramble-crawled away just in time to get behind a bigger fir tree before she threw up.

"Fenn, you okay?"

She was shaking from head to toe, head spinning, chest tight. "I...think I...should go home."

Eric dragged a hand through his hair and nodded. "Yeah. Okay. I'll walk you."

Just then the back door of the Hemlock cabin squeaked, and the man in dark clothes darted out. He jumped down the steps to the back landing and sprinted away. Up the hillside, weaving through the young Christmas trees.

Eric placed a hand on Fenn's back and shoved her to the ground. He flattened himself next to her, his breathing ragged. Fenn couldn't breathe at all. Terror had balled in her throat, choking her.

The man ran past them, cutting at an angle toward the crest of the hill before disappearing on the far side. Even after the trespasser was gone, she and Eric lay motionless, silent. After a few seconds, he seemed to realize how scared she was, and he wrapped her in a hug. Held her while she shook and cried quietly.

"It's okay. He's gone," Eric said, although his tone didn't match the assurance of his words.

"Do you think he saw us?" Fenn asked, her own voice cracking.

He hesitated, then shook his head. "Nah. I doubt it."

"Oh, God, Eric," she whispered, her voice cracking, "What do we do?"

Eric levered her back and met her eyes with a hard look. "Nothing. You can't do or say anything. Okay?"

"But—"

"I mean it, Fenn. *Please.* Promise me." Eric looked scared. Which scared her even more.

She gulped and bobbed her head in a nod. "I promise."

He exhaled and pulled her back into a hug. "Good.

Thanks." Then squeezing her tighter, he added, "Everything will be fine. You'll see."

Held close in his arms the way she was, the soap and clean-sweat scent of him filling her nose, she clung to his shoulder and sent up a silent prayer that he was right.

Chapter 8

The whine of sirens woke Matt at dawn the next morning. He rolled over to check his alarm clock, only to be reminded by the unfamiliar decor that he wasn't in his apartment in Charlotte.

The cabin. Cameron Glen.

The wailing sound continued, and the incongruity finally pierced the fog of sleep. The siren was out of place in this peaceful setting, unlike the busy city street he lived on.

Moving to the edge of the bed, he put on his prosthesis, a pair of jeans and shoes, and ambled to the front of the cabin. He peered out the window and saw Neil Cameron hurrying down the private lane, his expression distressed.

More than a little curious, concerned even, Matt stepped out on the porch for a better view of the property. The siren sounded close. Somewhere near the front of the property. Near Cait's cabin. He debated only seconds before heading down his driveway to the narrow road. He followed Neil around the curves of the wooded lane to the valley where the fishing pond shimmered in the pearl gray light of morning. At the foot of the hillside where the Fraser and Douglas fir trees grew in neat rows, an ambulance pulled up to the Hemlock cabin.

Matt's pulse spiked. Hadn't Cait said the cabin had been reopened for rent? A couple from Nashville had booked it for a long weekend. He walked faster, anxiety tightening his gut.

"Cait!" he called when he saw her jogging toward Hemlock from the opposite direction. She paused to wait for him, her face free of makeup and lined with worry. "What's happened?"

"I don't know. I came when I heard the sirens. The Gilbreaths are staying there. They must have called the ambulance."

Matt placed a hand at the small of Cait's back as, together, they made their way to the stairs of the cabin.

"Stand clear!" an EMT called as they rolled a stretcher inside.

He guided Cait back, out of the emergency workers' way. She was trembling, and he longed to pull her into his arms and soothe her shaking. But she bustled inside, following the stretcher, and he trailed in her wake.

An older woman in a thin nightgown and robe hovered near a prone figure on the floor. The older woman, Mrs. Gilbreath, he presumed, clutched a tissue, dabbing at her eyes and nose as she wept. Cait rushed to her and gave the older woman a hug.

"Oh, Mrs. Gilbreath, what's happened?"

"When I got up this morning and…and went in to make the coffee," she paused to draw a quavering breath,

"I found George on the floor. His head was bleeding—" she motioned to her own temple "—and I couldn't wake him up."

Cait cut a glance to Matt that needed no words. He gave a slight nod and eased inside, careful to stay out of the way of where the EMTs were working. "Is he alive?"

One of the paramedics glanced over her shoulder and bobbed her chin. "Just. You family?"

"Asking for his wife. She's understandably distraught. Anything encouraging you can tell me would help her."

The female EMT continued working, hanging an IV bag and helping her partner place a neck brace on the older man before they moved Mr. Gilbreath to the gurney. "His pulse is weak, and he's unresponsive. But he's alive. That's as encouraging as I can be at the moment, I'm afraid."

"Any idea what happened to him?"

"Not really." She pointed to the bleeding wound on the older man's temple. "He took a hit to the head, but until we get him to the ER we won't know much more than that."

"Does it look like the head wound is from a fall or did someone hit him?" Matt asked.

As the medics raised the stretcher, preparing to roll Mr. Gilbreath out, the second EMT glared a warning to the first.

She jerked her head. "Sorry. That's not my job to determine. I've said too much."

"Stand clear," the second medic called to Matt.

Cait walked with Mrs. Gilbreath as they followed the stretcher outside.

The whoop of another siren and crunch of tires on gravel signaled the arrival of the police. Before he was ordered off the grounds for the cops to investigate the scene, Matt cast his gaze around, memorizing as much as he could. He might have left the Army, but he still had an instinct for investigation, an eye for detail, a compelling need for answers. Especially when innocent people were being injured.

His attention moved from the small spot of blood on the hardwood floor, where Mr. Gilbreath had bled for an undetermined length of time, to the tidy living room. Every book on the mantel and pillow on the couch seemed in place. Nothing untoward.

A uniformed officer appeared in the front door. "What have we got? Sir? Are you family of the injured man?"

"Uh, no. Friend of the cabin owners." He hoped that explanation was true enough. He wanted to believe he and Cait were at least friends, that her kindness toward him wasn't just about professional hospitality.

"Can you wait outside, please? We need to take a look at the scene," the officer said.

"Of course." Matt gave the room one more sweeping appraisal, his gaze snagging on the only sign of disruption in the perfectly ordered cabin. The area rug in the kitchen was rumpled, a long lump indicating there was either an uneven spot in the floor or a long flat item underneath. He didn't have time to study the irregularity more closely. The uniformed cop cleared his throat and stepped aside to let him pass. His experience with military policing told him the cop wouldn't take kindly to Matt's stalling or poking around what could be physical evidence of what happened to Mr. Gilbreath.

Matt gave the officer a nod and smile as he passed, and headed out to join Cait and Mrs. Gilbreath.

"George! George, I'm here, dearest!" The older woman

crowded as close to the ambulance as she could, trying to catch a glimpse of her husband.

Cait spotted Matt and eased toward him. "Well?"

"We'll talk later," he said quietly, earning a concerned and curious frown from Cait. Moving closer to the older woman, he put a comforting hand on Mrs. Gilbreath's frail shoulder.

She looked up at him, her eyes full of tears…and hope. "Is he…?"

"He's alive but still unconscious. They'll make further assessments at the hospital. Would you like me to drive you? To follow the ambulance?"

Mrs. Gilbreath sent another worried look to the back of the ambulance, just as the medics slammed the doors shut and then clutched at Matt's hand. "Oh, dear boy. Yes, thank you. Thank you, I—"

"Which hospital?" Cait called to the EMTs.

"St. Mary's."

"I'll wait with her while you get your car," Cait said.

After giving Mrs. Gilbreath's shoulder an encouraging squeeze and nodding to Cait, Matt trudged down the gravel drive to the narrow, paved road that circled the property. Had the older man tripped on the loose rug and fallen, hitting his head? The location of the rug bump Matt had noticed seemed too far from where Mr. Gilbreath had landed for that to be the case. And it didn't escape Matt's attention that this was the second tragic discovery in the Hemlock cabin in a week.

While the coroner and police couldn't specifically point to foul play in Mary's death, and very little seemed awry in the cabin this morning, Matt didn't believe in coincidences. Maybe it was his military career, his police training or his cynical nature as a crime fiction writer, but he couldn't shake his suspicion that something more than a second unfortunate mishap with an older person was to blame for Mr. Gilbreath's head injury. When he got back from driving Mrs. Gilbreath to the hospital, he intended to have a look around Hemlock cabin for himself. Ask questions. If something sinister was happening at Cameron Glen, he intended to root it out.

A police officer arrived at the hospital about an hour after Matt and Cait did. They answered the officer's questions as best they could. No, they hadn't seen anyone unauthorized on the property. No, they didn't know why anyone would want to harm Mr. Gilbreath. No, they hadn't touched or disturbed anything at the scene, although Cait and her sister had been in the cabin cleaning the day before and had surely left prints. The officer said the scene had been photographed and released. Cait took the officer's card in case she thought of anything else that might be helpful, and the officer moved on to interview Mrs. Gilbreath.

Cait's shoulders slumped as she settled back in her waiting room seat. In just the few days he'd known her, Matt had seen dark circles appear under her eyes. He reached for her hand, and she smiled at him as he laced their fingers. He meant it as a simple gesture of support, but the contact, the warmth of her soft hand in his, filled him with a tender ache he hadn't experienced in many years. Part longing, part intimate connection, part quiet camaraderie. He was definitely forming a bond with Cait Cameron.

Once Mrs. Gilbreath's son and daughter-in-law had arrived from Nashville to sit with her at the hospital and they had a report that the senior Mr. Gilbreath was stable, Cait and Matt headed back to Cameron Glen. As soon as they were in the privacy of Matt's Jeep, she pinned a hard look on him. "Okay. Tell me what you couldn't say in front of Mrs. Gilbreath. What did you see?"

He seemed startled by her question at first, sending her a blank look. Clearly his mind had been elsewhere. But when he turned his gaze back to the road and had time to process her query, his dark eyebrows beetled. "It may be nothing. Main reason I put you off was that the priority at the moment was Mrs. Gilbreath, and it seemed insensitive to talk about anything else in front of her."

"But there was something of note in the cabin? Something that might indicate what happened to him?"

He offered a shrug. "Maybe. Could be nothing."

"Tell me anyway." She shifted on the seat as far as her seat belt allowed, facing him at an angle. "Did you find something suspicious?"

He grunted and pursed his lips. "*Suspicious* may be too strong of a word. It's just that while everything else in the cabin was neat as a pin and in perfect order, the rug in the kitchen was crumpled, a corner flopped back. And there was a lump under it, as if the floorboards were uneven somehow."

The floorboards...

As soon as he said the words, an image popped into Cait's head. Mary on the floor. Her skin waxy pale. And a plank of the hardwood floor loose, pried up and sitting cockeyed. That was the oddity that had struck her but gotten shoved to the back of her brain amid the tragedy of Mary's death.

"What? Cait? You look like you've seen a ghost." Matt's voice brought her out of her thoughts.

"I—" She chewed her bottom lip a moment. "It's just that the day you found Mary, when I first arrived at the cabin and we were waiting for the police, I noticed that there was a plank of flooring loose and sitting crooked in the kitchen. I wondered for a moment if she might have tripped over it and the fall caused her death."

His dark eyes narrowed on her. "I suppose she could have tripped, but I thought you said the coroner's report said she had a massive heart attack."

"Right. But it's still odd the floorboard was loose. Why was it angled up like that? And why was a floorboard loose again when Mr. Gilbreath was injured?"

The crease in his brow deepened. "I see your point."

She gnawed her lip some more as she mulled the odd coincidence. "I mean…the broken lamp was closer to Mary, suggesting she'd reached for something near the bedroom door as she collapsed. But she was too far away from the kitchen for the floorboard to be connected to her fall. Mr. Gilbreath's head injury could have been from a fall, I suppose. Tripping on the loose board."

"Mmm…" He tapped his thumb on the steering wheel as he stared at the road, but his expression reflected deep thought. "Wouldn't someone have seen the rumpled rug and loose board and fixed it before the Gilbreaths checked in?"

"Absolutely. Isla and I went in to clean and organize everything ourselves on Tuesday. I'm sure I'd have noticed if something was amiss. I swept in the kitchen myself!"

"So how'd the board get loose?"

"Good question."

"Could it be as simple as someone stepping on one end of a warped plank, making it flip up like a seesaw?"

"I don't know. But I intend to find out." Cait squeezed her hands into fists and drew in a few slow breaths, trying to set aside the tension and worry that had twisted her in knots for days. "Did you mention the lump under the rug to the police when you gave your statement?"

"I did. They made note of it. He didn't act surprised when I mentioned it, so I'm guessing they saw it, too."

She clicked her tongue as she thought. "With Mrs. Gilbreath at the hospital, no one will be in Hemlock when we get back. If the police are through with the scene, I'm going to check those floors for myself."

He shot her a look across the front seat. "If you're willing, I'd like to take a look too. I used to do police investigations while I was in the Army. I might see something telling your eye misses due to your familiarity with the cabin."

Police investigations. A detail about his military career he'd not mentioned before. No wonder the incidents at Hemlock interested him so.

Cait considered telling him to leave the business at the Hemlock to her. Did she want a crime writer, a former military policeman involved in her family's business?

She exhaled a weary breath. "Matt, while I appreciate you volunteering this morning to drive Mrs. Gilbreath and me—"

"I promise not to use anything we find in a way that could hurt you or Cameron Glen."

She snorted mildly. "Are you a mind reader?"

"You've mentioned your concerns about a true crime book before, and I saw the doubt in your eyes. But I swear, I just want to help. I know you have questions the police and doctors haven't answered, and if I can help settle your mind or find answers that will speed the investigation, then why not let me use my skills?"

She lifted a shoulder, glanced out the side window at the haze-shrouded mountains in the distance. "Am I making too big of a deal out of a little thing like a buckled floorboard?"

He skewed his mouth to the side. "I guess we'll see once we take a closer look. It could be as simple as a warped board, but we won't know until we check. What do you say? Want my assistance?"

She studied his chiseled profile, the square cut of his stubble-dusted jaw. When he shot another inquisitive glance toward her, his dark espresso eyes stirred a shimmering heat in her belly. Spending more time with Matt would only fuel this maddening attraction she had for him. Why feed that fire if she knew nothing could come of it? Yet the thought of missing an opportunity to get to know Matt better poked her with fingers of disappointment. So she nodded. "Okay. I accept. Thanks."

"Do you think Eric's been worried about you and where you've been?"

"When I went back for the Jeep, I left a note telling him where I was going. But honestly," Matt said checking his watch, "I'd be surprised if the kid is even out of bed yet. It's only ten-thirty. Typically he sleeps until the crack of noon."

Cait chuckled politely at his joke, and they headed inside via the back porch door.

To his amazement, not only was Eric up and eating a bowl of cereal, but he had company.

"Fenn?" Cait said, her tone reflecting the same surprise. "What are you doing here?"

"I can't hang out with my friend?" the girl asked, defensiveness in her tone.

"Of course you can," Matt said. "It's just early for Eric to be up and about, and we weren't expecting to see you here."

"I guess the sirens and activity down at Hemlock woke you?" Cait asked.

The teens exchanged an inscrutable look.

"No. She woke me knocking on the front door." Eric rocked his head from side to side, stretching his neck muscles, then shoveled in another large bite of cereal.

"Did you offer Fenn anything to eat?" Matt asked, tossing his car keys on the table.

"No thanks. Not hungry," Fenn said, flicking Eric another strange glance. Nervous. Uneasy. "Is the old man okay?"

"So you heard?" Cait walked over to her niece and squeezed her shoulder.

"Grandpa told Mom. I overheard. Did he die?"

Cait shook her head. "No. Bad bump on the head, but he's stable."

Fenn glanced at Eric again, and Eric gave his head a small, almost indiscernible shake that seemed, from Matt's perspective, to upset the girl. She clamped her mouth tight and stared down at her hands.

"Fenn? You okay?" Matt asked, cocked his head as he studied Cait's niece.

Her gaze shot to him. Guilt. Panic.

Head bowed over his cereal bowl, Eric angled his friend a subtle dark glare.

Curiouser and curiouser.

Fenn shifted her feet and looked away.

Matt cast a glance to Cait, who was also studying her niece's edgy behavior.

"Fenn, do you know something about what happened to Mr. Gilbreath?" Cait asked.

The teen's nose flared, and her throat worked as she swallowed. She sighed, then said, "It's just that last night, Eric and I saw—"

"—the old man sitting on the front porch," Eric said, cutting Fenn off. "You know. In one of those rocking chairs? We waved, and he waved back. He seemed like a nice guy. Fenn and me were just talking about how it was a shame that he got hurt. That's all."

Matt let the grammatical error he'd normally have corrected slide in deference to the bigger picture. "When did you and Fenn see him? You were in the living room here with me last night watching that movie after dinner."

Eric only took a fraction of a second before he answered. "Before dinner. Not really night, so much as afternoon. Right, Fenn?"

Matt was sure Eric was lying. And he hated that lies rolled off his son's tongue so easily. The question now was, why was he lying about Mr. Gilbreath and about when he and Fenn saw the older man?

Fenn stared at the floor.

"Fenn?"

The girl lifted her head to meet her aunt's gaze. Nodded. "That's right. Just sad about the old guy. And just a few days after Ms. Mary died. In the same cabin. It's… freaky."

Cait folded her arms over her chest and divided a skeptical look between the two teenagers. Matt intended to press his son for the truth later, but he decided he wouldn't win any points if he called Eric out in front of his new friend and Cait. Instead, he faced Cait, raised an eyebrow and said, "Well, shall we go run that errand we were talking about earlier?"

"Sure."

"Let me grab something from the back room."

"What errand?" Eric asked, his expression suspicious.

"Nothing to concern yourself with. Finish your cereal." As he turned to leave, he added, "And don't leave your bowl on the table. Put it in the dishwasher. Got it?"

"Yeah, yeah," Eric groaned.

Matt hurried to his bedroom and got the small LED flashlight from his nightstand, jammed it in his pocket then headed back to join Cait.

Putting a hand on Cait's back, he steered her back outside and down the porch steps.

"Was it just me or was something odd going on with those two?" Cait asked as they started toward Hemlock.

"Not just you. I'll broach the topic with Eric again later, but didn't see any reason to belabor the issue with an audience. That wouldn't win me dad points."

"True enough." She slanted a look to him. "If it turns out to be related to the Hemlock cabin or Mr. Gilbreath, you'll let me know what he says?"

Matt nodded. "Sure."

"Or something out of line concerning Fenn? I'm not her mother, but if she's up to something she shouldn't be—"

"If my wayward son has led her down a thorny path?" he asked with a crooked smile.

"I didn't say that!"

He took her hand again and gave it a consoling pat. "You didn't need to. I did. He'd never get her in any real trouble, but he might drag her into some mildly rebellious acts." *He hoped.*

"Thing is, I've been worried about Fenn lately. Emma and Jake have been going through a rough patch—as you overheard the other day at lunch—and Fenn has been moody and withdrawn."

"Sounds like she has teenager-itis to me. Isn't moody and withdrawn a requirement for teenagers?"

Cait shrugged. "Not having my own kids, I can't say. But Fenn was always outgoing and happy in the past. I just want to be there for her if she needs someone to talk to. If something is bothering her, whatever it is."

He acknowledged her comment with a smile and nod. "It's really terrific that you have so many family members all living so close, part of each other's lives. A big network of love and support."

She laughed. "Yeah, sometimes it is fantastic. A real blessing. Other times… I want to run screaming for the hills. It's like living in a small town within a small town. Everyone knows everyone's business. Or tries to. It can be overwhelming at times."

They'd reached the gravel drive up to Hemlock, and Matt slowed his pace, studying the cabin from a distance before they approached. "You know, something Fenn said has me thinking. I'm not a believer in coincidence. I can't get past the fact that two people in a week met tragedy in the same cabin. What if the bottom line in all this isn't about Mary's death or Mr. Gilbreath's head injury? What if we're overlooking the most obvious common denominator? The cabin itself."

"What?" Cait gaped at him as if he'd suggested evil-doing gremlins lived in Hemlock.

"Who has access to this cabin day-to-day?"

"Well, I do. I keep the keys to all the cabins in the office."

"Locked up? Or could someone who knew where to look get them?"

She scowled and cocked her hip, propping one hand there. "You don't really think someone from Cameron Glen is involved do you? The few people we have working for us from outside of the family might as well be family. They're trustworthy people who've worked for us for years. People we've grown up with, gone to church with, gone to school with—"

"Easy, partner." He raised a hand and offered a grin. "I'm not casting aspersions on your friends. Just trying to get a feel for how things operate, who had opportunity…" He waved off the rest of the thought. "Maybe we're getting ahead of ourselves. Let's go have a look at those floorboards and see what shakes out."

He started up the drive, then stopped when he realized she wasn't following. "Cait?"

"I need you to promise me you won't write a true crime piece that casts Cameron Glen in a bad light or puts people off visiting, renting the cabins, fearing for their safety here."

He coughed a startled laugh. "I have no intention of writing anything about Cameron Glen." *At this point.* He didn't say the last aloud, knowing it would only upset her further. Her continued suspicion of his motives stung. He thought he'd earned her trust. To appease her, he added, "I would never write anything malicious or sensational that would harm you or your family." That much he could swear to—even if he wanted to keep the possibility of a true crime write-up in his back pocket, depending upon how these mysterious circumstances played out.

* * *

"Cait, don't you trust me?"

Matt's question caught Cait off guard, and she expelled a harsh sigh. "I…do. It's just…" She continued walking slowly toward the Hemlock cabin, adding in a calmer voice, "Obviously, I'm very protective of my family and what we've built here at Cameron Glen."

"Understandable." He followed her up the steps to the porch and waited while she keyed open the front door.

"It's not personal, Matt. But with Emma and Jake's trouble at the construction company, and the things happening here—" she waved a hand inside the cabin "—and a retreat guest landing in the hospital, my nerves are frayed and my lizard-brain warning signal is blaring. I'm trying to muddle through a most unusual and confusing time without a map."

He touched her cheek, cupping her chin in his palm. "Deep breath."

She inhaled the suggested cleansing air and released it. Cracked a quick lopsided grin.

"I'm here for whatever you need."

Her chest filled with an unexpected sense of comfort, assurance, companionship. His promise lifted a portion of the weight of her worries from her shoulders. Trying to shield her parents and siblings from the bulk of her concerns left her feeling isolated in her stress. Knowing Matt was willing to support her, assist her, be a sounding board meant the world to her.

With renewed confidence, she stepped just inside and stopped there to survey the living room and adjoining kitchen area. He stood beside her, making his own mental notes.

"It all appears pretty much the way I recall from earlier. Everything is extremely tidy. Nothing out of place to suggest a struggle or that the room has been searched."

Cait's pulse jumbled when her attention snagged on the small bloodstain from Mr. Gilbreath's head wound still on the hardwood floor. She shifted her gaze and furrowed her brow in consternation. "Matt, the area rug has been smoothed out."

He exchanged a confused look with Cait. "Then someone's straightened the rug and replaced the loose floorboard since this morning."

"You're sure it was—"

"I'm positive." He moved to the kitchen and crouched. "This is the spot where I saw the loosened board."

When he knelt on his good knee to get a closer look at the wood, Cait crouched beside him. The clean, woodsy scent of the retreat-provided soap clung to Matt and filled her nose, distracting her briefly. On Matt, Alpine Spice smelled far sexier than she'd ever known it to.

Refocusing on the task at hand, she rubbed her fingers at the end of one of the floorboards. "Look. It's all scratched and scarred."

"You're right. The scrapes looked recent, too."

Cait studied the pale, raw marks in the aged wood—the antique floors of her beloved family property—with a deep ache inside, as if claws were leaving similar scrapes in her heart. "Damn it, these floors are original. Over one hundred and thirty years old!"

"Really?" Matt grunted and cast his gaze over the polished wood with a new appreciation. "The craftsmanship is amazing."

"I know. Right? My family has worked hard to preserve the cabins. They are art as much as they are shelter." Her voice cracked, and she glanced away to gather her composure.

"Unfortunately, someone didn't share your appreciation of art. It looks like someone used a tool to pry it up," Matt said with a solemnity that seemed to understand her hurt over the damaged wood. "So…I guess we can rule out a simple warped plank getting dislodged. These boards had help coming up. Someone did this intentionally. Likely hiding something."

Cait muttered an uncharacteristic curse. "I was afraid of that." Gritting her teeth, she swallowed the bitterness that rose in her throat and waved a hand to the damaged wood. "All right. Let's see what the contraband is."

Cait fingered the end of the board as if to lift it, and Matt pulled out his pocketknife. "Here. Let me. I promise to be careful."

He wedged the tip of the blade in the crevice and pried up the floor plank.

Leaning forward, Cait looked into the small space that was exposed. "Hand me the flashlight. It's too dark to see anything and I'm *not* sticking my hand in there without looking first."

He passed her the flashlight he'd brought, and she shined the light all around the empty crevice. The relief that flashed across her face would have been comical if the situation wasn't shadowed by the recent incidents in the cabin.

"Okay, so there's nothing there. Now. But there could have been earlier." He arched an eyebrow, not wanting to alarm her but knowing they needed to be thorough. "Whatever was there could have been moved."

"Plenty of other boards in the floor, and this isn't even

the board I saw loose." She turned to point at another area of the floor. "The day Mary died, I saw a board sitting cockeyed over there."

Matt bobbed a nod. "All right." He replaced the first floorboard and flipped the rug back in place before moving across the kitchen.

Cait moved with him, and after pulling out a chair from the breakfast table, she tugged back the other side of the area rug. "Here."

They both leaned down to examine the floor more closely, their heads touching, and Cait's sweet floral scent filling his nose.

Concentrate, pal. He mentally shoved the sexy distraction aside as he studied the wood planking.

"Yep. Right here. Look." She pointed to a similar set of scratches and chips in the wood. "Damn it! If I find the person who did this, I'll tan their hide if for no other reason than messing up the floors."

He paused with the blade hovering over the crack between boards. "Are you sure you want to keep prying up planks? Whoever did this could have loosened any number of boards in this floor."

The truth of his comment clearly daunted her. Her shoulders dropped, and her expression sagged with sorrow. "Yes. Continue. At least with this one, where I know something was amiss earlier." She raised a hand, adding, "But carefully."

He ducked his head in understanding, "Of course."

An apologetic grin flickered over her forlorn features, softening the tension, and he took an extra second or two just to stare at her. Sunlight streamed in from the window above the kitchen sink and highlighted the auburn streaks in her hair and the faint freckles on her upturned nose. The bright beam reflected in her pale blue eyes, reminding him of sparkling water in the stream by his cabin. A throb of emotion grabbed at his chest.

"Matt?"

"Do you know how beautiful you are?"

She blinked. Blushed.

"What?" The word sounded strangled.

"You are." He stoked her cheek with the back of his left hand. "Beautiful."

Her throat worked as she swallowed, and she glanced down, shyly. "Um, thank you. I—"

"Anyway…" He withdrew his hand and turned his attention back to the floorboard. He eased the pocketknife blade in the small crack and gently levered the plank up.

As he moved the board out of the way, Cait shined the flashlight in the hole beneath.

She gasped at the same moment he muttered, "Holy hell."

In the dark space they exposed was a small plastic bag. Cait moved the light closer, illuminating the contents of the clear bag—a large bundle of cash, bound by a white paper band with "$7458" written on it.

When she reached for the bag of money, he caught her wrist. "No. Don't touch it."

When she frowned a query at him, he added, "Fingerprints. That's evidence."

Chapter 9

*E*vidence.

The word churned through Cait's gut as she watched the uniformed cop use tweezers to lift the plastic bag of money from the underfloor crevice. The word implied criminal activity. *Seven thousand, four hundred, fifty-eight dollars' worth of criminal activity.* And while she couldn't explain why such a large bundle of money was stashed under the floor of the Hemlock cabin, she could no longer deny the frightening truth that Cameron Glen was being used for some nefarious purpose.

"Could it have been left there by a guest?" she asked no one in particular, still trying to justify the discovery with a more palatable explanation.

Beside her, Matt sent her a dubious frown. "There's several thousand dollars in that bag. You really think someone forgot it?"

"I know. It seems hard to fathom someone could forget such a large sum of cash, but you might be surprised at the valuable property sometimes left behind. Cameras, laptops, jewelry."

He lifted a shoulder. "Considering the other recent incidents in this cabin, I don't think the owner of this money forgot it at all."

The police officer, whom she recognized from his earlier trips out to the property this week, stood from his crouch. After dropping the money in an evidence bag, he said, "I'm inclined to agree with the gentleman. In fact, I recommend you close this cabin until further notice. Whoever put this money here doesn't know we know about it. They could well come back for it, and we don't want anyone coming between mama bear and her cub." He raised the bag indicating the cash was the cub.

"You think that's what happened to Mr. Gilbreath? Someone hurt him when they came looking for the money?" she asked, her agitation growing.

The officer said nothing. Only gave a mild shrug and a flipped-up palm.

Of course, he wouldn't comment on an open investigation. But the lack of answers weighed on Cait. This was her family's property. The rental cabins were more than a main revenue stream. Cameron Glen was their heritage. Their home.

Now their retreat had been breached. Violated. Tainted.

"I need air," she muttered as she trudged to the door and out to the cabin lawn.

Matt followed, and when she paused to gather her composure, he put a hand at the nape of her neck, gently massaging the tension coiled there. Which was exactly what she needed at the moment.

As a second police cruiser pulled up, Matt hitched his head toward the side yard. "Shall we get out of the way?"

Cait nodded, and they moved from the front yard and the heat of the noonday sun to the shade of the walnut tree at the side of the cabin. There, she sank onto one of the wooden benches situated around the Hemlock cabin's firepit. Matt settled beside her and draped an arm around her shoulders, tugging her close. She leaned against him, resting her head on his shoulder. At a time when her world seemed to be built on shifting sand, she took solace from his strength and solidity.

As Matt studied the area, he seemed to be looking for something.

"What?" she asked, after a few moments when a low, puzzled hum rumbled in his chest. "Is something wrong?"

"What's over that rise?" He pointed to the hillside behind the Hemlock cabin, lined with Fraser firs.

"More trees. Some farm property. Eventually the highway that leads to the property's front drive. Why?"

"I'm wondering how the person that attacked Mr. Gilbreath arrived at the cabin."

She drew a shallow breath. "We don't know that he was attacked. Maybe he tripped and—"

The look Matt sent her said, *You don't really believe that, do you?*

"How do we know the culprit didn't just drive in from the highway and walk through the front door?" She pinched the bridge of her nose. "God, I hate to say it, but I think the outside world has spoiled Cameron Glen. It's time we invested in security cameras. Past time."

Matt put a consoling hand on her knee. "I think you're right."

"I've fought the idea for so long, because they seem like such an intrusion on people's privacy. The point of this place is to be a peaceful, private escape from the hubbub and noise of daily life."

"They can feel obtrusive, but for safety's sake—yours as well as your guests—I'm afraid they are a reality of today's world."

She groaned. "I hate this. All of this." She waved a hand toward the Hemlock cabin. "Injured guests. Illicit money. Police swarming the property. Geez. Great-grandpa Cameron must be rolling in his grave."

Matt said nothing for a moment, then, giving her leg a pat, he rose. "Wait here. I'll be right back."

He headed toward the back porch of the Hemlock cabin. Curiosity stung Cait. No way would she wait on the perimeter if Matt felt there was something important to discover. She trotted across the carpet of grass to catch up to him as he traipsed up the steps of the back landing.

"What is it? What are you looking for?"

He glanced over his shoulder to her and smiled as if saying he wasn't surprised she'd followed. He bent at the waist and examined the doorknob, the door frame, all without touching anything. "This."

He pointed to the door, and she moved closer to see what he'd found.

"More fresh scratches around the lock. Signs of forced entry," he said.

Bile crept up her throat as the signs of illegal activity centered around the cabin piled up. Straightening and pressing a hand to her swirling stomach, she sighed. "I'll go get the police officers. They should see this."

Chapter 10

That evening, Matt's cell phone rang while he and Eric were sharing their umpteenth pizza, and he pulled it out to check the screen. *Cait.*

"No phones at the table," Eric said with a smug grin.

Matt hesitated a beat. In truth, he should ignore the call and abide by the same rules he asked Eric to follow. But he had promised to be available to Cait and her family, night and day. He wiped his mouth with his napkin, and as he thumbed the answer icon, said, "This could be important."

Eric rolled his eyes. "What a crock."

"Hey, Cait. What's up?"

"I shouldn't bother you with this. I know I shouldn't, but…" The distress in her voice set off alarm bells in his head.

From the charging stand on the kitchen counter, where

Eric's phone resided the twenty-three hours he was not allowed to use it, his EDM-song ringtone blared.

"No bother. What's wrong?" He gave Eric a warning glare that said, "Don't answer that."

"It could be important," his son said, and pushed his chair back to retrieve his phone.

Matt shook his head, choosing to ignore Eric's recalcitrance in light of the worrying tone of Cait's voice.

"The police are at Emma's house. She just called me in a panic. They're questioning Jake about the money we found today."

"Jake? But why—"

Cait started to respond, but he was distracted by Eric's muttered curse. He glanced at Eric. His son's face was dark and full of anxiety as he said sotto voce, "You can't. Fenn, no…"

"Never mind why. I'll be right there." Matt disconnected with Cait and narrowed his attention on Eric, who met his gaze with barely concealed panic.

"I gotta go," Eric said into his phone in a quick, quiet whisper. "Everything will be fine. I promise." His son hung up his call and raised his chin defiantly. "It was important."

If Eric's call was, in fact, Fenn, he knew what had upset the girl.

Matt nodded and rose from the table. "So was mine." He grabbed his jacket and the key to the cabin. "In fact, I'm going out. Don't know when I'll be back."

"To Cait's?"

"Her sister's house, actually."

"The Turners'?"

"Yeah." He jabbed his arms in his sleeves and crossed to the front door.

Eric snagged his own jacket from the back of his chair. "I'm coming with you."

"No. Not this time."

Squaring his shoulders, Eric returned, "Yeah. This time. Cait is upset, and you're going to help her. Well, Fenn is upset, too, and I'm going to help her."

How did he argue with logic like that? Wasn't he trying to raise a young man who thought of others and showed compassion?

"All right." He sighed and hitched his head. "But the adults have business to handle that you two don't need to be involved in. You need to stay in her room or outside somewhere while we talk. Got it?"

Eric loped down the porch steps without waiting for Matt while he locked the front door. Although Eric walked beside him most of the way to the Turners' house, Matt could tell his son was itching to race ahead at a pace beyond what Matt was capable of any longer. "Go on," he said finally. "I'll catch up."

"Thanks." With that, Eric peeled off at an angle to cut through the woods, uphill to the Turners' home.

By the time Matt had negotiated the steep driveway, Eric was in the yard with Fenn, hugging the crying girl. A Valley Haven police cruiser was parked in the driveway behind Jake's Turner Construction truck. When Eric spotted Matt walking up the sidewalk, he guided Fenn around the corner of the house, out of view.

"Matt!" Cait came out the front door, and the flash of anxiety in her eyes matched the stress he'd heard in her voice when she called. Following his son's lead, he drew Cait into his arms to hug her. She trembled in his embrace and rested her head against his chest. "This is a nightmare."

"What's happening? Why are they questioning Jake?"

Cait took a deep breath, raised her head and levered away in order to meet his eyes.

"Remember the argument we overheard the other day at lunch about some money that had gone missing from Jake's construction business? Apparently, every time he checked the books in the last few months, more money was gone."

"Damn."

"Yeah. Jake was trying to deal with it internally. He was hoping it was just clerical errors on the part of his bookkeeper, but then the bookkeeper began worrying she'd be held responsible, accused of wrongdoing, and she announced it at a staff meeting. Someone called it in to the police."

"And?"

"They're talking to everyone in the company that has any access to the accounts." Her jaw tightened, and she pressed her mouth in a taut line before adding, "Peter told the police that he saw Jake going in the company safe late one night when everyone else had gone home."

Matt furrowed his brow. "Okay, two questions. First, who is Peter? And how does it cast suspicion on Jake, the owner of the business, to be accessing the safe?"

"Peter is Jake's accounts manager." Her expression darkened further. "And my ex-boyfriend."

That piece of information stuck Matt in the gut. Harder than it should have. The guy was an ex after all, but something—jealousy—put him automatically on edge. "I see."

She sighed again and shook her head. "I'm not sure you do. Matt, the money we found in the Hemlock cabin was bound by a paper strip that had a number written on it. Remember?"

"Yeah." A cold suspicion growing in his belly. "Seven thousand, four hundred and fifty-eight dollars."

She nodded. "That's the exact amount reported to the police as missing from Turner Construction."

"They want to arrest my dad, Eric! We have to say something!" Fenn said, tears spilling from her eyes. She paced the packed dirt in front of the bench swing while a cloud of gnats buzzed around her head.

"We can't. If your parents find out you snuck out or my dad learns that I took his beer—" Eric raked a hand through his hair, knowing how selfish he sounded. But he was scared. He didn't want to get in worse trouble than he was, and he didn't want Fenn to pay for his encouraging her to sneak off that night. Damn it, why did doing the right thing have to be so hard?

"Look," he said with a calm he didn't feel, "your dad is innocent, right?"

"Of course, he is! He's not a thief!" Fenn's volume grew, and he had to hush her. She dropped on the swing beside him and drew a shaky breath before adding, "And we know it wasn't him we saw break into the Hemlock cabin that night."

"Well, if he didn't do it, they won't have any reason to hold him." Eric grabbed and squeezed her hand, hoping to instill a little reassurance. "They can't charge him with something without proof, right?"

Slumped on the swing, Fenn gnawed her bottom lip. "I don't know. What if someone framed him? Don't you watch those real-life crime shows on cable? Innocent people go to jail all the time!"

The sound of voices drifted back from the front yard, and Fenn sat straighter, her worried gaze flying to the corner of her house. Without saying anything, she jumped up and trotted toward the front yard, startling their black feral cat from her sleeping spot in the bushes.

Eric jogged after her. "Fenn, wait."

Fenn gasped when she rounded the flowering tree at the corner of her house.

"No! Daddy!"

She sprinted out of Eric's line of sight, and he ran to catch up with her. The front walk was full of people now. His dad and Cait were comforting Fenn's mom, a cop was talking to Fenn's grandfather, and another cop was putting Fenn's dad in the back of the squad car. Fenn threw her arms around her dad and clung to him, sobbing. "He didn't do anything! You can't arrest him! Daddy, please!"

Her father hugged her and kissed the top of her head. Eric's heart twisted, and his throat felt tight. He knew how it felt to fear you were losing your dad.

At least Mr. Turner wasn't handcuffed. Maybe he wasn't being arrested.

Cait walked over to Fenn and pulled her away from Mr. Turner, and Eric crossed the yard to his dad. "Why are the cops taking him in?"

His dad gave him a side glance. Hesitated. "They just want to ask him some questions. He's not under arrest."

Fenn's grandfather crossed to Cait and Fenn and tucked his granddaughter in a firm embrace, kissing her head and saying something quiet in her ear. Eric's gut wrenched. Was this huge misunderstanding all his fault? Because he'd sworn Fenn to secrecy about what they knew, what they'd seen?

He stared at the ground as the cops backed up the

squad car, Y-turned, and headed down the steep drive. Cait ushered Fenn's mom past him, and he caught a snatch of conversation.

"Call Bill Harris. He's not in criminal law, but he'll know who—"

Fenn and her grandfather passed him then, and he glanced up to give her an encouraging smile. But the accusing glare he met in Fenn's face stopped him. "Fenn?"

Bursting into sobs, she pulled away from her grandfather's grasp and ran inside.

Eric stared after her, his chest tight, his gut churning. *Do something.* He took a step toward the Turners' house, but his dad caught his arm, draped an arm around his shoulders. "Give her some space. She needs her family right now."

Cait returned from the porch, hugging herself as if cold, despite the warm muggy night. "I— Thank you for coming." She bit her lip the way Eric had seen Fenn do so many times when she was worried.

"Tell me what I can do. I want to help," his dad said.

Cait spread her arms now, then let them flop loose at her sides. "There's nothing any of us can do except wait. Pray. Emma's calling a lawyer. Beyond that…" She sighed and glanced away. "I don't know why I called you. I shouldn't have bothered you, but—"

"No bother."

"I guess…" Cait lowered her voice to almost an apologetic mumble, "I just wanted another ally close by. A friendly face…"

His dad eased forward so he could tug Cait into his arms for a hug. "I'm glad you think of me as a friend and ally."

Eric watched how Cait sank against his dad, the way

his dad's face transformed as he held Cait and brushed his mouth against her temple. Maybe his dad and Cait wouldn't say it, but he saw the truth. They'd become much more to each other than *friends* or *allies*. Awkward with the affection his dad was showing Cait, Eric turned away, his hands fisting in his pockets.

A different sort of disturbance rumbled in Eric's core. Not that he didn't like Cait. He did. She was about as cool as adults came. But he'd been dragged here this summer to have time alone with his dad. Now his dad was coupling up with Fenn's aunt. Was his dad going to push him aside again in order to be with his new girlfriend? Story of his life.

Forget that Eric needed a dad who was there for him. There was a war to fight. Leave the country for two years. Can't get along with his wife? Get a divorce and leave the kid again just three years after you get back stateside.

Eric swallowed the bitter taste of resentment that burned the back of his throat. He should be used to it by now. His dad's part-time commitment to him. Putting him second. Or third even. Had he ever been a priority in his dad's life?

"I should go in," Cait said. "Emma's got her hands full with the girls and calling the lawyer and her own upset over all this."

"Right. Well, you know where I am if I can do anything. And I mean anything, Cait."

Eric glanced back at his dad in time to see him kiss Cait's cheek. Without waiting for his dad, Eric marched across the dusk-shrouded yard toward the driveway. The image of Fenn's tearstained cheeks and panicked eyes flashed in his memory, knotting his emotions all over again. *Crap.* What was he supposed to do? He hated think-ing he'd caused Fenn's anguish. Divided her loyalties.

Your choices determine your character. You need to have the inner strength and moral fiber to make good choices. Not just for yourself, but for others. He'd heard the lecture, or similar words, too many times to count. From his dad, from his mom, from his counselor.

At the foot of the Turners' steep driveway, he slowed to wait for his dad, dread curdling inside him. He'd screwed up—again—and for Fenn's sake, for Mr. Turner's sake, he needed to 'fess up.

He took a deep breath as his dad neared. Cleared his throat. "Dad, I…have to tell you something."

Chapter 11

Matt had been preoccupied, mulling over the twist of events tonight, when Eric approached him. Jake Turner, in his limited interactions with the man, seemed like a good guy. Jake claimed to be innocent of wrongdoing. How did the money found in the Hemlock cabin connect to Jake's construction company? It seemed pretty obvious the person who'd stolen the cash had hidden it at Hemlock, but who—

The distress in Eric's face registered as he closed the distance between them. "What's wrong, Eric?"

"I, um…" Eric wouldn't look at him.

Concern spiked with a punch to Matt's gut. "Eric?"

His son rubbed his hands on the seat of his shorts and stared at the ground.

Matt fought for patience. If Eric was ready to volunteer information, the last thing he wanted to do was send his son's hackles and defenses back up by pushing him.

Matt hitched his head. "Let's walk. You can tell me on the way back to the cabin."

Eric fell in step beside him, matching Matt's slower pace. "Um...the other night, Fenn and I were out late, hanging out close to that cabin...the one where the lady died and the old man was hurt."

"Hemlock?"

Eric nodded. "Yeah. Hemlock."

When was this? Why were you out late? What were you doing? Matt bit the inside of his cheek and made himself swallow the barrage of questions. Give him a chance to talk...

"Well, we saw this guy."

Matt's pulse leaped. "What?"

"I don't know who he was. Neither did Fenn. But he came over the hill, out of nowhere, and crept down to the Hemlock cabin. The back door."

The door that had been forcibly jimmied open. Matt stopped walking and faced his son, stunned. "Go on."

"He snooped around for a little bit then, like, broke in, I guess. That's what it looked like."

"When was this?" He couldn't help it. The question had to be asked.

"The night before the old man was found hurt."

Matt's breath stuck in his lungs, and he swiped a hand over his mouth, muffling a curse.

"The guy stayed inside a few minutes before he ran out the back and up the hill behind the cabin. Back the way he came."

"Then where'd he go? Did he have a car? Was anyone with him?"

Eric shook his head. "He was alone. Didn't see a car. Fenn was scared, and we didn't follow him. She said the other side of the hill was more Christmas trees and a pasture, then woods before reaching the highway."

That matched what Cait had told him earlier in the day.

Dear God, give me strength not to strangle my son and the wisdom to handle this the best way. Matt took an intentional breath. Released it. *Stay calm. Yelling helps no one.*

"Eric, why didn't you tell me this before now? Didn't you realize how important what you saw was?" There. Good. Firm and disappointed without being ballistic. Even though inside him skyrockets were firing all over the place.

Eric sighed. "I guess so." He turned and started walking back down the road again, and Matt had to hustle to catch up.

Don't walk away from me! He wanted to shout, but he *had* suggested they talk as they returned to their cabin. "And the first question? The why?"

Eric didn't answer for a moment, clearly weighing his words. "I didn't want to get Fenn in trouble."

"Why would Fenn be in trouble?"

Eric blew out an exasperated breath. "She snuck out without telling her parents."

"I see." Matt read into the answer what wasn't said. He'd been young and adventurous once. "How late was this?"

"Not too late. Eleven maybe."

"So you snuck out, too." A statement not a question.

A groan. "Yeah."

"And?"

"And what?"

"Anything else you want to tell me about that evening?"

Eric shrugged. "We didn't get a close look at the guy. And it was dark, so we couldn't really see his face. Just that he was a white guy. Clean-shaven. Average height and weight. Dark clothes."

Matt made a mental note of the description. Not much to go on, but it was something. "All right. Thank you for that. What I meant, though, was whether you have anything else you want to share with me about your outing with Fenn."

Eric sent him a guilty side glance. "Like what?"

"I'm giving you the chance to take responsibility. To volunteer the information, not be cornered and have to admit to or deny my accusations. Isn't that how you've said you wanted it?"

Eric gave an exaggerated moan and scrubbed both hands on his head. "I took a couple beers with us. Okay? Is that what you wanted me to say?"

Matt blinked. He'd actually been expecting to hear that his son and Fenn had snuck out more than once. Or that he'd used the car without permission.

Matt flexed and clenched his hands, trying to burn off the frustration and anger, fighting hard to keep his temper in check. "I wanted the truth, so if that is the whole truth, then I'm glad to get it. But you can't imagine I'm pleased to hear you were drinking again. Or that you stole them from me. Or that you, presumably, offered it to Fenn."

They were nearing the cabin, and he could sense Eric's desire to run the rest of the way back and lock himself in his room to avoid the fallout of his admission.

Eric stalked silently beside him with his shoulders hunched forward, his hands in his pockets and his face pulled into a scowl.

Matt pinched the bridge of his nose. "There need to be consequences, Eric. I can't let this slide. I'm glad you were honest with me, but it shouldn't have taken Fenn's father being questioned by the police to force your hand." He gritted his teeth and grumbled, "There really shouldn't have been any misbehavior to confess, but—"

Eric shot him a dark glower and peeled off from the road, marching across the grass to the Fraser cabin's front porch. When he found the door locked, Eric growled and smacked his hand against the solid wood. He paced the length of the porch until Matt reached the steps.

"We'll take a little break, you and I, to calm down. No point letting this devolve into a shouting match. Huh?"

Eric gave him a grudging nod.

"But we will discuss it later." Matt reached in his pocket and pulled out the key. Tossing it to Eric, he said, "I'm heading back over to the Turners'. They need to know what you've told me."

Eric's eyes flared wide with betrayal and alarm. "Dad, no! Fenn will get in trouble. I didn't tell you so that you could rat her out!"

Matt scratched his chin. Fenn's parents deserved to know the truth about what Eric and their daughter had been up to, but maybe that matter could wait. He'd give Fenn a chance to confess once she learned Eric had done so.

"How about this? I'll leave Fenn out of it. I'll tell them you were the one out late without mentioning Fenn. But they need all the facts about the guy at the Hemlock cabin in order to defend Jake." He hesitated. "You're sure it wasn't Mr. Turner?"

Eric rolled his eyes. "I think Fenn would recognize her own father."

"A little less sarcasm please, mister. We're trying to keep this civil. Right?"

Eric took a breath, visibly collecting himself, before saying calmly, "It wasn't Mr. Turner. We didn't recognize him. Either of us."

Matt experienced a moment of pride. His son's ability to put aside his snark and speak rationally to the matter at hand might seem small, but it was a first step in the right direction.

"Okay." Matt squared his shoulders, ordered his thoughts. "You go ahead and finish your dinner. Don't wait for me. I don't know when I'll be back."

"'Kay." Eric unlocked the door.

"And, Eric?" Matt said before his son could shut the door. "Thank you." When Eric furrowed a puzzled brow, he added. "For the information. For being honest. For doing the right thing." *Even if belated.*

A flash of something—contrition? humility? relief?— passed over Eric's face before he schooled his expression, nodded and closed the door.

Cracking his knuckles as he turned back toward the road, Matt headed back to the Turners' house with the new information.

"Matt?" Cait said, startled to see him on Emma's front porch again. Even before he said anything, her gut clenched. His knitted brow, tight mouth and dark eyes told her something was wrong. *Something else* was wrong. She'd heard trouble came in threes, but wasn't her family well past that number now?

"Can we talk?"

She stepped out on the porch and was closing the door

behind her when he added, "Actually, Emma needs to hear this, too. Can we go inside?"

"Well, but…Emma's getting ready to go down to the police station. What's going on?"

"I have new information that could clear Jake. She needs to hear this before she goes. In fact, Jake's lawyer needs to know this, as well."

Cait gaped at Matt. "New information? In the last fifteen minutes?" And then she got it. "Eric told you something."

He nodded.

"Something Fenn said?"

"No. It's…" He motioned to the door. "Let's go in, and I'll explain to everyone at once."

She led him into Emma's living room and gathered Emma, her mother and father. Isla stayed with Lexi in the little girl's room, but Fenn came to the living room door, spotted Matt, and her eyes rounded. She hovered at the door, and Cait wondered if what Matt had to say was appropriate for her niece's ears. She signaled Matt with a glance and subtle hand motion toward the teen. He gave a nod.

Once everyone was assembled, he began.

Cait listened with dismay as Matt relayed the story Eric had told of being out late one night and seeing a stranger enter the Hemlock cabin. As rapt as she was by the disturbing new information, she made a point of watching Fenn. The girl's face paled. She shifted her weight nervously. It didn't take Sherlock Holmes to figure out Fenn had been with Eric, even if Matt made no mention of her. Emma, already flustered by the police taking Jake in for questioning and the ramifications of what Eric had seen, didn't seem to notice her daughter's unease. Possible guilt.

"He needs to give an official statement to the police," Cait's father said.

Matt nodded. "I know. I'll take him to the station in little while, but I thought Emma should know—" he spoke directly to Emma now "—before you left to meet with your lawyer."

"Yes." She pressed a hand to her mouth, her face wan.

"I really wish I'd called sooner to have security cameras installed. Next week doesn't seem soon enough," Cait said to no one in particular.

"You're installing security cameras on the property?" Cait's mother asked, her expression stunned. "What about privacy? And can we even afford that?"

"Can we afford not to?" Neil returned.

"I should go now." Emma shoved to her feet and glanced to Neil. "Jake'll be waiting on me. Dad?"

"Right. Let's go." Cait's father escorted Emma out to his car, and no one said anything else until Fenn turned to go back to her bedroom.

"Fenn," Cait said.

Her niece stopped, turned, her shoulders stiffening.

"If you know something, you need to tell us."

Fenn wet her lips and stared at them, wide-eyed.

Cait drew a slow breath for patience. "Fenn?"

Her niece glanced away then whispered, "I was with Eric. It all happened just like he said."

Cait exchanged a look with Matt.

"Will I have to talk to the cops, too?" Fenn asked in a tiny, frightened voice.

Matt sighed. "Yeah, I think that would be for the best. To corroborate what Eric has to say."

Tears welled in Fenn's eyes, and Cait rushed to her niece, embracing her. "You're not in trouble, honey. Not with me. And I'll talk to your mom, get her to go easy on you. Especially since you were brave enough to come forward with this. Your statement will definitely help your dad."

She sniffed. "But I didn't come forward. Eric did. I'm a horrible daughter!"

Oh, boy. Cait hugged Fenn tighter and murmured re-assurances to the distraught teenager.

Matt rose from his seat and headed to the front door. "Well, I'm going to go have a talk with Eric, and I'll call you when we're ready to head down to the police station."

Chapter 12

Matt disconnected his call to his ex-wife, having reported the latest happenings with Eric, and headed back to the small waiting room of the Valley Haven Police Department. He took the empty chair next to Cait and rubbed his eyes with the pads of his fingers.

Cait squeezed his shoulder. "You okay?"

He angled a tired smile toward her. "Sure. Jessica wanted to drive over, but I talked her down."

"I can understand her worry. You two have had an… interesting few days."

He snorted. "Yeah."

"Not really the peaceful vacation retreat our brochure promised, I'm afraid." She scowled. "I'll be sure we make it up to you. Somehow. Free nights or—"

"Hey." He cut her off with a hand around hers. "None of this is your fault. You owe us nothing."

"But…"

He squeezed harder. "But nothing." Despite the warm night, Cait's hand was cold. He pressed it between both of his and rubbed warmth into it. She didn't take her hand back until her phone beeped, and she checked the incoming text.

"That was Isla," she said. "While you were talking to Jessica, I updated her on things here. She said Lexi woke up once, but she read her a story and curled up on the bed with her until she went back to sleep. Brody will take over babysitting in the morning if Em and Jake aren't back yet."

Matt nodded. "I think it's great that you have a big family and can look out for each other."

She smiled as she covered a yawn. "It is pretty great. Holidays get crazy, but…I love it."

Matt checked his watch and settled back in the uncomfortable chair. "This could take a while. Small police department. Small staff. Several people to interview. You sure you don't want to wait at home?"

"Are you saying you don't want my company?" Cait said with a teasing grin.

"Not at all, but…" He sent a meaningful glance to Emma and their father, who waited on the other side of the room. "I'm not alone."

"True, still…" She pitched her volume lower. "I wanted to ask you something."

He arched a black eyebrow and matched her whisper. "Do we need to step outside?"

She hesitated, then bobbed a nod. As she stood, she told her sister, "Be right back. Matt and I are going to grab a cup of coffee from the diner before it closes. Can I bring you anything?"

Emma shook her head, and their father said, "Coffee would be great, Cait. Black."

The humid summer night embraced them as they left the station, and crickets filled the air with song. Matt waited until they were in the parking lot before he prodded Cait. She seemed to be struggling for a way to open the conversation she wanted to have.

Finally she said, "I have to do something. I can't sit on the sidelines and watch my sister and her husband go down for something I know he didn't do."

Shoving his hands in his pockets, Matt cast her a side glance. "I can understand why you'd want to help, but what can you do?"

"Well…" She chewed her bottom lip as she strolled across the blacktop to the edge of the road. Across the street, the nondescript brick building with Ma's Mountain Kitchen painted on the large plate-glass window beckoned with the scents of fried chicken and barbecued meats. She checked for traffic before hustling across the two-lane road.

"The fact that the kids saw someone breaking in the cabin got me thinking. Who else might have seen something or overheard a conversation or…" She raised both hands then let them drop as she shrugged. "Who knows what? Valley Haven is a small town, Matt. People talk." She twisted her mouth in a wry grin. "People eavesdrop. People know each other's business. Heck, by the time Ma's switches from serving pancakes to pulled-pork lunch plates tomorrow, half the town will know Jake was brought in tonight for questioning. And the whole town will know by supper. Somebody knows something that will help clear Jake and find the guy who broke into the Hemlock cabin. They have to."

His flipped up a palm. "All right. So you ask around town what people know." When he started to pull the diner door open for her, she braced her arm against it to stop him.

"What if *we* asked around?" Her voice was quiet again, even though there was no one around to overhear. "Are you still interested in investigating the break-ins and what might have happened to Mr. Gilbreath?"

"Well…sure. I'll help you out however I can. What do you have in mind?"

An older couple exited the diner, and Matt and Cait had to step away from the door to let them pass. Once the couple was out of earshot, Cait said, "I want to start with Peter."

Matt frowned. "Peter?"

Her sigh sounded unhappy. "My ex."

"I remember who he is. But why him?"

"Because he works with Jake at the construction company," she said as if the answer should be obvious. "He's in as good a position as anyone to have the inside scoop on what's really going on at Turner Construction."

Matt scratched his ear, telling himself he was *not* jealous that Cait wanted to go see her ex. He certainly had no right to have any opinion on her relationship with her ex.

But there it was again, like the first time she'd mentioned him. The gnawing niggle in his gut.

"Do you think he'll talk to you? And maybe more important, do you think he'll be honest with you?"

Cait chewed her lip again, her brow furrowed in consternation. Reaching for the door handle, she exhaled a frustrated sigh. "I guess we'll see."

The next day, when Peter answered the door, Cait's first reaction was a gut punch of surprise. He'd shaved his beard and mustache since she'd last seen him.

"Cait!" Peter's eyes widened, and his smile seemed genuine…until his gaze flicked to Matt, standing behind her. The joy of his initial greeting dimmed, and a dent of confusion furrowed his brow. "What's up?"

"Can we talk?" She bobbed her head toward his living room.

"Uh…" He rubbed his chin, floundering a bit before opening the door wider and stepping back. "Sure."

Matt stuck his hand out and introduced himself. Peter shook the proffered hand and reciprocated the introduction, his expression still confused.

"Matt is a guest at Cameron Glen who's helping me with a…project. Lending his experience and expertise, you might say," she explained.

Peter led them into the living room, and Cait's gaze swept the familiar room where she'd once lived. Matt took a seat on the couch, and as she made her way to the space next to Matt, her eye snagged on a picture on the mantel. Between a picture of his family from twenty years ago and the ugly glazed ceramic piece his brother had given them for Christmas two years ago sat a photo that featured her and Peter from a skiing weekend at Maggie Valley. Her heart thumped with surprise—and perhaps a grain of irritation. She crossed the room to take the framed photo down. "Why do you still have this out?"

Peter lifted his chin. "Why shouldn't I? It's a good picture of us. We had a nice time that weekend. I like having the memento where I can see it and remember the trip."

"But…" She replaced the photo and sighed. "Isn't it awkward or inappropriate or something since we're no longer dating? I'd think it would be a—"

She hesitated. *Painful* implied he'd cared about her,

suffered after their breakup, and, therefore, felt presumptive of her. "*Unwelcome* reminder of me."

Peter flashed her a wry grin as he settled in an overstuffed chair catty-corner to the couch. "Any more so than showing up at work every day and seeing your brother-in-law? The family photos on his desk that include you?"

"I, uh—"

"Besides, maybe I'm glad to have reminders of you around. Maybe I miss you. Maybe I cared about you more than you gave me credit for." Hurt infused his tone.

She swallowed hard, glanced away long enough to gather her composure. "When did you shave?"

Peter raised a hand to his face as if he'd forgotten he'd removed his beard, stroking his smooth cheek. "Few weeks back. Summertime and all. It was hot, and I thought I'd give it a rest until next winter. Why?"

She shrugged his question off, even though Fenn's description of the man she'd seen breaking into the Hemlock cabin scratched in her brain. Clean-shaven. Dark hair. Average height. Average weight. Fenn could have been describing Peter. Quashing that thought, Cait said, "Just...curious. The new look surprised me."

Cait took a seat next to Matt, catching the disgruntled look from Peter that she surmised was jealousy. She *had* sat rather close to Matt. Rising a bit, she tugged the skirt of her sundress and resettled a few inches farther away from Matt. Not that she cared what Peter thought of her new relationship with Matt, but because she figured he'd be more cooperative and forthcoming if they didn't actively provoke ill will from him.

"So I know you didn't come to discuss my facial hair or criticize my choice of home decor." Peter propped an ankle on his opposite knee as he leaned back in his chair. "What is this project you need help with?"

Cait took a deep breath. "I know you have to be aware of the fact that Jake was questioned by the police recently over money missing from the business account at the construction company."

Peter laced his fingers, resting his hands on his chest and tapping his thumbs together. Despite his casual pose, Cait saw the tic of the muscle in his jaw and knew him well enough to recognize the slight waggle of his propped foot as a sign of anxiety. Restlessness. "I'm aware."

"I was hoping you could shed some light on what was happening in the construction office. To give us a different perspective than Jake's."

"What kind of *perspective*?"

"Just an account of what you've observed in the office. He's stumped as to who might be pilfering the money."

"You want me to be a spy?" Peter asked, raising an eyebrow.

"Not a spy," Matt said. "But if you know of any grievances someone has with Jake concerning the way he runs the business, an employee with financial troubles, someone who has been acting suspiciously or out of character lately—"

"Besides Jake, you mean?" Peter pulled a sarcastic face. "Because Jake's the one whose behavior and temper has been unpredictable lately. Grumpy. Short with people one minute then humble the next, letting people leave early or take long lunches as his means of apology. Bringing in doughnuts and coffee for the office to try to ease the tension he's created."

Cait folded her arms over her chest and huffed. "Can you blame him for being tense and stressed? Someone is stealing from him, and when he tried to deal with it internally and give the culprit the opportunity to rectify the matter without police involvement, someone calls the police on him and throws Jake under the bus!" She heard her volume growing, the frustration knotting her gut and tightening muscles.

"I didn't throw him under the bus. I like Jake. Really, I do. But the police needed to know the money was gone. Jake's handling of the matter just made him look guilty."

Cait narrowed her eyes and gave her head a little shake. Had she heard him correctly? "Wait. Are you saying *you* called the police? *You* implicated Jake?"

Peter uncrossed his legs and scratched his eyebrow. "Don't sound so offended, Cait. I reported a crime. I gave an honest account to the cops when they asked me questions. I did nothing wrong."

"Nothing wro—" Her temper spiked. "What about loyalty to the man who employed you when no one else would because of your past drug use?"

He scoffed. "Really? Is that like the kind of loyalty you had for a man you lived with for three years?"

She stiffened. "Low blow, Peter. And unrelated. In fact, it was your lack of commitment that—"

A shrill whistle cut her off, and she cut a startled glance to Matt, who made slashing motions at his throat. "We're getting off topic here. Instead of turning this into a rehashing of your past regrets and disagreements, can we focus our discussion on the situation at the construction company?"

Cait sighed and sank back on the couch. "You're right." She waved a hand toward Peter. "Sorry. I was wrong to bring up your past."

He nodded an acceptance of her apology and muttered

what she chose to assume was his own, adding, "Look, I already talked to the police. They've got copies of the company's books. I really think you two should leave this to the professionals. Don't muddy the waters with your own poking around."

"I don't consider it poking around where my family is concerned. And Matt has professional experience in police matters."

Maybe not civilian criminal investigations, but she didn't bother to elaborate for her ex.

Peter shot Matt another suspicious look. "Really?"

Matt gave a nonspecific hand flip and a shrug. "We're really just looking for some answers to questions the police won't tell us. Her family needs some peace of mind."

"Jake didn't take that money or hide it. I'm sure of that much, Peter. I thought you could help us figure out who might have done it. We just want the matter resolved with as little brouhaha as possible. I don't even think Jake is looking at pressing charges if the thief will come forward. He wants to settle it quietly. Not make matters worse with lawyers and cops and all that."

"So I'm the bad guy because I called the police?" Peter asked.

"I didn't say that."

Peter grunted, looked away.

"The question is simple enough." Matt leaned forward, keeping his tone even and calm. "Do you have any idea who is behind the missing money? Having had more time to think about all the personnel at Turner Construction, everyone who had opportunity to take the money, anyone who voiced a complaint with Jake or the company or had financial troubles… Does anything come to mind that would help us?"

Peter divided a cool glance between them. "I know it's not what you want to hear, but the only person who has been acting erratically and also has access to the books and deposits is Jake. Everyone at the office knows he's having trouble with Emma. He's been moody for weeks. He wouldn't be the first company owner to try to secretly dip into company funds for personal gain."

Cait clenched her teeth. Shook her head. "No. It's not Jake. There has to be someone else behind this! What about someone from outside the office? A customer who was unhappy? A competitor? Anyone like that?"

From his chair, Peter gave her a flat, pitying stare, which only frustrated and annoyed her all the more. Finally, he said, "All right. For old times' sake, I'll keep an eye out around the office for anything suspicious. If anyone says or does anything that gives a sniff of rotten, I'll let you know. Good enough?"

"We'd appreciate that," Matt said, sounding more reasonable than Cait felt at the moment.

She wanted to scream, wanted to shake Peter until he told her a name, gave her something that would clear Jake and bring order back into her family. Grudgingly, she nodded. With a sigh of exasperation, she shoved to her feet. "If that's all you have, I guess it will have to do."

She looked to Matt, telling him with a lift of her eyebrows that she was done here.

"You surprise me, Cait," Peter said, drawing her attention again. "I'd have thought your own problems at Cameron Glen would be enough to keep you busy."

Her pulse spiked with a heavy throb from her chest. "Sorry?"

"I heard someone died. And some old guy was attacked. That the cops have been out there more times than they've been to the doughnut shop in recent weeks."

She couldn't say if his grin was for what he must have considered a clever quip about the police or smugness over the rash of trouble at Cameron Glen. Either way, his schadenfreude over the recent tragedies and his snarky cops-and-doughnuts comment irked her. She didn't bother asking how he'd heard about the events at the cabins. If living in a small town with an active grapevine wasn't enough, she had no doubt he'd heard at least bits of the story from Jake.

She propped her hands on her hips and sent him a look of disgust. "I am worried about the things that have happened at Cameron Glen. Especially since I'm not one hundred percent sure the events there aren't related to the missing money at Jake's company."

Peter snorted. "Jake's company? I should have known that's how you'd see it."

She frowned. "I'm sorry. What did I say wrong?"

As if sensing the escalating tension inside her, Matt stood and moved close enough to put a hand on her shoulder. Dipping his head close to her ear, he whispered, "Breathe."

Peter's frown said he clearly noticed Matt's intimate attention to her and understood more than they'd admitted about their relationship. The tic of the muscle in his jaw spoke for what she read as jealousy. Or pettiness.

Narrowing his eyes, Peter said, "Jake's last name may be on the construction company, and he may be president and CEO, but his investors own equal shares in the business. It's not just *Jake's* company."

She hiked her chin up, shook her head. "Investors? He doesn't have investors."

His smug look returned. "You see? You really don't know what you're talking about when it comes to Turner Construction. So again, my advice is not to meddle where you shouldn't be."

Matt gave her a side glance. She knew he had a thousand questions for her that he was saving for the privacy of their ride home.

Peter moved to the front door and opened it. "I think we're done here. And while I'd like to say it was good to see you again, I'd rather not lie."

Cait marched toward him, settling her purse strap higher on her shoulder. Stopping in front of him, she clamped her mouth tight as she exhaled harshly. "This side of you is unattractive, Peter. I thought you were better than this."

"Yeah, well…life is full of disappointments, isn't it, Cait?"

Matt strolled up beside them and had the courtesy to offer his hand to Peter. "Thank you for your time. We'll get out of your hair now."

Peter glanced at Matt's hand but ignored it. Finally, Matt moved the proffered hand to the small of Cait's back, possessively ushering her to the passenger side of his Wrangler. He opened the door for her but before she could climb in, he caught her around the waist, drew her close and dipped his head for a long, smoldering kiss.

Chapter 13

Cait caught her breath, stunned. Intrigued. Aroused.

When Matt lifted his head and gazed deeply into her eyes, he said, smiling, "If he's going to act like a jealous ass, I figured we might as well give him a reason to be jealous."

She laughed and rose on her toes to kiss him again. "I like the way you think."

Her insides thrummed with a pleasant trill in her veins as she climbed into the car. She lifted a hand to her tingling lips and smiled. Amazing how Matt's kiss was able to drive out the sour note Peter had left and fill her so quickly and simply with a feeling of warm honey at her core.

After Matt had settled in the Jeep and they were headed back to Cameron Glen, he gave her an inquisitive gaze. "After that visit, how convinced are you of Peter's innocence in this whole matter? Could he be

guilty of the theft? Could he have done it out of re-
venge? Because you broke up with him? Or jealousy?"

"Oh…you buzzkill."

"Huh?"

"Here I was riding high on that kiss you gave me, and
you spoiled it by mentioning *him*." She flashed him a
teasing grin to soften her admonishment.

"Riding high, were you?"

She reached for his arm and gently squeezed his wide
wrist. "Absolutely. You are a magnificent kisser, Matt
Harkney."

"Good to know. I'm a bit out of practice." He stopped
for a red light and faced her, his eyes warm and full of
affection. "You're pretty skilled yourself. I know that
kiss will distract me from my writing this afternoon."

Her heart gave a soft *lub-dub*, and she could have
stared into his fathomless eyes forever. But an impatient
driver behind them honked when the light changed, and
Matt turned his attention back to the road and his previous question.

"Could Peter be involved?"

"Of course he could." Her gut swirled at the possibility. Despite his hurtful comments and rudeness today,
she'd cherished the relationship they'd shared and their
happy times in the past. "It's hard to imagine the Peter I
thought I knew doing something illegal, something that
would hurt Jake and the construction company. I mean…
if we're to believe him, and it's easy enough to verify,
he's the one who called the police to report the theft."

He raised his fingers from the steering wheel in ac-
knowledgment. "But it wouldn't be the first time someone tried to throw the cops off their scent by playing the
victim or the helpful witness."

"Huh. True. And before today, I wouldn't have thought Peter was upset about our breakup. He didn't seem that torn up when I moved out. But today…" She buzzed her lips in dismay.

"Maybe before today he thought he had a chance to get you back. When we first arrived, he seemed genuinely glad to see you. It was only as your allegiance to your family over him became more apparent and your resolve that things were over with him crystalized that he grew more hostile. And my presence, my touching you and sharing secret comments annoyed the hell out of him. That much was plain as day."

"But he didn't know about you—I didn't even know you—when the theft from Jake's happened. This isn't about jealousy."

"Not even jealousy of your relationship with and loyalty to your family? A lot of people wish they had a big loving family around them like you have. What kind of family ties does Peter have?"

"A brother and a sister. His mom lives in Georgia near his sister. I met her once. They aren't close."

"Where's his brother?"

"Uh…" She gnawed her bottom lip as she searched her memory. "Asheville, maybe? Or he was. He's younger than Peter and kinda wayward. Drifts from job to job. Has a drinking problem, like their father did." She twisted her mouth, raked her fingers through her hair. "He's the one that got Peter mixed up in drugs way back when."

Matt gave her a long, hard look that needed no verbalization.

She shook her head vehemently. "Peter's been clean for years. Always regretted his foray into that life. He and David entered rehab together when Peter was twenty. For

Peter, it stuck. For David, not so much. He's been in and out of clinics ever since. I shouldn't have brought it up."

"But his brother…"

She lifted a shoulder. "I'm guessing he's still around somewhere near here. Peter always felt a stronger connection to his brother than his sister because…well, they were brothers. More in common growing up, you know? Peter wanted to 'save' David." She wiggled her fingers to make air quotes. "But you can't help someone who doesn't want to be helped. At least not helped the way you or I would think was best. At least Peter has stopped giving him money. Once I convinced him he was only enabling his brother's bad habits and addictive disease, he cut David off. David was not happy about that, and a pretty big rift split them up about a year and a half ago. Last I heard, they were still not speaking."

"Hmm." Matt drummed the steering wheel again with his thumbs. After a few moments of silence, he said, "I thought you were going to ask Peter what he knew about the break-ins at Hemlock."

"Yeah. Well, I was. But then, when he copped the attitude about it, it felt too much like showing him my cards. And he didn't volunteer any helpful information when he raised the subject, so…" She sighed. "Do you think I should have? Did I miss a chance because I was miffed at him?"

Matt scratched the back of his head and sent her a lopsided grin. "Considering his mood and general unhelpfulness, I don't think he had anything useful that he'd share."

She leaned her head back against the seat, a sinking sensation weighting her gut. "So this whole trip was a waste of time."

Matt reached over and brushed his knuckles softly along her cheek. "Not entirely. Goading Peter did give me the excuse to kiss you the way I'd been aching to for a very long time."

She grinned toward him. "For what it's worth, in the future, you don't need to wait for an excuse."

As before, Matt and Eric were invited to join the Cameron family for Wednesday lunch. Unlike before, Eric seemed genuinely happy to be going.

When Matt commented on Eric's improved mood, his son shrugged it off. "Why not? You gotta admit, the food's a lot better than what we've been eating. I'm getting tired of sandwiches. Plus I know Fenn now. She's cool. And so's her cousin, Daryl. We went fishing together yesterday."

Matt's spirits lifted. What was that—four, five whole sentences from Eric at once, and no sarcasm, either. Progress! "Oh? Catch anything?"

"Just a few small ones. We threw 'em back."

"Maybe the two of us could cast a line together later. I used to be a pretty good fisherman in my day."

Eric cast him an unenthused side glance as they walked from their cabin. "Maybe. I had planned to hang out with Fenn and Daryl. They're going to a movie later."

"Oh. After the movie then?"

Eric shoved both hands in his pockets and walked a bit faster. "Might be too dark by the time we get back. We may get burgers after the movie."

Message received. Eric's mood may have improved but his dad was still *persona non grata*. Matt didn't bother pointing out the sun didn't set until after eight-thirty. No point starting an argument. "Okay, another day then."

And maybe he'd take advantage of Eric being out for dinner to have Cait over for a quiet meal alone. Now that idea put a little pep in *his* step.

As they approached the front porch, a black cat stood from where it had been curled up napping.

"Hi, Magic," Eric said to the cat, approaching the porch slowly, his hand out toward the feline.

"Magic, huh?"

"The Camerons' feral cat. Fenn says she won't let them—"

Before he could finish the sentence, Magic gave the two men a wary look and bolted off the porch into the shrubs.

Eric grunted. "Won't let them pet her."

"Pity. Handsome cat."

"Pretty cat," Eric countered. "She's a girl."

Fenn answered their knock, but she only had eyes for Eric. Matt smiled to himself as they disappeared into the living room together. Eric could do a lot worse for a summer romance. Fenn was a pretty girl and clearly as smart and kind as her Aunt Cait.

"I thought I heard your voice," Cait said, emerging from the kitchen. "Join me in the kitchen? Lunch is almost ready."

Matt glanced in the front room as he passed the door and spotted Eric and Fenn talking to Flora, Neil and Daryl. From her wheelchair, the elderly matriarch laughed at something Eric said. Matt prayed his son was reining in his sarcastic sense of humor to match his audience.

When he entered the kitchen, he found Cait's mother and Isla, heads together at the stove, stirring pots of something that smelled delicious. Emma was preparing a garden salad at the table, and Cait returned to her post at the counter where she was slathering butter on biscuits with a pastry brush. He was about to make a comment about busting up their hen party when Jake tromped up from the basement and entered the kitchen with a dusty jar in his hand.

"Is this what you mean? It's the only one I saw that wasn't grape, blueberry or strawberry." He set the jar of something brownish on the table by his wife.

She turned the jar so that the faded label showed. "Yep. Says right there, apple butter." She gave Jake a withering look.

He pulled a face. "I didn't see that. It was dark in that corner of the cellar."

Emma opened her mouth to reply, and Cait cut her off.

"Thank you, Jake. It will be the perfect complement to the pork chops and biscuits." Cait leaned over and muttered to her sister, "No sniping allowed."

Emma shot her sister an initially defensive look, but quickly schooled her face and nodded.

Jake wiped his dusty hand on the seat of his jeans then extended it toward Matt. Though Jake smiled, Matt noticed the creases in his tanned face that spoke of stress and bleary eyes that hinted at lack of sleep. "Hey, buddy. How's the book coming?"

A tug of guilt for his ignored manuscript wormed through Matt as he shook Jake's hand and frowned. "Rather neglected in recent days, actually. I've been a little distracted by other things."

"What kind of distractions? Has Fenn been over to your place too much?" Jake asked.

"No, no. Fenn's great. She and Eric have really hit it off, and I'm glad he's found a friend this summer." Matt glanced to Cait. "But Cait and I have been looking into a few matters…" He kept his reply intentionally vague. What had she told her brother-in-law about their inquiries on his behalf?

Jake shifted his attention to Cait, as well, suspicion furrowing his brow. "What kind of matters?"

Cait hesitated, and her sisters turned to her. "Oh, uh… we…" She divided a look among the women and Jake, then sighed. "I went to see Peter. Matt and I went, rather."

Emma lay down the knife she'd been chopping cucumbers with and groaned. "Oh, Caitie, why? You're not having second thoughts about breaking up with him, are you?"

Cait waved her hands dismissively. "No. Oh, no, no, no. Especially not after this past weekend."

"Why especially not? What happened?" Emma asked.

"Em, let her talk," Jake grumbled, earning a glare from his wife.

"We," she started, then cut a side glance to Matt. "Well, *I* wanted to ask him what he knew about the missing money from your construction account."

"Cait!" Jake plowed a hand through his thick dark hair and shook his head in irritation.

"Considering the money was found in one of the property's cabins, which Cait manages, it seemed reasonable to *us* that the missing link had to have ties both to Cameron Glen and Turner Construction," Matt said, deliberately using the plural pronoun to deflect some of the attention from Cait's role. "Other than Jake, Peter had the strongest dual link until recently."

"But he only dated Cait," Emma argued. "He didn't have any real access to the cabins." She faced Cait more fully. "How could you not know going to see him again would be a mistake? A step backward in your healing."

"But it wasn't, Em. I'm over him. Really, I am. And his rudeness and the unfair allegations he made when we saw him only cemented for me *how* over him I am."

"Allegations?" Jake said. "Like what?"

Again Matt could see Cait was reluctant to speak about the case to Jake, so he elaborated. "He admitted he was the one who called the police about the missing money."

Jake's mouth compressed in a hard line, and he jerked a nod. "Yeah. I knew that. He claims he was just doing what he thought was right, and I can see his point. But…"

"But it was disloyal of him to point fingers at you without any proof," Cait said hotly.

Jake blinked. "What? He's accusing me of taking the money?"

Cait flattened her hands on the tabletop, clearly choosing her words carefully. Her caution, Matt guessed, was more for Jake's feelings than any loyalty to Peter. "He claims you are the most obvious person. That no one else has as much access and opportunity as you have."

Emma scowled and slapped her hand noisily on the table. "That's ridiculous. More access doesn't mean more guilt. Jake didn't do anything wrong."

Jake arched an eyebrow as he glanced at his wife. "Huh, nice to hear you defend me for a change."

Emma shifted her scowl to her husband. She seemed to be debating whether to take Jake's comment as a compliment or a slam.

Matt jumped in to derail the sidetrack squabble. "For what it's worth, I'm not wholly convinced Peter isn't involved." All eyes in the kitchen swiveled to Matt. "Like we said earlier, he's got the connection to both Cameron Glen, where the money was found, and the company accounts. Cait wasn't just dating Peter." He directed this toward Emma. "They were living together, remember? That involves a much more intimate knowledge of a person's habits and routines. Makes sense he could have learned her routines regarding Cameron Glen, as well. Enough to know the best time to break into an empty cabin. Things like where she kept the schedule of when people checked out, when the cabins were cleaned, when people moved in, where the logbook of which cabins had been rented was kept in the office."

"It's not in the office per se. It's on my laptop, but I back it up to the cloud every night." Cait swallowed visibly, her expression falling. "Peter knew my password. He could have easily logged on as me and gotten any information regarding the property he wanted."

"You didn't change your password after you broke up with him?" Jake asked, aghast.

"I broke up with him because we had different plans for our future, not because I thought he was a criminal. I still trusted him. I didn't really think—" She stopped herself. "I will change it right after lunch."

Emma mumbled something about a horse and a barn door, and their mother swatted at her. "Not helpful, Em."

Jake narrowed a dark look toward Matt. "Go on. What else did you learn from Peter?"

He cut a quick glance toward Cait, who shrugged, before he added, "Well, he did sound bitter about their breakup. It's possible he wanted to strike out at Cait through her family. Through you and the business."

"Are you saying he wanted to frame Jake for the theft? To hurt Cait?" Emma asked, her face paling.

Matt turned up both palms. "I'm just speculating here. I have no proof. What I do know is Peter was none too happy today about my presence or the questions we were asking. He dodged most of our direct questions about other possible suspects by turning things back to Jake."

"As in, 'He doth protest too much?'" Isla asked.

"Mom, when's lunch?" Daryl asked, appearing at the kitchen door. "We're hungry."

"Um, yeah. I hate to be a nag," Isla said, "but I have to be at the airport in Asheville in two hours. Can we eat now and y'all finish this conversation later?"

"The airport?" Matt asked.

"Isla has a conference in Denver. She's presenting a research paper she worked on," Grace said proudly.

"Mom?" Daryl huffed and pantomimed eating.

"All right, Daryl. Go wash your hands and tell the others we're putting the food on the table," Grace said, wiggling her fingers toward her youngest child.

Jake sidled closer to Matt as the women busied themselves getting the serving bowls to the table. "Tell me truthfully—what's your reading of Peter? Should I be watching my back with him? Do you really think he's trying to sabotage the company?"

Matt raised a palm. "I can't speak to more than the one conversation I had with him. But definitely be on guard at work. Not just with Peter, but all your employees. If the thief wasn't you and wasn't Peter, then someone else is pilfering funds. In my experience, once this kind of strife hits a business, everyone's going to distrust everyone else and be looking to cover their own butts. Even the innocent may stab others in the back to protect themselves."

Jake groaned. "Yeah. The office is already in upheaval. I hate it."

"Sorry, man."

Jake's expression hardened, and he gestured with one

hand. "Look, I know you and Cait meant well, but I think your asking questions is just adding fuel to the fire. Could you stand down?" Cait's brother-in-law raised his eyebrows, his expression saying his request was really just a polite command. "Please."

"I think you were right to talk to Peter," Emma said quietly to Cait as they carried the food to the table. "The police act like they don't care. They're moving at a snail's pace. We have to get to the bottom of this and clear Jake's name as soon as possible. He's bringing home the tension at his office, and we've been fighting far too much lately. I hate it!"

"We all see it. Have you thought about counseling?" Cait asked.

"I asked him to go, and he said no. He said everything would be fine as soon as the embezzler was found and the company settled down." She sighed. "But I'm not so sure."

Cait's heart sank. "Emma?"

Her sister shook her head, signaling with a flick of her gaze that the family was gathering and they didn't have privacy anymore. "Later." She clamped a hand on Cait's wrist, though, and leaned close to whisper. "But any more information you can gather by asking around discreetly would be so helpful. Maybe Sandra Greer or Freddy Hall?" she said, naming two other members of the construction company office staff. "People at the office like you. They remember you as the extroverted student body president and girl voted 'most friendly' in high school. They're more likely to talk to you than me, seeing as I'm Jake's wife."

Cait drew and released a slow breath, buying herself

a second or two to consider her sister's request. "Sure. Of course, Emma. I want things resolved for you and for Cameron Glen, too. I'll see what I can do."

As the family took their seats around the lunch table, Cait cast a glance toward Matt. She hated to draw him deeper into her family's problems, and *really* hated to give him more fodder for a true crime book that would put the Camerons in the spotlight, but his unbiased observations, his training as an MP and his writer's attention to detail had already proved valuable.

The family joined hands to say a blessing over the food, and Cait confessed to herself that she also wanted an excuse to spend more time with Matt. She could only hope that her personal desire to get closer to the handsome and charming single father would not come at the cost of her family's peace and privacy.

Chapter 14

The mood around the conference table took a nosedive. He tapped the photographs, the evidence of Hart's treason and—

"And...what?" Matt grumbled, leaning back in his chair and lacing his fingers behind his head. Words had been slow to come today, and his ideas felt cold and flat. Glancing at the window, he chuckled in amusement as a chipmunk scampered along the split-rail fence of the side yard. He admired a male cardinal that swooped down to perch on the low branch of a Fraser fir, then, beyond the cabin yard, he spotted three figures walking by the large pond with fishing poles. Eric, Fenn and Daryl. He smiled to himself, glad to see his son trying the activities the retreat offered and making friends with the other teenagers.

A knock at his door pulled his attention away from the idyllic view, and he found Cait on his porch.

"Sorry to interrupt. I know you were trying to write today," she said quickly.

He shrugged and raised both palms. "You're not interrupting. In fact, my muse is on hiatus today, it seems. I'm finding the scenery here far too distracting to get any work done."

"Good," she said then winced. "I mean…not good that you're distracted, but that you're enjoying the scenery and…well, that I'm not—"

He opened the door wider to admit her. "I knew what you meant. Come on in. I was just about to get some iced tea. Want some?"

"Actually, I was thinking of going to lunch down at Ma's Mountain Kitchen. They have great home-cooked meals there, but more important, they're near the construction company office. The office staff and crew often eat there. I was hoping to talk to some of the other folks from the office and see what I can decipher about the missing money."

Matt angled his head. "Are you sure that's a good idea? Jake didn't seem happy to know we'd questioned Peter. In fact, he asked me to back off our informal investigation."

Her chin twitched up in surprise. "Did he?" She laughed awkwardly. "I guess I'm not surprised. Emma and Jake haven't agreed on much lately. Emma asked me to find out as much as I could. She wants things resolved same as I do, and she's unhappy with the manner in which the police are handling things. I don't like the idea that Peter is laying all this at Jake's feet. I feel like, because of my connection to Peter, it's my responsibility to straighten things out."

"But…it's not." Jamming his hands in his pockets, he eyed her. He didn't like the idea of her mixing herself up in bad business at the construction company any more than Jake did.

She scowled at him, and her shoulders drooped.

After a beat, he said, "However…if the food at Ma's Mountain Kitchen is as good as the coffee we got the other night, it sounds like someplace I need to dine. Nothing says we can't go grab a bite, and if we just happen to run into someone you know, you can introduce me. Sound good?"

Her smile was tinged with both gratitude and relief. "I'll get my car and be back to pick you up in five minutes."

Matt walked a short way down to the pond where he'd seen Eric, Daryl and Fenn fishing, stuck two fingers on his tongue and whistled for his son. He read the embarrassment in his teen's body language, but Eric met him halfway. "Geez, Dad. I'm not a dog."

"But you came up to talk to me, and that's what I needed, so…"

"So…what?"

Matt explained that he was going to lunch with Cait, handed Eric the key to the cabin and offered to bring him back a plate from the restaurant.

"Naw. I think Fenn, Daryl and I are going to order a pizza later."

"More pizza? Don't you ever get tired of it?"

Eric shot him a look that said he'd just asked the stupidest question ever. Matt shrugged. "Whatever. But try to eat some fruit later today, okay?"

"God, you sound like Mom," Eric grumbled.

"Good. I'm glad we agree on your nutrition." He ruffled Eric's hair and received a glower for his efforts. "Good luck with the fish."

Treat Yourself with 2 Free Books!

GET UP TO 4 FREE BOOKS & 2 FREE GIFTS WORTH OVER $20

See Inside For Details

Get ready to relax and indulge with your FREE BOOKS and more!

Claim up to FOUR NEW BOOKS & TWO MYSTERY GIFTS – absolutely FREE!

Dear Reader,

We both know life can be difficult at times. That's why it's important to treat yourself so you can relax and recharge once in a while.

And I'd like to help you do this by sending you this amazing offer of up to FOUR brand new full length FREE BOOKS that WE pay for.

This is everything I have ready to send to you right now:

Try **Harlequin® Romantic Suspense** books featuring heart-racing page-turners with unexpected plot twists and irresistible chemistry that will keep you guessing to the very end.

Try **Harlequin Intrigue® Larger-Print** books featuring action-packed stories that will keep you on the edge of your seat. Solve the crime and deliver justice at all costs.
Or **TRY BOTH!**

All we ask in return is that you answer 4 simple questions on the attached Treat Yourself survey. You'll get **Two Free Books** and **Two Mystery Gifts** from each series you try, *altogether worth over $20*! Who could pass up a deal like that?

Sincerely,

Pam Powers

Harlequin Reader Service

Treat Yourself to Free Books and Free Gifts.

Answer 4 fun questions and get rewarded.

We love to connect with our readers! Please tell us a little about you...

	YES	NO
1. I LOVE reading a good book.		
2. I indulge and "treat" myself often.		
3. I love getting FREE things.		
4. Reading is one of my favorite activities.		

TREAT YOURSELF • Pick your 2 Free Books...

Yes! Please send me my Free Books from each series I select and Free Mystery Gifts. I understand that I am under no obligation to buy anything, as explained on the back of this card.

Which do you prefer?

❏ **Harlequin® Romantic Suspense** 240/340 HDL GRCZ
❏ **Harlequin Intrigue® Larger-Print** 199/399 HDL GRCZ
❏ **Try Both** 240/340 & 199/399 HDL GRDD

FIRST NAME   LAST NAME

ADDRESS

APT.#   CITY

STATE/PROV.   ZIP/POSTAL CODE

EMAIL ❏ Please check this box if you would like to receive newsletters and promotional emails from Harlequin Enterprises ULC and its affiliates. You can unsubscribe anytime.

▶ DETACH AND MAIL CARD TODAY!

© 2022 HARLEQUIN ENTERPRISES ULC
and ® are trademarks owned by Harlequin Enterprises ULC. Printed in the U.S.A.

HI/HRS-520-TY22

As he jogged away, Eric grunted something unintelligible. Matt chuckled wryly and called, "Love you, too!"

Giving the sunny day and grassy lawn appreciative notice, he strolled back up to the driveway. Another of the retreat's renters was walking their dog, and he exchanged pleasantries with the woman until Cait arrived.

Matt settled in the front seat of her small sedan, and once they were on the highway headed down the mountain toward the little town of Valley Haven, he asked, "What do you plan to do if we see Peter or Jake at the diner?"

"Jake takes his lunch most days, so I doubt we'll see him. As for Peter—" she shook her head "—I'll play it by ear. I owe him nothing. You and I are entitled to eat at Ma's if we want to."

"So you have no more questions for him?"

She hesitated before twitching a sardonic smile. "Not ones I want to ask in public."

The conversation shifted to the scenery, to the lack of word from the police regarding the evidence from the Hemlock cabin and to speculation over the nature of Eric and Fenn's relationship.

"She's never had a steady boyfriend, so I hope he'll be kind, not lead her on if he doesn't like her that way," Cait said, gripping the steering wheel harder.

"I hope so, too. But considering how much time he spends with her and the look he gets in his eyes when he talks about her, I think he's rather smitten."

"Smitten?" She chuckled. "Do teenagers still use that word?"

"Probably not." He flashed her a teasing grin. "But antique fathers who study language for a living do. It's a good word!" *And one I'd use to describe how I feel toward you.*

"Agreed," she admitted, chuckling. "And you are not an antique. Far from it."

Matt sighed and rolled his shoulders. Rubbed his injured leg. "I feel like an antique some days."

Cait drew her bottom lip between her teeth for a moment before asking, "Does your leg still give you pain?"

Matt shrugged. "Yes and no. The pain from the amputation is gone, but I get ghost pains some days, and the prosthesis chafes sometimes. I need to see the doc about adjusting it. And I get remnant pain from other injuries I acquired in the bombing—backaches, headaches, etc." He waved a hand. "I don't like to talk about it, and I never want to complain. I survived the attack when others, friends of mine, didn't. I was lucky."

"Lucky?"

Before the conversation devolved into a pity party or deeper discussion of a time he chose to put behind him, Matt shifted his gaze out the front window and down the main street of Valley Haven. "Looks like Ma's is hopping today."

Cait nodded, silently saying she understood his desire to change the topic.

Matt pointed out an empty parking space in the side lot, which Cait took, and once they'd secured the car, he ushered her inside the quaint diner.

The hostess showed them to a small table with two seats near the center of the room. "So," he said, lifting the plastic-encased menu and scanning it, "do you see anyone here from the construction company?"

She lifted her own menu as if to examine it more closely, but her gaze traveled around the room. "No. Not at the moment. But lunch hour just—" Cait's expression reflected surprise, then dread.

He resisted the urge to spin around and look for what had upset her, drawing attention to them. Matt leaned forward, whispering. "What is it? Or should I say, who?"

Cait dragged her attention away from the woman in the corner booth as her stomach flip-flopped. She dropped her eyes to the menu and rolled her shoulders. "The blonde at the table in the corner."

Matt didn't look. "What about her?"

"Her name's Jane. Peter used to date her. Rumor mill has it, two weeks after I moved out, she and Peter hooked up." Cait closed her menu and laid it on the table, making eye contact with Matt. "Not that I care. I left him. He can do what he wants. But she has a reputation for being an opportunist. She's broken up more than one marriage in town."

"In my experience, that's not called being an opportunist. It's being a—"

"Hello, folks." The waitress set two glasses of ice water on the table. "Have you had time to decide what you— Oh, hi, Cait. I didn't realize that was you. How are you?"

Cait glanced up and recognized the waitress as someone with whom she'd gone to high school. "Hi, Linda. How are you?"

After exchanging introductions and the usual pleasantries with Linda, she and Matt each ordered the hot plate special of meatloaf with tomato gravy and homemade biscuits. Once they were alone at the table again, she grinned at Matt. "You were saying about Jane?"

He waved her off. "Nothing polite. So anyone else in here that might have information we want?"

"Hmm. Where to start?" Her attention returned to Jane as the blonde stood and headed to the ladies' room. Cait let her shoulders drop. She knew where she should start. Jane might not be her favorite person, but she was a key figure in the Valley Haven grapevine. "I'm going to the restroom. Be right back."

He glanced over his shoulder and must have figured out her target, because he caught her arm as she passed his chair. The warmth of his fingers against the sensitive underside of her wrist shot ribbons of sweet sensation through her blood. When she met his dark gaze, she could tell he was affected by the contact as well. He wet his lips before warning, "Try not to ask leading questions."

Cait bobbed a nod. "Right."

"And remember, you decided you're better off without Peter, so don't let anything she says about him get under your skin."

Standing there, gazing into Matt's eyes, his thumb stroking her palm, she could easily have said, *Peter who?* For the space of a few seconds, she shut out the other diners, the sound of conversations and clinking utensils, the savory scents from the kitchen. She forgot everything but Matt.

My God, how I want to kiss him! Her heart thumped double time when the thought tripped through her brain. If another diner hadn't bumped her with her purse as she passed, snapping her out of the trance, she might have acted on the impulse. Then Matt dropped her hand, and the spell was completely broken.

She released a shaky breath and flexed her fingers,

trying to clear her mind as she wove through the tables toward the restroom.

In the ladies' room, she stepped up to one of the sinks and turned on the water to wash her hands and kill time until Jane finished her business and came out of the stall. She caught a glimpse of herself in the cracked mirror and did a double take. She wished she'd taken more time to do something besides a lazy ponytail with her hair. Plus, her face was flushed, and she'd apparently nibbled off all her lipstick. She was a mess. Biting her lip was a bad habit she really had to break. As for the color in her cheeks, she could only blame the recent intimate moment with Matt. Which meant he'd undoubtedly seen her physical reaction to him, leaving no secret to her attraction to him.

A toilet flushed, and the door of the stall opened. Using the mirror, Cait watched as Jane approached the sink beside her, straightening her clothes. Putting on a pleasant smile, she chirped, "Jane! Hi. How are you?"

Jane glanced over and gave a perfunctory smile and nod. "Oh, hi, Cait. I'm fine. You?"

"I'm good." *Think, think, think...* She scrambled to come up with a conversation starter that would lead to helpful information without being leading or setting off warning bells.

As Cait fumbled mentally, Jane said, "I hear you and Peter broke up."

"Um, yeah. Where'd you hear that?"

Jane flashed a smug look as she washed her hands. "If you're asking if I've slept with Peter since you dumped him the answer is yes. You'd have no room to complain. You let him go. You have no claim to him anymore."

Wow. Cait blinked, surprised by the not-so-subtle

hostility. She tamped her desire to snap back. *Keep it civil or you won't get anywhere with her.* "No, I do not. Peter is free to date whomever he chooses."

Jane lifted one over-tweezed eyebrow. "You don't seem to be hard up though, judging by the tall drink of water you came in with just now. Who is that guy? I don't recognize him."

Cait couldn't help the grin that rose on her lips when she thought of Matt. "His name's Matt. And we're not an item. He's a friend. A guest at Cameron Glen. He's helping me with a project, so I offered to buy him lunch." Cait ripped a paper towel from the dispenser. "But you're right. He is awfully handsome. Isn't he?"

"Just friends, huh?" Jane turned off the water and pointed to the paper towels. Cait tore a couple off and passed them to Jane. "If I weren't here with Gene, I'd stop by and introduce myself to your *friend*. You know, welcome him to the area?"

Jane's sultry smile made Cait want to claw at her in an old-fashioned catfight. Instead, she swallowed the sour taste in her throat and replied, "Gene who? I didn't recognize your lunch companion either."

Jane flapped a dismissive hand at her. "Oh, you wouldn't. He's from out of town. Gene Gibbs. He's fallen in love with our little neck of the woods and is investing heavily in real estate and land tracts around here." She cocked her head. "In fact, I bet he'd buy Cameron Glen for the right price."

Cait stiffened. "Cameron Glen is not for sale."

Jane smirked. "Honey, for the right price, everything is for sale." She flipped her hair and studied herself in the mirror. "Say, I bet your brother knows Gene, being in the construction business. Or he should. Gene will be needing builders and renovators for his hotels and restaurants."

Gene Gibbs. Cait tucked that name away as she said, "Brother-in-law. Jake is my sister's husband." *Lest you have any ideas of trying to get your claws in him...*

Jane finished drying her hands and tossed the wadded paper towel in the open trash basket. "Oh, that's right. Your brother is that cutie-pie Brody. I've seen him around town working on landscaping jobs. All hot and sweaty and shirtless." Jane flashed a goading grin. "Yum. Is Brody married?"

Cait curled her fingers into fists to keep from slapping the lecherous smile from Jane's face. "No. He's not. What he *is* is a minimum of ten years younger than you."

Jane clearly caught the implied warning and scoffed. "Some men like an older, more experienced woman." With that, Jane sashayed past her to the door and wiggled her fingers in a flippant goodbye.

"*Much* more experienced," Cait grumbled under her breath as the door swung closed. Taking a moment to regain her composure, Cait turned back to the mirror, released her hair from the scrunchie and finger combed her hair around her face. Better. She was not—*not*—primping for Matt, she assured herself as she headed back to the dining room.

But a little voice in her head whispered, *Liar.*

Over lunch, Cait shared with Matt the conversation she'd had with Jane. When she told him about the real estate developer Jane was dating, he sensed something in her voice that alerted him. "Cait? You suspect something is amiss with this guy?"

She tucked her hair behind her ear and twisted her

mouth as she thought. "Not really. He obviously has poor taste in women, but beyond that...who knows?"

Matt snorted. "While a person's known associates can't be dismissed when analyzing a situation, I'm not sure his relationship with Jane is relevant."

"She also made a reference to him trying to buy Cameron Glen, and it set me on my heels."

He hummed sympathetically. "Still, you have to be careful not to let your personal feelings taint your perspective."

She waved her fork toward him. "Which is why I brought you on board. Your experience and unbiased opinion."

He sipped his sweet tea, then cast an encompassing glance around the dining room. "So who's next? Do you recognize anyone else?"

She snorted a laugh. "This is Valley Haven, Matt. Not Charlotte. I recognize half the crowd. The other half is almost assuredly tourists on family vacation."

"Well, even if you don't talk to anyone else, eating here was a good idea. If for no other reason than this is the best meal I've eaten—besides the lunches with your family—in quite a while."

"You can always count on Ma's for good food," Cait said, nodding her agreement. Then her shoulders drooped. "But beyond lunch, I feel like this venture was a bust. I can't see where we've gleaned anything useful."

"Don't lose hope. We can try some other businesses before we go home."

She buzzed her lips in frustration. "Maybe we should head over to the Cut and Curl. Don't they say beauty parlors are a hive of gossip?"

Matt raked his fingers through his hair. "Well, if you're serious, I suppose I could use a trim. For the cause."

Cait gave a breathy chuckle and shook her head. "Well, I was semi-serious. But not at the expense of your hair. I like the way it curls under at your nape and around your ears. It's sexy."

He sat taller in his chair. Despite knowing she was teasing—she was teasing, right?—her characterization set his pulse thrumming. He hadn't forgotten the color that rose in her cheeks or the fire that had lit her eyes when he'd held her arm and stroked her wrist earlier. For a brief moment, something powerful and evocative had passed between them. He was sure of it. He'd thought of little else as they ate, wondering if he should address the spark of attraction growing between them.

Linda, their waitress, appeared with the check, and his chance to press her about her "sexy" comment dissipated. After leaving their bill on the table, Linda directed a hesitant look at Cait. "I know I shouldn't ask, but seeing as my brother was good friends with Jake in high school...well, I heard that he was questioned by the police this week. Something about a theft at the construction company?"

Cait's gaze flicked from Linda's to Matt's and back to the waitress. "Um, he was. But just questions. He wasn't arrested. He's done nothing wrong."

Linda laughed awkwardly and raised a hand. "Oh, honey, I know he's not the sort to do anything criminal. My brother used to tease him about being so saintly. Jake wouldn't let him cheat off his test papers, never cut school, never even shared the same music files with Gregory because he said it was stealing from the artist."

"That's Jake," Cait said. "Honest to a fault."

"So someone stole something from the company? Like what? Was it tools? Building supplies? Wait, I've heard of people stealing the copper wire from buildings because the resale value is so high."

Cait shook her head. "No. I mean, yes, that happens, and Jake has to take precautions to secure sites, but…" She glanced at Matt again, and her expression seemed to ask what to do. Protect the truth or confirm it?

Matt jumped in. "There has been some trouble at the company, yes. Jake was trying to help the police resolve the issue."

Linda shifted her curious and concerned gaze to him. "What kind of trouble? If I may ask?"

"What have you heard?" Matt volleyed back. "And from whom?"

"Well…" Linda shifted her weight and sent Matt a wary gaze. "Seein' as how we're pretty much across the street from the police station, everybody who works here, from cashiers to the cooks, knew about Jake getting brought in by a cruiser the other night. And when most of the family followed…" Linda shrugged and glanced back at Cait. "Look, I like your family and I don't mean to be nosy—" she frowned "—although I guess that's really what I'm being—but if I can shut down the speculation and keep the record straight with all the gossipers that come through here…"

When Linda let her voice trail off, Cait drew a slow breath. "What you know is really all anyone needs to know until we get to the bottom of things. Tell people, yes, the police are investigating a theft at Turner Construction. Jake was questioned to help the police solve the theft. Most of all, Jake is innocent of any wrongdoing."

Cait's assertion about her brother-in-law shot an uneasy quiver to Matt's gut. Other than faith in her family, Matt had seen no proof Jake wasn't involved in the theft in some way. He didn't relish suspecting the man, whom he liked based on his brief encounters with him. But his training, both as a military police officer and as a writer, was not to rely on speculation or faith. He needed facts. Proof.

He hated to think of Cait's heartache should her belief in and trust of her brother-in-law be broken.

Chapter 15

"Just a trim," Matt told the hairdresser at Cut and Curl, who'd introduced herself as Madison. "I've been told that a bit of length curling at my collar and ears is sexy."

He sent Cait a grin.

The twentysomething hairdresser with pink streaks in her own hair and bright fuchsia fingernails patted him on the shoulder. "Definitely sexy. In fact, I wouldn't do more than shape it up a bit."

Having merely been teasing Cait, and certainly not digging for a compliment, Matt was startled by Madison's reply. He hadn't thought of his own attractiveness—or not—in years. In the past several years, he'd gotten married, become a father, served as a soldier and dealt with the aftermath of traumatic injury, scars and emotional baggage.

Cait's see-I-told-you grin burrowed to his core. Forget Madison, who was threading her fingers through his hair and deciding what to cut. Having Cait look at him with that bewitching lopsided grin and come-hither expression in her eyes made him *feel* attractive. And hopeful. He hadn't forgotten the sparks that fired in his blood when he'd kissed her outside Peter's house.

The prospect of pursuing this mutual attraction with Cait left him impatient to finish their business in town and get back to the cabin, where they might find a bit of privacy for—

Snip!

The first lock of hair dropped in his lap, and he snapped his attention back to his image in the mirror. *Best pay attention so you don't leave with a hipster style you hadn't intended.*

"Madison," Cait said, "I'm sure you've heard about Jake being questioned by the police."

The hairdresser nodded as her scissors flashed and snipped. "Everyone has by now. You know how small towns are."

"Hmm, I do. It's just hard when someone you love is at the center of the gossip. I want to do my part to dispel the lies and keep misinformation from spreading."

"This day and age?" Madison cackled a laugh. "Good luck with that."

Cait raised her eyebrows in a you're-not-wrong gesture and nibbled the corner of her lip.

"So what were you gonna say about Jake?" Madison asked, turning the barber's chair to access another part of Matt's hair.

He continued watching both women via the mirror as Cait restated her faith in Jake's innocence, downplayed the significance of his interview with the police and corrected Madison's misinformation regarding Mary's death.

At a brief lull in discussion, Matt took a chance and asked Madison, "Do you know someone named Gene Gibbs?"

Cait's chin jerked up, and her eyes widened. Madison didn't seem to notice Cait's reaction as she tidied the hairline at Matt's nape.

Madison screwed up her face. "Hmm. Naw. Should I?"

Matt grunted. "Not necessarily. I was told he was the guy to see if I wanted to invest in property around here."

Madison paused and slapped the comb in her hand against the opposite palm. "Wait a minute. I do remember David Fanton—" She hesitated and glanced at Cait. "You know. Peter's brother." A statement, not a question.

Cait nodded, her expression saying Madison was stating the obvious. "Yeah. I know David."

Madison, reassured Cait was on the same page, flapped her hand and went back to work trimming Matt's hair. "Right. Of course. Anyway, David was in here getting a cut a couple weeks ago, and he—"

"David's in town?" Cait blurted.

"Yeah. Moved back a few months ago, I think."

"Oh. Huh." Cait schooled her face, obviously trying to play down her surprise over this bit of information. Well, obvious to Matt. Madison didn't seem to be paying attention to Cait's body language the way he was.

"So…" Madison picked up again, her eyes trained on Matt's head and her scissors, "David was talking about some investor guy Peter said was buying the empty lot down by the Pump-N-Save to build a motel or something. I told David what we needed was a movie theater. And a bowling alley. There's nothing to do around here within twenty miles." Madison traded her scissors and comb for an electric razor. "Anyway, I wonder if that Gibbs guy is the same one building the motel. I could ask Peter for you, if you want."

"Uh, no," Cait said, quickly, then with a chuckle and a light tone, added, "I do still have Peter's number. But thanks."

Madison shrugged. "Whatevs. Didn't know you were still speaking to him."

"Our breakup was civil."

The hairdresser put away the razor and used a tiny brush to clean Matt's neck. "All done. What do you think?"

Matt examined his image in the mirror, surprised to find he liked what Madison had done. A lot. "I think I need to send my son down here to get a cut from you. This is great. Thanks."

As he dug out his wallet to pay for the cut, he sorted through the information they knew about the case and what they still needed to know. Was there anything else they needed to ask or confirm before they left the Cut and Curl? Could he ask anything else without raising suspicion?

Cait stood, settling the strap of her purse on her shoulder, a clear signal that she thought they should go. They thanked Madison again and left the shop together, stepping into the baking summer heat, reflected from the asphalt, and stifling humidity.

He waited for the shop door to close before asking, "Well, what do you think?"

With a side glance, Cait replied, "Very nice. I'd say she improved upon the sexy." She reached up and fingered the hair behind his ear. "I like it. A lot."

A rush of pure pleasure shot through him, from his scalp, where her fingers toyed, to his groin. The spark of interest in her eyes and seductive smile tugging her mouth only heightened the sensation.

He chuckled and cleared his throat. "Thank you. I was actually talking about what she had to say. Does any of it ring alarms for you?"

She dropped her hand from teasing his hair and strolled toward her car, parked in a side lot. "Well, David is an unknown factor. I didn't get to know him that well, myself, but according to Peter, he's always been rather unpredictable. Drifting from place to place, job to job. Struggling to stay sober. Going where the wind blows him. But is he tangled up in all this?" She lifted a hand, her expression saying she was at a loss. "Why would he be? I don't know." She clicked her key fob to unlock her car. "Why did you ask about Gibbs? And so...directly?"

Matt twisted his mouth in thought as he walked to the passenger door. "Your reaction to Madison mentioning David. David's interest in Gibbs. The fact that this Gibbs guy is in a business that aligns with Turner Construction. And...a gut feeling. Seemed a valuable risk to take, and being an out-of-towner, my asking seemed less likely to raise questions."

Cait gave a hum that indicated she was considering his reply, then climbed in her car. Before Matt followed suit, he gave the small-town business district a quick appraisal. Diner. Police station. Auto repair shop. Real estate office. Bakery. Quiet. Calm. And yet...

A prickling sense of being watched, which he'd honed while in Afghanistan, crawled up his spine and bit his neck. He let his gaze drift back over the area he'd just scanned, but still nothing leaped out at him.

"Matt?" Cait called from inside the car. "Something wrong?"

He sighed and settled in the passenger seat. "Guess not."

But despite his reassurances to her, as they drove out of town, he couldn't shake the sense that they'd attracted someone's notice. And things were not as quiet and calm in Valley Haven as appearances might suggest.

He climbed in the front seat of Gibbs's truck, flop sweat pouring off him, and without preamble, Gibbs handed him a cell phone with the screen opened to a slightly fuzzy photograph, one that had been clearly taken from long range and zoomed in, losing pixelation. "Know him?"

He studied the photo carefully. Shook his head. "No. Never seen him before."

His answer clearly displeased Gibbs, so trying to win points, he added, "But I know who she is. That's Cait Cameron. Her family owns that property off the highway north of town called Cameron Glen."

A muscle in Gibbs's jaw flexed. "I already knew who she was. Jane told me all about her. It's the guy I'm interested in."

He handed the phone back to Gibbs. "Why?"

Gibbs's expression grew flinty, and for a moment he worried he'd crossed a line by asking. Then the land developer said, "Jane said her friend Avery was in the break room at the Cut and Curl eating her lunch when she overheard one of the other stylists discussing recent events with a couple in the front of the shop."

"Cait and this guy?" he guessed.

"Exactly. Avery told Jane she didn't pay much mind. They talked about Cait's brother some, and Avery was payin' more attention to texting her husband when she heard the guy ask about me. Point-blank."

He blinked. "You?"

"Yeah. Me. And I don't like folks knowing about me when I don't know them. Right?"

"Yeah, right." He'd agree to anything Gibbs said if it meant he got out of that truck alive.

"So I got two jobs for you." Gibbs angled his body toward him. "You take care of these jobs for me, and I'll give you some more time to pay back that money you owe."

He sat taller. "How much more time?"

"Is that a yes?"

He swiped at the perspiration rolling down his temple. Any extra time to find the money he needed to pay off his debt was worth it. He nodded. "Yeah. What do ya need me to do?"

Chapter 16

That night, Cait tossed and turned, unable to sleep as she stewed over how little information they'd learned in town, the unanswered questions about how the money got in the Hemlock cabin and her confrontation with Peter earlier in the week. Had he always been that petty and sarcastic and she'd turned a blind eye? After all the years he'd worked with Jake, how could Peter possibly think that Jake had anything to do with the stolen money?

David was in town. Peter might have an alibi that passed muster with the police for the night the teenagers saw a man break into the Hemlock cabin, but could his brother be involved with this whole frustrating, confusing situation? Why would he?

She heard Jane's taunting tone when she'd mentioned her current boyfriend making a bid to buy Cameron Glen. *Honey, for the right price, everything is for sale.*

Cait huffed and gritted her teeth. *Wrong, Jane. My family's heritage, my home is priceless. I will never let it be sold.*

With a restless sigh, she tried to shove the ill ease and circular thoughts from her brain and quiet her mind. But what took the place of her distressing ruminations shot a new jolt of adrenaline and wakefulness through her.

Matt's kiss. The tenderness. The crackling energy and tingling pleasure that had surged through her blood from the instant his lips touched hers. The desire that lit his dark eyes when he looked at her afterward, making her feel like the most beautiful woman in the world. He was a skilled kisser, that was certain. And she'd wanted to go on kissing him, wanted to explore his body with her hands and savor the feel of his hard body pressed close to hers. For a few precious moments, she'd been able to block out the world, stressful family issues, and all the reasons she'd told herself getting involved with Matt was a bad idea.

He said he'd been wanting to taunt Peter. Maybe he didn't have the same interest in her she had for him. Maybe…

Maybe she could indulge in a fling before he left and keep her heart out of it?

Cait grunted and rolled to her side, knowing flings were not and would never be her style. She needed love and loyalty before she could be that intimate with a man. Another reason why Peter's lack of commitment and true passion had stung her so deeply. She punched her pillow and tried to ignore the throb at her core when she replayed Matt's kiss in her mind's eye.

Sleep. Again she tried to clear her mind. Quiet the clamor. But the night was filled with its own symphony of noises.

The low creak of the cabin settling. The chatter of a raccoon—*that better not be in the trash, dang it!* The rustling wind in the trees. Pickles and Petunia bleating. She'd never noticed before how noisy her house and yard could be at night. Maybe she was just jumpy because Isla was out of town and the sanctity of Cameron Glen had been breached by the recent intruder. Trying to blank her mind and get to sleep seemed impossible tonight. With a resigned sigh, she tossed back her covers, stumbled to the kitchen for a cup of chamomile tea and dug a pair of earplugs out of the bathroom drawer before returning to bed.

Finally sleep came—

Only to be interrupted by a firm hand pressed to her mouth.

Cait's eyes flew open, panic surging as she struggled against the grip of the ski-masked man hovering over her in the dark bedroom. She smelled tobacco on his fingers and cigarette smoke on his breath as he leaned close. He ripped the earplugs from her ears by their tiny plastic cord and hissed, "Keep your nose out of things that aren't your business, or next time I visit you—" She heard a metallic *snick*, then the sharp tip of a knife poked her neck. "I'll slit your damn throat. Got it, chickadee?"

She gave a feeble nod, tears stinging her eyes.

He released her with a brutal shove and darted out of her bedroom.

For several shocked seconds, all Cait could do was gulp oxygen and tremble. His threat replayed in her head, sending ice to her core.

She heard the back door close and, mustering the wherewithal and courage to act, she slipped to the floor by her window to peek out. The dark-clad figure of her intruder crossed the yard, passed the goat pen and disappeared into the shadows of the trees behind her house.

Adrenaline buzzed in her ears. Slowly her shocked brain cleared and shouted, *Do something!* She needed to call 911.

Fumbling her phone from her nightstand, she woke the screen. But instead of the police she found herself calling Matt. First and foremost, she wanted Matt, to hold her, to reassure her. His number was the last one she'd dialed, and her thumb hit redial without a second thought.

His groggy voice answered, and her heart leaped.

"Someone b-broke in. He—" Her voice cracked. "I need you."

"What! Cait? Oh my God!" His tone was alert now and full of alarm. "Are you all right? Is he still there?"

"He's gone, b-but I— Can you come?"

"I'm on my way."

Matt disconnected, and she stared at her phone numbly for a few more seconds, shaking head to toe. After a few more seconds to collect herself, she called the police. She was still on the phone with the emergency operator when Matt pounded on her front door.

"Cait! Open up. It's me."

She dropped her cell phone on the slim table in the foyer and snatched open the door. Immediately, he pulled her into his arms. There was a loud clatter as he hugged her. When she finally released him and took a step back, she surveyed the man standing on her porch. One bare foot peeked from beneath the right leg of his sleep pants. The left pants leg flapped loosely. He'd come without taking the time to put on shoes…or his prosthetic foot. A pair of crutches lay discarded on the porch. She bent to retrieve the supports for him.

When she straightened, his hands smoothed the hair back from her face, and his gaze raked over her. "What happened? Did he hurt you? Are you sure you're all right?"

"I am now." She stepped back into his embrace, feeling warm tears leak onto her cheeks. "Oh, Matt, it was terrifying. He had a knife at my throat! I've never felt so vulnerable. So violated. He—"

Matt stiffened and pushed her to arm's length again, his grip on her arms tightening. "What? Are you saying he…?"

She shook her head. "No. No, poor choice of words."

Except they weren't. A strange man had been in her bedroom, had touched her, had threatened her both verbally and with a weapon. Her home, privacy and personal safety *had* been violated. She shuddered, and as Matt guided her inside, she retrieved her phone from the foyer table. "Yes, I'm sorry. I'm here. My friend just arrived."

After being assured the police were on their way, Cait put the call on speaker and set the phone aside. She sank onto the couch beside Matt. He held her hand as she explained about being woken from her sleep, the hand over her nose and mouth, the man's threat.

Matt grumbled darkly, a ridge in his brow as he frowned. "It's settled then. Until we know who that bastard was, who has been breaking in the cabins—and they're behind bars—I'll be staying here with you. I don't want you alone."

She levered back to regard him with a quirked eyebrow. "Oh? And what about your son? You plan to leave him alone at your cabin?"

Matt's mouth compressed in a firm line. "No. I—" He scrubbed a hand on his stubbled cheek. "But I can't leave you alone here."

"Isla will be back in a few days. I—"

"A few days is a few days too many. Go to your parents' house. Or Emma's."

She shook her head. "Emma has enough on her plate to worry about. And I don't want to upset my parents. They, and Nanna, don't need to know about what happened tonight." She scraped her bottom lip with her teeth, searching for courage. If she hadn't just been attacked, maybe it would be easier to quell Matt's concerns. But she was still shaking at her core. She gave him a false smile. "I'll be fine."

He twisted his mouth in thought. "Yeah. You will. Because Eric and I both will stay with you until I'm convinced the danger has passed."

"Wha…? Matt, no. I—"

He silenced her protest with a kiss. The sweet shock of his lips on hers sent a different kind of quaver to her core. Cait clung to his shoulders. The solid strength of him calmed the jitters that danced along her nerves, and the gentle caress of his kiss blotted out the looping images of the intruder. When he raised his head and met her gaze with passion firing in his eyes, she muttered huskily, "You make a very convincing argument, Mr. Harkney."

After an initial grin, he sobered, his eyes narrowing. "I don't want you to feel I've pushed my way in or manipulated you. That kiss was just because… Hell, just because I've thought of nothing else since the last time I kissed you."

"Same here," she admitted. "Well, kissing you and the trouble my family is going through. But certainly your kiss was the more pleasant option."

He leaned in to brush his mouth against hers again, then, with his forehead touching hers, he sighed. "So Eric and I will sleep here for the next little while. Okay? We'll be fine on the couch and in that recliner." He jerked his head toward the comfy chair across the room.

"What's Eric going to say about this?"

"If he's half the man I've raised him to be, he'll understand and be in full agreement. If not, it will be a lesson to him on doing the right thing and looking after the people you care about."

"I'm not a damsel in distress, Matt. You don't have to do this."

"No. I don't mean to imply you are helpless or needy or anything like that. But answer me this. Will you feel better, safer, calmer, knowing we're here instead of being alone?"

She opened her mouth. Closed it. The truth thumped through her chest with heavy beats of her heart. The reality was, she wanted Matt close, protective detail or not. She enjoyed his company. Savored his kisses. Wanted... more. She stroked a hand along his cheek. "When you put it that way..."

He flashed a triumphant smile, and with a hand cupped behind her head, nudged her closer for a nuzzle, a light kiss. Then a deeper, more urgent kiss that reverberated in her soul. She sank against him and draped her arms around his neck. Her fingers burrowed through his hair, and she inhaled the familiar, woodsy scent that surrounded him. The complimentary soap that Cameron Glen provided in the cabins. On Matt the spice-and-pine aroma was sexy as hell. Or was it just that Matt, his touch, his lips on hers, was so incredibly intoxicating to her?

A pounding on her front door jolted her from the blissful diversion, rattling her nerves anew.

"Ms. Cameron? It's the police," a male voice called.

"Coming!" Regret for the lost moment weighted her chest as she pulled away and hurried to the door. She recognized the officers immediately. The same ones who'd responded to previous calls in recent weeks. "Well, Officer Smith, Officer Martinez, this is becoming an unfortunate routine, you making trips out to Cameron Glen."

Officer Smith flipped up his palm. "We'll come as many times as needed. That's our job."

Matt hobbled over on his crutches and stopped behind Cait. "Your job is also to find the creep who's been breaking in the buildings on the property so that the Camerons are safe in their own beds at night. Some guy got into Cait's bedroom tonight and threatened her." Matt's tone spoke for his frustration, irritation and impatience with the police.

"How long ago was this? Is he still on the premises?" Officer Smith asked.

Cait shook her head. "As far as I know, he left the way he came in. I heard the back door, saw him head into the line of trees so I assumed—" She shuddered, reliving the suffocating hand over her nose and mouth. The terror of finding the dark-clad figure in her room. His gravelly, menacing voice. "I was in shock. Scared. I really haven't taken the time to search the property, check any windows…"

"Did he have a weapon?"

She nodded. "A knife. A switchblade, I think, because I heard him open it. It was dark, so I can't say what the blade looked like."

Officer Smith unsnapped the holster where he wore his service weapon and glanced over his shoulder. With a nod, he sent Officer Martinez toward the back of the house to begin searching. "Did you recognize him?"

She shook her head. "He wore a ski mask and talked in a low, whispering voice." She told him everything she could about his size, the smell of cigarettes, the clothes he wore.

When she'd given the officer all she could remember, he flipped closed his notepad and nodded to her. "I need both of you to please stay in the living room while we search the property. Is anyone else here?"

"No, my sister is out of town. It's just us."

When the officer gave her and Matt's dishabille a quick up-and-down glance and a knowing twitch of his eyebrow, she felt Matt tense. She placed a hand on Matt's arm to still him. An active gossip mill was part and parcel to living in a small town. And she really didn't care what anyone thought or whispered anymore. She was *done* with judgmental people.

Besides, she wasn't opposed to a relationship with Matt like the one Officer Smith probably assumed she had.

"Were you here when the intruder confronted Ms. Cameron?" Officer Smith asked Matt.

Matt blinked, squared his shoulders. "No."

"Where were you?"

Matt narrowed his eyes, clearly unhappy with the questions. "At my cabin, asleep. The Fraser cabin. Before you ask, I can't prove it." His tone was civil. Barely. "My son was asleep, as well."

"I called Matt, woke him up, before I called the police, and Matt was here within a couple minutes." She tightened her grip on Matt's arm, and he covered her hand with his.

Officer Smith made a notation on his notepad, then gave them a long, steady gaze.

"I was just so scared. And I knew Matt was close by. That he'd come, that he could be here quickly," she explained without being asked.

Matt squeezed her hand, and Officer Smith dipped his head in a nod. "Okay. I'm going to take a look in the house. All right?"

"Yes. Of course." She sidled out of the officer's way, and he headed down her hallway, checking rooms one by one, his hand on his service weapon.

Despite the warm night, a chill slithered through Cait, and she rubbed her arms.

"Hey," Matt said, moving closer. He raised his hand to her cheek and stroked his thumb on her bottom lip. "Stop abusing that beautiful mouth. Everything's going to be fine."

She hadn't even realized she was chewing her lip until he touched it. A different sort of tremor rolled through her then. One far more pleasant.

"Come on." He hitched his head toward the couch. "Sit with me and let them work."

She followed Matt as he returned to the couch, his crutches thumping on the hardwood floor. When she dropped on the cushions, he snuggled her close and kissed her head. "You're okay."

Something in his tone made her wonder if he was reassuring her—or himself.

Several anxious minutes later, the two Valley Haven police officers returned to her living room to report no sign of anyone on the premises. Neither had they found evidence of forced entry. "Did you lock your doors tonight?"

"I—" Cait blinked. "I don't remember checking them. I'm not in the habit of locking our doors yet."

The police officer lifted an eyebrow in a silent rebuke.

"Cameron Glen is a safe retreat in a safe town," she said in her defense, then added in a mumble, "At least, it used to be. We saw no need."

She heard Matt's disgruntled sigh.

"Well, from now—" Officer Martinez began.

"I will lock my doors and see that my family does as well."

After seeing the police officers to the door, Cait returned to the front room where Matt waited for her.

"Cait…" His tone was incredulous.

She held up a hand. "Our lax security habits haven't been an issue in all the years my family has lived at and operated Cameron Glen."

"It's a different day and age."

Sitting on the edge of the sofa cushion, she propped her arms on her legs and let her head droop forward. With one hand, she pinched the bridge of her nose as she sighed. "Yes, it is." She felt the warmth and weight of Matt's hand on her shoulder. "Geez, I'm exhausted. And yet I don't think I'll sleep another wink tonight. Every time I close my eyes, I see that man's masked face. Hear the flick of the knife. And I feel the terror all over again."

"Perfectly understandable. And one hundred percent normal. Especially this soon after it happened." Matt scooted closer and slid his other strong, wide hand to her shoulders. His thumbs dug into the tense cords of her neck as his fingers and palms squeezed her taut shoulder muscles.

A moan of pleasure escaped her throat, and when he tugged her to his lap, she went willingly. He continued to work his magic, kneading the stiffness of the recent weeks' stress from her back and nape and arms. She relaxed by degrees, growing limper and more pliant with each heavenly stroke and healing rub. When he brushed her hair away from the back of her neck and placed a soft kiss there, she thought her body would go up in flames. Never had one simple kiss been so enticing and erotic for her. Until he repeated the kiss, nipping lightly at a tendon with his teeth before soothing the spot with a deeper kiss.

"Do something for me?" he asked, his voice a husky whisper.

"Mmm, anything. Right now, I'd promise to give a speech to my high school class while naked if it would keep you doing what you're doing with those talented hands."

He laughed quietly, a rich, seductive rumble from his chest. "Nothing quite as daunting as that." He paused, and she heard him inhale deeply. "Although the naked part sounds intriguing."

A fresh ripple of awareness skittered over her skin and left her tingling. "What then?"

"Expedite getting those security cameras installed around the retreat?"

The reminder of the evening's danger shot a streak of cold to her belly, and she grunted her disapproval. "I've got the work order in, but I'll call and put a rush on them tomorrow." She turned so that she was facing Matt at an angle. "But thanks for the mood killer."

He arched one black eyebrow. "We had a mood?"

She sent a telling glance to his lap, where his own arousal was obvious. "Didn't we?"

Smoothing his hand along her cheek to cup her jaw, he smiled. "Well, then, allow me to repair the damage."

Matt leaned in and pressed his lips to hers. The contact sent sensation like lightning through her blood.

She wrapped her arms around his neck and slanted her mouth over his, deepening the kiss and sinking against his sturdy frame. When his tongue darted out to tease the seam of her lips, she opened to him, greeting his foray in kind.

When they finally came up for air, Matt rested his forehead against hers and whispered, "Now how's the mood?"

She swallowed hard and rasped, *"Crivvens."*

He chuckled. "I'm going to take that in a good way."

She licked her lips and sighed happily. "Very good."

His palms framed her face, and he canted back far enough to lock his gaze with hers. "If I had two good legs, I'd scoop you in my arms and carry you down the hall to your bedroom right now."

Her heart jolted. Cocking her head to one side she sent him a scolding frown. "For one thing, I think your legs are perfectly good, in every way that matters to me."

His answering smile was humble and touched.

"And second," she added, "I don't need caveman theatrics to get me to my bedroom. As long as we end up there together, I'm perfectly happy to walk."

"Caveman theatrics? I thought he-man gestures like that were romantic."

"Oh, well, I did swoon a little when Rhett swept Scarlett up the stairs. But romantic gestures are really more about what's important and thoughtful for each couple."

He nodded. "I agree there."

She nestled in close again, trailing her fingertips along his scratchy jaw. "For example, you showing up on my porch so quickly after I called tonight, in your PJ pants and without your prosthetic leg?" She raised both eyebrows and nodded. "Very romantic."

When he wrinkled his brow dubiously, she kissed his nose. "Because it said to me—" kissed his cheek "—how important it was to you—" kissed his chin "—to get to me—" kissed his mouth "—as fast as you could."

She felt the shudder that raced through him.

He threaded fingers through her hair and traced the shell of her ear. "That was my single focus." His smile twisted with irony. "So much so that I didn't process in the moment that I could actually have reached you faster if I'd put on my leg. Crutches were not built for speed."

She laughed and rewarded him with another lingering kiss. "I was still touched. And now…" She bent to retrieve the crutches from the floor where they'd fallen and flashed a seductive grin. "I'll give you a head start and race you to my bedroom."

"No head start needed." He jammed the crutches under his arms and rose nimbly. "Readysetgo!"

With a happy squeal, she scampered after him.

Chapter 17

Cait kicked at the sheet that trapped her legs and sent it to the floor to lie in a pile with her nightshirt and Matt's sleep pants. Their bedclothes had landed on top of each other, much as she and Matt had, the moment they reached her room.

Now, some indeterminate and blissful time later, her ceiling fan sent a gentle breeze to cool her sweat-slicked skin as she wiggled her way on top of Matt. Free of the sheets that had hampered her movement, she could explore the feast for her senses that was Matt's lean torso and broad shoulders. She ran hungry hands over his chest, then bent to steal a kiss from the mouth that smiled up at her like the Cheshire cat. "You look smug."

"Not smug. Just happy. Satisfied."

She quirked a grin. "Satisfied? After one round? I was only getting started."

He gave her fanny a playful pat. "Satisfied, my dear,

does not mean finished. Even a little bit of you pleases me in a big way."

"Mmm, likewise," she purred as she snuggled against him again and stole more kisses. When she angled her head toward him, his expression was pensive. "Matt? What?"

"So…does that—" he nodded toward his damaged left leg "—bother you?"

She was so surprised by his question that for a moment she could only stare blankly at him. How could he think she'd care anything about his amputation? Especially after…

Clearing her throat, she levered back and pointed to a pale pink line on the right side of her lower abdomen. "Does this bother you?"

He frowned, squinting at the spot she pointed to. "Does what?"

"My scar. I had my appendix removed when I was eighteen."

He snorted. "Cait, be serious."

"I am serious! If you think I might be disturbed over your lack of a shin and foot, maybe you're the sort who'd be bothered that I don't have an appendix." She knit her brow in thought. "Or my tonsils, come to think of it."

He tugged her closer and propped his chin on the top of her head as he hugged her. "Okay! Point taken. But a leg is a little different. I just thought—" He sighed. "Well, I haven't been with a woman other than Jessica since it happened. I guess I was…a little self-conscious."

"Well, stop. It's a nonissue for me." Twisting her mouth in a playful grin, she added, "Especially when you are so skilled with, uh…other parts of your anatomy."

Matt barked a laugh. "Umm…thank you…for that."

Cait drew little circles on his chest with her finger, so-bering. "However, it occurs to me that the real issue may be that you want a chance to talk about it."

"My anatomy?" he said in a tone that let her know he was being purposely obtuse.

"The explosion. You said you lost the leg because of a roadside bomb while you were stationed in Afghanistan?" She used her tone to turn the statement into a question, inviting him to fill in the blanks, tell her as much or as little as he wanted about the events that had left him an amputee.

"Huh, right." He folded one arm behind his head while he traced lazy patterns on her bare arm with the fingers of his other. "I don't have a lot of detail. The explosion knocked me out."

She burrowed close to him, her body pressed to his despite the sticky warmth in the cabin from the day's remnant summer heat. Above her, the ceiling fan clicked a steady cadence as it rotated. A drowsy lethargy stole over her as she listened to his deep voice whisper in the darkness. So at peace. So happy. So secure. Amazing to her that mere hours before this same spot had been a scene of icy fear and dread.

The difference, clearly, was Matt. She accepted that truth at face value, knowing she'd have to examine it more closely by the light of day. But for now, she simply wanted to savor…

"I can remember joking with some of my patrol mates about the awful Italian movie we'd watched the night before. The subtitles were way behind the action on the screen, and after a while we just turned off the closed-caption translation and made up our own dialogue."

He chuckled, and she felt the vibration from his chest beneath her hand.

"One guy in particular, Billy Nash, was aces at improvising one-liners for the actors."

She smiled, imagining Matt cutting up with his fellow soldiers.

"Anyway, it was just business as usual one minute, then the ground shook and my ears rang, and the next thing I remember is waking up in a field hospital, about to be loaded on a helo and transferred to an Army hospital in Germany."

Cait tightened her grip on his shoulder. "Oh, Matt."

"It's probably a blessing I don't remember anything else about it. The guys who survived it said it was…bad."

She caught her breath. "You said earlier you lost friends in the bombing. How many?"

He nodded slowly. "Three casualties. Two men and a woman. All friends. All good people."

She touched a puckered scar at his waist. "Did you get this then, too?"

"Nope." He grinned at her look of surprise. "That's from a skateboard accident when I was nine. Tony Hawk, I am not." He pushed the sheet out of the way and pointed to several red scars on his thigh, his hip and the small of his back. "These are from the bomb. I also lost part of my liver and have some hardware reinforcing my right knee. That, more than the prosthesis, is why I have a stiff gait."

She lowered her eyebrows and shook her head. "Hardware in your knee? Really?" She threw her hands up and grunted. "Now, *that* is a deal breaker for me! I can't possibly be in a relationship with someone whose knee needs reinforcement." She flashed a teasing scowl and pretended to be getting out of bed. "I mean, really! A girl can only take so much."

He seized her wrist and tugged her back. "Get over here, Miss No Appendix."

She laughed and smacked a kiss on his lips. "Well, okay."

As she stared down at his handsome face, a rush of emotion caught her off guard. Tears filled her eyes, and she nestled at his side again before he could see them. She chewed her bottom lip, and knowing how close she'd come to never meeting Matt caused acid to puddle in her gut. "You know… I'm as guilty as anyone of taking for granted the service and sacrifice of our military overseas every day. I blithely go about my life without thinking about roadside bombs or snipers or losing a cohort in the blink of an eye."

"Hey." He ruffled her hair and jostled her with a nudge from his shoulder. "While vets do appreciate recognition for what they do and being told 'thank you,' we also do what we do *so that* you can go through your day without thinking about roadside bombs or snipers. You should feel that safe in your home. And, ideally, we're making the *world* safer…in the long game."

A lump swelled in her throat, and she pushed up to her elbow so she could look him directly in the eyes. "Well, sir, I thank you. For your service and your sacrifice. *Oorah!*"

He twitched a grin. "That's the Marines, love. You're looking for *hooah*!"

She pulled a face. "Oops. Okay, then *hoo—*"

He kissed her before she could finish the battle cry, and she fell against him, wrapping her body around his. Their kisses lingered, then heated. Her hands explored his warm skin and burrowed into his hair, leaving it sexily mussed.

He made love to her again, his touch tender and his attention to her needs thorough. She didn't want to compare his careful and loving technique to Peter's, but the differences were so obvious. Matt was so much...*more*, she couldn't help but think to herself, "*This.* This is what was missing. What I've been looking for." Not just the sex—though it was certainly great—but the care to detail, the obvious feeling in his kisses. His respect for her, his affection for her, his—her heart jolted—*love* for her was in his eyes and every touch. *Oh, crivvens and help ma boab!* Her grandmother's favorite Scottish expression sprang to mind. Was he falling in love with her? She realized the idea didn't upset her as much as she'd have thought. In fact, it stirred a warmth in her core.

Good grief! Was *she* falling in love with *him*? That was a complication she hadn't factored in when she acted on her desire for him. She shoved the thought aside, refusing to spoil this moment with recriminations or what-ifs.

Cait drifted to sleep at some point, sated and comfortable in his arms, until she heard the bleating of her sister's goats and cracked an eye open to see the first light of morning peeking through her venetian blinds.

Matt stirred as well, and she whispered, "Good morning, handsome."

His eyes popped open, and he jerked his wrist up to check his watch. "Crap."

She snorted, then in a deep voice said, "Good morning to you, too, Cait."

He scrubbed a hand over his face, then rolled to his side, pulling her closer. "Sorry. Good morning, beautiful. This has been...so very—" He kissed her soundly.

"But I didn't mean to stay this long. I need to get back to my cabin before Eric wakes up."

She grinned and nodded. "You're excused."

With a final lingering kiss, he slid out of bed, fumbled for his clothes and crutches and was gone in a matter of minutes.

The loneliness of the silence after he was gone spoke volumes. She was getting in over her head.

By the time Matt got back to his cabin, Eric was already up, holding a cup of coffee between his hands as he sat on the sofa, glowering.

Nabbed. Matt squared his shoulders and entered the kitchen, determined not to let on that anything was different. That Cait Cameron had just rocked him to his core and made him feel truly alive for the first time since he'd almost died in the explosion that took his leg.

"You're up early," Matt said, heading to the coffeepot to get his own dose of caffeine.

"Not the only one. Where were you?"

Matt heard accusation in his son's tone. He could fudge and say he'd gone out for an early-morning walk... With his crutches? In his sleep pants? No. He wouldn't lie to Eric. "Cait's."

Eric scoffed as he eyed his father's dishabille. "So this is your walk of shame? Did I spoil things by being up already so you couldn't sneak back in unseen?"

Matt plunked his mug down harder than he intended and sloshed coffee on the counter. "No, it is not a walk of shame." Because he didn't regret one minute of the night with her.

But he could see why Eric thought so when he took a moment to see the situation through his son's eyes.

"She had a prowler last night and called me." He with-held the bit about the creep holding a knife to her throat and threatening her. No point upsetting Eric more than he obviously already was.

"And you couldn't wait to run to her side. Forget that you had a kid back in your own cabin."

"Usually you argue that you're old enough to drive, so you're old enough to be treated as an adult. This is far from the first time you've been home alone." Matt blinked. "What's up with the attitude this morning?"

Eric shrugged and raised his cup to drink. "What's up with leaving in the middle of the night without tell-ing me where you're going, then ignoring all my texts?"

He knew he shouldn't laugh, but the irony was too rich. His guffaw earned a darker glare from Eric.

"You think it's funny? I didn't know where you were, what had happened to you."

"Oh, Eric," Matt said, limping into the living room with one crutch and his cup of coffee. "I'm sorry for laughing, but you have to admit the turnabout is ironic. You chastising me about not answering texts."

He sipped his coffee, sensing he'd need the fortifica-tion for this conversation. "I didn't answer you because I left my phone here in my hurry to get to Cait's. I didn't know you'd texted. I assumed you were asleep the whole time. You should have been." He raised one eyebrow, si-lently asking, *And why weren't you in bed?* In deference to Eric's mood, he schooled his expression. "I apologize for scaring you."

Eric's brow dipped lower. "I wasn't scared. I was pissed."

Matt dropped into a chair opposite his son. "Why were you angry?"

"Because you did it again. *Are* doing it again. You talk a good game about *wanting to build a better relationship with me*—" the last part he said in a mocking tone "—but as soon as something better, something more important to you comes along, g'bye, Eric. You're gone." Eric gulped the last of his coffee and set the cup aside.

Matt screwed up his face and gave his head a little shake as if to clear it. "Say what?"

"Don't try to deny it." His son folded his arms over his chest and turned his dark gaze toward the window.

"I can't deny something I don't even understand. What are you talking about?"

No response—other than a noticeable escalation in his son's breathing, an agitated wiggling of his bare toes.

Matt set his own drink aside and leaned forward. Something besides his late-night disappearance had his son stirred up. "Eric, buddy, what are you saying?"

"Buddy? Is that what I am to you?"

"Okay, you don't like buddy?" Matt sized up his son. What was he missing? Did Eric need reassurance? Affirmation? Encouragement? He took a breath and said quietly, "How about my one and only child, whom I love and treasure more than anything and anyone on Earth?"

Eric snorted and gave a humorless cackle before facing Matt with a bitter glare. "Bullshit!"

Matt sat back in his chair, stunned both by his son's vulgarity and by the acrimony behind Eric's dismissal of his affection. "Excuse me?"

Eric pointed to his mouth. "Read my lips. *Bull. Shit.*"

Pain lanced Matt's heart, as much for the harshness of Eric's rejection as for the pain he saw reflected in his son's eyes. Moisture gathered in Eric's dark gaze, a heartbreaking counterpoint to the anger and ice in his expression and tone.

"Eric." Matt struggled awkwardly to get out of his chair and move to the couch beside his son…only to have Eric bolt away as soon as he'd settled next to him. "Eric, stop! Look at me! Please!"

His son stopped in the middle of the floor and swiped at his face before spinning around and nailing a steely gaze on him, mouth pinched.

Matt held his son's gaze, wanting, praying he could reach him now when nothing else he'd ever said seemed to have penetrated the stubborn boy's hard head. "I. Love. You. I have always loved you, and I always will. Please believe that, because nothing else is more true."

Now his son's chin did tremble, reminding Matt of when Eric was much smaller and he'd rush to his father for comfort when life hurt him. And his heart cracked.

In a small voice, Eric rasped, "If you love me, why do you always abandon me?"

Matt could only stare at Eric, gobsmacked. Finally he managed a weak, "What?"

"If you love me, why do you always abandon me?" Eric shouted, his body shaking with rage and sobs.

Matt shot from the couch, fumbling with his crutch, and in two lurching steps, he grabbed Eric into his arms and clung to him. The crutch clattered to the floor, but Matt ignored it. Eric was all that mattered.

Eric fought him, writhing and pushing to get loose, but Matt held tight. He clutched him against his chest as if letting go meant his son would be lost forever. Broken.

When Eric stilled finally, Matt whispered, "I've had to leave you in the past, but surely you know I'd never abandon you."

"Do I? It certainly seemed like abandonment when it happened. You put yourself first, what you wanted, over your kid. Why should I believe anything you say now?"

Matt held Eric at arm's length so he could meet his son's dark, wounded glare. "What I wanted? I never wanted to leave you!"

"Seemed that way. When I was just a little kid and I stood there at the airport, crying, begging you not to go overseas, but you turned around and got on that plane. How was I supposed to understand?"

Matt struggled for a breath. Had Eric been carrying this resentment and hurt for ten years? "I tried to explain what was happening to you. I had no choice about deploying! Surely in hindsight you understand that?"

Eric shrugged as if it didn't matter, glanced away, but Matt could see the tears his teenager was fighting.

He took a slow breath. "Eric, look at me."

His boy set his mouth in a grim line.

"Look at me. Please."

His son turned a grudging gaze to his.

"I'm going to let you in on a little secret."

Eric's brow furrowed.

"Ten years ago, when I got on that transport plane, I was crying, too. Because I didn't want to leave you. Or your mother. You are my little boy, my heart, and it hurt me to see you crying, hear you pleading with me to stay when I had no choice but to deploy. It hurt me to be away from my family for so long. To miss your first day of school and your first baseball game. To miss tucking you in at night and birthday parties.

"And when I came back from my tour overseas, I was crying when I got on that transport plane, also. And not because of the injuries I'd sustained or the fact that I had lost the bottom half of my leg. I was crying because I was happy that I was going home to my little boy. That I was alive, and able to see you again, and hold you, and hug you, and kiss you, and tell you how proud I am of you."

Eric's shoulders jerked as he lost his battle to muffle his sobs.

Matt squeezed his son's elbows. "You're old enough now to understand that I had a duty to serve my country, and sometimes duty means sacrifice."

Eric scoffed and his expression soured. "So you sacrificed me. That's what you're saying. Aren't you proving my point? You cared more about your stupid job than your family!"

Matt took another slow, patient breath. "No. That's not what I'm saying. You know it's not."

"Do I? 'Cause you left again six years later."

Matt's shoulders sank, realizing the depth of the hurt and misconception Eric had struggled with for years.

"Yeah. But that had nothing to do with you."

Again, Eric looked away, his mouth drawn tight as if holding back the weight of the world. His world. His deep and heavy grief.

"So guess what? When my marriage to your mom ended and I moved out of the house, I cried in the car as I was driving away. Because I already knew what it was like to miss you and be separated from you. And I hated that I was not gonna see you every day." Matt had to pause to clear the emotion clogging his throat. "And because I felt like a failure to you and to your mother. I hated that we couldn't make the marriage work, that we couldn't find a way to patch up our differences, and that I had to be an absentee father for fifty percent of your life going forward. I hated that I only saw you every other weekend. It killed me, Eric. I didn't *want* to leave you."

"Then why did you?" his son asked, sounding more like a hurt little boy than a teen on the verge of manhood.

"Because…" Matt scrubbed a hand in his hair. How did he explain? He couldn't undo the scars his choices had left on his son, but he had to find a way to bridge the gulf between them if they were going to move forward. "Because being an adult means making hard decisions sometimes. Choices where you feel stuck between two impossible scenarios. Ones where you have to make a hard call and do things you don't like for the greater good."

"How was leaving your family for the greater good?" Eric snarled.

He took a deep breath. "Eric, you're almost an adult now yourself. What choice do you think I should have made? Think about it. Not as a kid who missed his dad, but as the responsible, thinking adult your mom and I have tried to raise you to be."

The muscle in Eric's jaw flexed as he gritted his teeth and considered the question put to him. "In my head, I know why you left. I'm not dumb. I heard you and mom arguing. But it still hurt. I still felt like trash you'd tossed aside."

Pain speared Matt's chest. "Geez, Eric, I'm so sorry. I never wanted you to feel that way. You are as far from trash as possible. You are gold to me. Irreplaceable treasure. I love you so, so much."

Eric twisted his mouth and wiped his eyes as he shrugged. "Yeah, okay. Whatever."

"No, not *whatever*. We need to finish this. Resolve things between us."

Turning, Eric shuffled to the couch and flopped onto it with a grunt.

Matt pointed to his crutch on the floor and wiggled his hand. "Would you…"

Eric picked up the crutch and handed it to his dad. "Where's your leg?"

"In my room. When Cait called, said someone had been in her bedroom, threatened her life, I didn't take the time to put it on. I just wanted to get to her as fast as I could. Protect her."

His son seemed ready to make a sarcastic quip, but Matt could see the moment Eric decided against it and instead nodded slowly. "You really like her, don't you? I mean…*really* like her."

Matt eased onto the sofa next to Eric. "I really do." He measured his teen's expression. "And what do you think about that?"

Eric's mouth twisted as if he were thinking hard. Finally he lifted a shoulder. "I like her. She's cool."

Relief, like the release of a pressure valve, loosened Matt's chest. He hadn't realized how much he wanted Eric's approval until that moment.

Because you're falling in love with her. A different sort of tension torqued inside him.

As if reading his father's mind, Eric asked, "Do you love her?"

Chapter 18

Matt exhaled a puff of breath through pursed lips. "Loaded question."

Eric shook his head. "Not really. Seems simple enough to me. Either you do or you don't."

"Yeah, well, but…there are different kinds and levels of love and—" Matt started, still trying to grapple with his own revelation.

Eric groaned and pushed off the couch.

Catching Eric's arm and tugging him back to the cushions, Matt said, "Wait! Don't go… I—" He found himself searching for words, but the simple truth was too plain to ignore. "Yeah. I think I do love her. I'm just not sure what to do with that reality yet. It's…new."

Eric settled back in, folding his arms over his chest as he faced his father. "Tell me about the guy in her room. Did he hurt her? Did she know him?"

He made the decision in that moment to treat Eric not as a child to be protected but as an adult who deserved honesty. Clarity.

"She didn't recognize him. He left a tiny cut on her neck. Nothing too serious. But scared the hell out of her."

"I guess so!"

"He was wearing a mask and..." Matt related the whole encounter, her panicked call to him and the fruitless police search. "And so, because Isla is out of town, I'd like for us to move in with her, so she's not alone."

Eric blinked. "Oh."

"I know it's asking a lot of you, and if I didn't feel like her life was in danger, I wouldn't—"

"No. You're right."

Now Matt blinked. Was his son actually cooperating?

"If someone broke in and threatened her last night, she should definitely not be alone. But why doesn't she go stay with her family? I mean, her parents and sister both live on the grounds."

Matt turned up a palm. "I guess she could, if she would. But I want to be sure—"

Eric's scoff interrupted him. "Don't bullshit me, Dad. I know perfectly well why you want to move in with her."

A self-conscious prickle swept over his skin. He narrowed a warning glare on his son. "Don't be crass."

"Look, you said yourself a minute ago, I'm not a kid anymore. I'm not stupid. And what's more, I agree. I think someone should protect her. I think *you* should protect her."

"You do?" Matt lifted both eyebrows. "Who is this reasonable person and what have you done with my son?"

Eric ignored his teasing and asked, "What if I just stayed here by myself while you're protecting her?"

Matt wrapped an arm around his son's shoulders and tugged him close for a hug. "Nice try. But no."

Later in the morning, while Matt was trying fruitlessly to focus on his writing, he heard male voices outside his cabin. And Cait's. He rose from his seat at the table and went to his front door, opening it before Cait could knock.

"Hi." The sight of her, his first since their emotional and passionate night together, stirred something deep in his core. *Yeah, Harkney. You're falling in love with her.* "What's, uh…" He waved a hand to the men and blue van behind her.

"They're here to install the security cameras. They just finished at Hemlock, and I told them I wanted your cabin to be next. I'm sorry for the intrusion. I know you're probably trying to work."

"Trying is the best I can say." He stepped back and opened the door wider. "Please, do what you need to."

Cait helped the men find all the outlets and breakers they needed, then found Matt in the kitchen. "Walk with me?"

He set his third cup of coffee aside. "Sure. Any destination in particular?"

"I saw Jake driving back in for lunch a moment ago, and I thought we could ask him what he knows about that developer, Gene Gibbs. Or if he's heard anything from Peter about his brother being in town."

"I thought you were unconvinced of his brother's significance in what's been happening."

"Honestly, I don't know what to think. Anyway, I want to check in on Jake, see if they've heard anything new from the police about the company theft, and asking him about the developer is an excuse to drop in."

Matt followed her down the porch steps and out to the paved drive that looped through the property and back to the front entrance.

"So," she said as they strolled, "Eric came down to the office earlier looking for Fenn, and he gave me a strange look."

"Strange how?"

She furrowed her brow. "As if he were just seeing me for the first time. Really seeing me and was sizing me up."

Matt grunted. "Yeah, well… I told him what happened last night."

She sent him a startled look, and he clarified, "About the break-in. And that I went to stay with you while the cops looked things over."

"And…"

"And he guessed the rest." He drew a deep breath. "He asked me about my feelings for you."

He heard her breath catch. "Oh. What did you say?"

He caught her hand in his and kissed it. "I told him the truth. That I'm falling in love with you."

Cait raised a trembling smile. "Oh. Matt, I—"

He didn't want to hear that she didn't reciprocate his feelings so he rushed to add, "We also had a good talk about what's been bothering him. About why he'd been acting out. I can see now it was a cry for attention, for boundaries, for proof of where he stood with his parents. I think we're finally on the same page about some things. Or I hope so." He explained all the hurt Eric had expressed and the discussion they'd had over breakfast about how to make a fresh start with their new understanding.

"Wow. That's— I'm glad, Matt." She squeezed his hand. "I'm so happy you two worked everything out."

"So does that mean you and your dad worked everything out? That you're off all those harsh restrictions?" Fenn asked as they walked through the fir trees to the back door of the Hemlock cabin.

Eric buzzed his lips. "No. He said we'd talk about the restrictions tonight after he'd discussed things with my mom."

"What a crock!"

He shrugged. "Yeah, well, at least he knows now I haven't forgotten everything he did and how he made me feel like he didn't care. Like I didn't matter."

Fenn faced him, bracing both her hands on his shoulders. "Hey. You do matter. Even if your dad doesn't see it. You. Matter."

A warm buzz filled his chest as he stared into Fenn's earnest eyes. "Ah, thanks. I know that. I know what you're thinking, and I'm not…" He waved his hand and chuckled a little. "But thanks. For caring. For saying that, anyway." He tugged his mouth in a bigger smile.

When she returned a grin, his pulse did a little jagged skipping thing, and he leaned in for a kiss.

Fenn sucked in a breath of surprise, and her cheeks colored. She looked all flustered then smiled at him again.

So he kissed her again. Longer. Deeper.

She leaned into him, wrapping her arms around his waist and returning his kisses. The more they kissed the more his body pulsed and tingled and ached for more.

He raised his head, trying to slow things down for

a minute so he could think straight. And there was the Hemlock cabin. Empty. Waiting. Private.

He stroked a hand along her cheek and leaned close to her ear to whisper, "Hey, I have an idea…"

"Gene Gibbs? Where'd you hear about him?" Jake asked, a frown denting his forehead as he looked up from his plate of leftover spaghetti.

"Then you do know of him?" Cait asked.

Jake wiped his mouth on his napkin and divided a look between her and Matt. "I know enough of him to tell you to steer clear of him. He came steamrolling into town in the last year, buying up land left and right. And from what I hear, his business practices and professional ethics are…questionable at best. I've even heard he's dangerous, that he's got side businesses and associates you don't want any part of."

"Dangerous enough to send a guy to threaten a woman in her bed at night with a knife to her throat?" Cait asked.

Sitting beside Jake, Emma gasped. "Cait? What are you saying? Were you threatened? With a knife!"

Cait kept her gaze on Jake, waiting for an answer. Rather than speak to her, Jake turned his focus to Matt and scowled. "I asked you to give up your digging and dissuade Cait from poking around any further. But I hear you did the opposite. You two went into town asking around about construction company matters and—" He waved a hand toward Cait. "And bringing dangerous men out to Cameron Glen to threaten my family!"

"Jake, don't take it out on Matt." Cait gritted her teeth and flattened her hands on the table. "I asked him to help me."

Jake sent Cait a disgruntled look. "I'm not happy with you either, but I specifically asked Matt—"

"And I specifically asked Cait to keep looking, to keep asking questions," Emma interrupted, placing a hand on her husband's arm. "So blame me if you have to blame someone."

Matt cleared his throat and turned both palms up. "Maybe we don't cast blame anywhere. Isn't that counterproductive? Can we just work together to figure out what's going on and all of us be alert so we can protect the family and the family's interests?"

"Yeah, well, the best way to do that, going forward, is to stay the hell away from Gibbs. I don't have proof he's anything but an aggressive businessman, but the rumors are enough for me to advise caution."

Matt nodded. "Understood." He leaned back in his ladder-backed chair and cocked his head to one side. "Any reason to think he's behind the theft from your company?"

Jake snorted. "None. This guy does deals worth hundreds of thousands of dollars. Millions, even. Why would he bother with a theft of a measly few thousand from a local business?"

"Worth asking," Cait said. "So…any more news from the police?"

"They've finished questioning everyone in the company. Still no significant leads. Helen Garcia bought a new car about the time the money went missing, but she could prove the down payment came from money she'd saved for years and the rest was financed through her bank. That's as close as they've come."

"Peter checks out?" Cait asked.

Jake narrowed his eyes on her. "You have new reason to suspect him?"

Cait sighed and rolled her eyes. "Not really. Just… I heard his brother was in town. Had been, at least. David's always been…erratic. A wild card."

Jake nodded. "I know. As a favor to Peter, I hired him for one of my crews last spring, and he only showed up to work about four out of five days. I fired him the day he came to work smelling of alcohol. Can't put my crew at risk having anyone under the influence near power tools and heavy equipment."

Cait sat taller and exchanged a look with Matt. "How did he take being fired? Did he or Peter give you any flak?"

"He wasn't happy, but he wasn't belligerent. I gave him a more than fair severance payment." Jake folded his arms over his chest. "I know what you're thinking, and I told this to the police. This all happened months ago, and well before the money started disappearing from the account."

No one said anything for several tense seconds until Jake slapped a hand on the table and rose from his chair. "Been fun, guys. But I have to get back to the salt mine." He directed a hard look to Cait and Matt. "Please. Just let the police deal with this." Then, bending, he gave Emma a quick kiss on the cheek.

As Jake left through the back door, Emma pressed her fingers to her bussed cheek, and the poignancy, the gratitude and heartache in her expression, brought a lump to Cait's throat. She prayed Jake and Emma could find a way through this turbulence in their marriage. It was obvious to their family they were still very much in love.

"Mommy?" Lexi called from the back of the house. "I can't find Lou Lou!"

Emma took a deep breath and flashed an obviously pasted-on smile. "Excuse me, please. I need to locate a missing lion."

Cait waved a hand as she shoved her chair back. "We'll get out of your hair. And, Emma…"

Her sister paused. "Hmm?"

Cait closed the distance between them and pulled her sister into a tight hug. "I love you."

Emma clung to her for a few seconds, then rasped, "Thanks." As she pulled away and left the room, Cait watched her sister wipe her eyes.

Matt walked silently to the door and didn't speak until they were almost at the end of Emma's driveway. "About Peter's brother…"

"Yeah?"

"That situation has the look and stink of a skunk. Better keep your guard up."

Chapter 19

"I don't know, Eric. It doesn't feel right being in here. It's like this cabin is...cursed." She trembled a little, and Eric took her hand in his.

"Aw, come on. You don't really believe in superstitious stuff like that, do you?" Eric tugged her hand, leading her deeper inside the vacant cabin. Toward the master bedroom.

"I don't know. But Aunt Cait and my parents would freak if they knew we were in here. Especially since the cops closed the cabin and all that bad stuff happened here."

"Cops reopened it, though. Right?" he asked, pretty sure he remembered Cait telling his dad as much a couple days ago. "We're not going to hurt anything. I just thought it'd be nice to have some..." He pulled her into his arms as they entered the master bedroom. "Privacy."

Though her brow dipped with a frown of worry, Fenn

kissed him back. Her stiff arms and legs softened the longer they kissed. Finally, she whispered, "Okay. Just for a little while."

Grinning, he walked backward, towing her with him, until he flopped onto the bed. She gasped a little as he rolled on top of her and resumed Frenching her. She was still pretty tense, probably because she was inexperienced, so he eased up, trying to calm her down. Trying to get his own head out of the strange mood he was in.

Don't overthink this, he told himself. *It's just a little fooling around.*

But the longer they kissed, the weirder he felt about the situation. He couldn't get the conversation he'd had with his dad out of his head. His dad had cried when he left for his overseas tour? When he'd divorced Mom? He'd just never thought about his dad being that...emotionally involved.

Eric raised his head and sighed. *Stop thinking about your dad, idiot! No wonder you can't get in the mood!*

"Is something the matter? Am I doing it wrong?" Fenn asked, a shy quiver in her voice.

"No, nothing like that." He flashed her a reassuring smile. She really was pretty. And nice. And funny, when they both let themselves relax. "Just...pacing myself."

He dipped his head to kiss her again. But after a minute, his stupid brain started nagging him again.

Dad and Cait were getting serious. Cait was the first lady his dad had cared about since his parents' divorce. If his dad and Cait got together, like married, then he and Fenn would be...*practically family.* That stopped him. He pushed away from Fenn and sat up on the bed, frowning.

"Eric? What—"

Being an adult means making hard decisions some-

times... Ones where you have to make a hard call and do things you don't like for the greater good, he heard his dad say.

"I can't... You're right. We probably shouldn't be in here. And..."

Fenn sat up and rubbed a hand on her opposite arm as if she were cold. Or scared. Or...

"It's not you," he rushed to assure her. "I just...was thinking about what my dad said earlier."

"Your dad?"

Huffing out a sigh, he faced Fenn, taking her hands in his. "My dad and your Aunt Cait have a thing going. A pretty serious thing, I think."

Her eyes widened. "Really? Like...how serious?"

"Like in love, or falling in love. And here's the thing..." He gripped her hands tighter as his weird feelings began to crystalize. "I like you, Fenn. A lot. But if my dad and your aunt do hook up, for real, for long-term, you and I would be—" He searched his brain for the right term to describe the relationship. But he didn't need to.

Her mouth dropped open, and she gasped. "Cousins! Oh my god."

"Well, step-cousins or something. But family. And I..."

"Wow..." she said, her gaze growing distant as if letting the revelation soak in.

"Whatever we'd be, the most important thing is, I want you to be my friend. I think that's more important than trying to be...anything else. I don't wanna risk hurting you if, in the future, we're maybe gonna be...related."

She nodded. "Yeah. I get that. Totally." She brought her feet up to sit cross-legged on the bed. "So...now what? What exactly did your dad say about Aunt Cait?"

* * *

Cait returned to the rental office after checking in with the men installing the security equipment. The video monitors for the first three cabins were up and running, and she went to her computer to click through the views, testing things out. When she reached the feed from the Hemlock cabin, the alert light was flashing, indicating motion had been detected and recorded. "What the—"

Her heart drumming against her ribs, Cait clicked to play the saved video.

Fenn. Eric. At the front door of the cabin. She gritted her teeth. Damn it! What did they think they were doing?

She watched with irritation as the teens broke into the cabin. No, not breaking in. The installers hadn't had a key to lock it back up after working on the camera installation. But still…they had no business—

Growling under her breath, she shoved her chair back. To maintain guest privacy, no cameras had been put inside the cabin. The best way to find out if Eric and Fenn were still in the cabin—and remove the opportunity for the kids to lie about their activity—was to go to the cabin and catch them out.

As she marched up the road, she considered calling Matt. But since he and Eric had reached a tentative truce that morning, she wanted to give the teen a chance to explain himself before she talked to Matt. Maybe, maybe, they had a reasonable excuse for—

She cut the thought off. Fenn knew better than to enter the unused cabins. And of all the properties on the grounds, the Hemlock! When she reached Hemlock, she opened the front door and cast her gaze around the living room. "Fenn?"

Hearing voices and scuffling from the master bedroom, her stomach swooped. Good grief! What were they doing in there? Cait swallowed hard and called, "Fenn, I know you're in there. I'm coming back."

Eric and her niece stood at the end of the rumpled, but still made-up bed, staring at her with wide, guilty gazes.

Cait braced a hand on her hip and shook her head. "Just an FYI. The security cameras outside the cabins are being installed today. This cabin was the first to be done."

Fenn shut her eyes, and her shoulders drooped as she groaned. Eric winced and muttered a curse word quietly.

"Is there any chance you have a legitimate, reasonable explanation that excuses this egregious disobedience, young lady?"

Fenn looked at her toes. "No, ma'am."

"Don't blame her. It's my fault. I talked her into breaking in. She didn't want to."

Cait gave Eric points for defending Fenn, taking the blame.

"Noted. I hold you both responsible for this lack of judgment."

Eric shoved his hands in his pockets and scowled. "Are you going to tell my dad?"

She folded her arms over her chest and studied Matt's son. "I'm not a tattletale. I think telling him should be your job."

"I know what you're thinking, but nothing happened," Eric grumbled.

"Regardless, he's your father, and when you break the rules, he needs to know."

"Honest, Aunt Cait. We were just kissing. What's wrong with that?" Fenn asked, pouting.

"What's wrong is that you snuck into a cabin. You've always known the cabins were off-limits, but *this cabin*?"

She huffed her frustration. "You know it's been at the center of an investigation by the police." Cait struggled to keep her tone calm. "You scared me half to death when I saw someone had broken in on the security system."

"I didn't know you'd put in security cameras," Fenn said as if that was an excuse.

"By the end of the week, all the cabins and the front entrance will have them. Your mom is talking to the company about putting a camera or two at your house, as well. Same with Gramps and Gran. This break-in stuff has us spooked, and we figured we needed to join the twenty-first century."

"But you always said the cabins were—" The crash of breaking glass in the mudroom stopped Fenn mid-sentence.

Cait's heart jumped to her throat, and she instinctively scurried closer to her niece, putting herself between the teenagers and the sounds that came from the back room of the cabin.

"Someone's out there," Eric whispered, when sounds of a rattling doorknob and squeaking hinges reached them.

Cait scrambled mentally. She had to keep the kids safe. And call the police. But she hadn't brought her phone from her purse which was in the office. And Matt had taken Eric's from him this summer. "Fenn, do you have your phone?"

Her niece nodded.

"Call Matt. Tell him where we are, what's happening. Then call 911," she whispered as she hurried them toward the master bathroom. "Stay in here with the door locked until the coast is clear. Got it?"

Fenn's eyes were wide, and her breathing shallow.

Eric took the cell phone from Fenn and started dialing. "What about you? Come in here with us!"

"I just want to have a look. The cabins are my responsibility." She shoved Matt's son into the bathroom. When she met the disgruntled expression she'd seen on Matt's face more than once, she almost laughed. Eric was so much like his father whether he liked it or not. "I'll be right back. Take care of Fenn."

The look in Eric's eyes morphed when she said that. Hardened. Intensified. Again, like Matt's. Like a soldier. A warrior. A protector.

Eric bobbed a nod. "I will."

When there was a loud thump in the front room, she closed the bathroom door and heard the *snick* as it was locked. Good.

Turning, she pressed her body against the inside wall of the bedroom and crept toward the door to peek out.

A man in dirty blue jeans and a baggy T-shirt was on his hands and knees prying up the floorboards in the kitchen. The intruder was back! She prayed the police could get here fast enough to catch him this time. They had him red-handed. This nightmare chapter could be over once and for—

When the man turned, trying a different plank, she caught a glimpse of his face. A familiar face. She gasped, and the intruder's head jerked up. His gaze clashed with Cait's.

"Cait?" said Peter's brother, David. He clambered to his feet, narrowing his eyes on her.

"What the hell are you doing?" she asked, moving into the living room and not hiding the bite of her anger and disappointment in David.

He stumbled toward her. "I'd think that was obvious. I want my money back."

She barked a bitter laugh. "*Your* money?"

"Yeah. My money," he growled, striding toward her. "Where is it?"

She took a step back when he crowded close, his six-foot-plus frame and barrel chest looming over her. Lifting her chin, she squared her shoulders. She knew David and didn't believe he'd harm her. He was irresponsible and without direction in life, but she couldn't believe he was dangerous. After all, because of Peter, she'd been almost family to him at one time. They'd shared meals. She'd spent a Christmas with him in the early days of her relationship with Peter. *That* David wouldn't hurt her. But had that David changed?

She drew a steadying breath. "It's not your money, David. You stole it from my brother's company. Didn't you?"

He glowered at her. "I didn't steal nothing. Peter got me that money. Said your brother owed him."

Her gut pitched. "*Peter* stole it?"

"He didn't steal it. Can't steal what is rightfully yours."

She smelled alcohol on David's breath, and a fresh arrow of alarm and discouragement pierced her. "You're drinking again, aren't you? What happened to your rehab?"

"Don't need it. What I need is my money." He grabbed her arm in a painfully tight grip, grating, "Where is it?"

"Ow! You're hurting me. Let go!"

"I'm gonna do a lot more than hurt you if you don't hand over my money. Right. Now!" He gave her a hard shake that made her head snap back and forward. Now, even closer to him, with him snarling right in her face, she smelled something else. Something that made her blood run cold. Cigarettes.

"You're the one who threatened me the other night, aren't you?"

He snorted. "What of it? I had a job to do to get the man off my back. If you'd just cough up the cash you took—"

She groaned. "I don't have it! And it's *not yours*!" She worked hard to fight back the swell of panic climbing her throat. If he was drunk—or worse…

Staring at him, she registered the dilated pupils and bloodshot whites of his eyes, both of which suggested he was high as well as drunk. Her heart sank. How did she negotiate rationally with a man who wasn't in his right mind?

With a growl, he yanked her arm behind her back, and she saw the flash of silver from the corner of her eye just before he pressed a blade against her neck. "I know you have that money. I know you found it. Give it back!"

"I don't have it. If you know I found it, then you should know I turned it in to the police."

He growled his aggravation, and his grip tightened. "Don't lie to me!"

"I'm not. David, you know the police will throw the book at you if you hurt me." She struggled to keep her tone calm, placating. "Now put down the knife, and we'll—"

"Shut up!" He shook her again, and sharp pains shot from her wrenched right shoulder down the arm he had twisted. "I'm giving the orders!"

She heard a scuffle of feet and hazarded a glance toward the bedroom. She'd told the kids to stay in the bathroom, but she saw a quick flash of movement near the door. *No, no, no!*

If Eric or Fenn tried something risky to save her and got themselves hurt in the process—

"Let me go, David!" Careful not to wiggle her body and let his knife cut her, she scooted her feet and turned her hips as he fought to keep her in his grasp. David's back was now to the bedroom door.

In a lightning-fast move she hadn't anticipated, he released her arm and snaked it around her waist, hauling her backward against his chest. "If it's not here, then we'll go get it. Together."

"What?"

"You heard me. Let's go." He shoved her toward the door.

"I— No!" Cait resisted as best she could. She braced her legs and tried to plant her heels firmly against the hardwood floor. But the polished wood was smooth, and the soles of her sandals slid across it. He pushed, dragged and lifted her while she stiffened and bucked her lower torso. Though she gave him trouble, slowed him down, she was all too aware of the hunting knife he held. It nicked her at the collarbone and scraped her arm when he shifted his grip to restrain her. Finally, he bent and hoisted her, throwing her over his shoulder in a fireman's carry.

Cait screamed and kicked. "No! Put me down! Help!"

As he lugged her out the door, her head banged against the door frame, sending a bolt of pain under her skull and making lights flicker in her vision. And then her view went black.

Chapter 20

The night was as black as any Bellingrath had ever seen back on his farm in Missouri. Every light was out, either bombed or extinguished by fearful civilians. As he made his way through—

Matt's phone buzzed for the third time in a minute. The same number. One he didn't recognize. Whoever wanted to sell him insurance was persistent. He was about to swipe cancel again, but he hesitated. Too much had been happening around Cameron Glen for him to ignore the possibility that there was trouble and one of Cait's sisters was trying to reach him. He moved his finger to Answer, but the call rolled over to voicemail. With a sigh, he turned to his laptop screen to read back over his last paragraph.

"As he made his way through…" he read aloud, then voiced as he typed, "the rubble in the street…"

The front door burst open. Eric charged in, shouting, "God, Dad! Why won't you answer your damn phone!"

Matt threw his hands up and groaned. "Because I'm trying to work!"

"Screw work! We need you!" Eric blurted, then bent at the waist, clearly winded and gasping for a breath.

"Hey! Watch the langu—" He stopped short when Eric's anxiety registered. He shoved his chair back and crossed the room to his son. "Eric? What's going on?"

"A man...took Cait!" Eric gasped. "He broke in...demanded money. Had a knife. Grabbed her."

Matt plowed a hand though his hair, his heart dropping to his toes. "What!"

"Picked her up," Eric panted. "Ran out...took her."

Matt darted to the front door, snatched it open. "Where'd they go? Which way?"

"Hemlock. Back way. Up...hill."

"Have you called the cops?" He jammed his feet in his shoes and tied them as fast as he could.

"Fenn has."

"Stay here." He aimed a finger at his son, praying for once Eric would do as told. "Wait for the police and tell them what you saw." He started down the porch stairs.

"Dad, wait!"

Impatience gnawed at him, but he turned back toward Eric. "What?"

"What are you doing? You can't go after them!"

"I have to!" How much of a head start did the guy have? Every second counted...

"But your—" Eric cut himself off. His gaze dropped to Matt's prosthetic leg. "How will you—"

"I didn't say it'd be easy. But I have to do what I can." He pointed at his son. "Now go inside! Lock the door."

He took off at a run—maybe not at the speed and with the agility he'd once had, but at a run.

He made calculations as he went. Back way, up the hill at Hemlock, Eric had said. The same way the intruder from a few weeks ago had disappeared according to the kids. Toward the highway that ran along the eastern edge of the property.

Matt didn't wait until he reached the Hemlock cabin. He started up the hillside where the Christmas trees grew, climbing at an angle toward the top of the ridge. He needed a vantage point as quickly as possible.

The trek was difficult, the ground uneven, the slope steep, but he didn't stop. Cait needed him. Each time he pictured a man with a knife carrying Cait off or dragging her as she fought him, his gut twisted. Bile surged in his throat. He loved her, and he could not, *would not* lose another person he loved.

In his haste, he slipped on damp grass where the automatic sprinklers had watered the trees that afternoon. Catching himself before he went all the way down, Matt stumbled back to a jog. He gulped air, refusing to slow his pace, even as his lungs labored. When he reached the top of the ridge, he scanned the grassy hill on the other side. A smattering of hardwoods obscured his view in spots and cast shadows that shifted as the breeze blew the branches. He kept moving along the top of the ridge, heading closer to the Hemlock cabin, listening, watching for a flash of color or a movement in the shade.

"Cait!" He held his breath, trying to silence the sawing of his own gasps so he could hear an answering cry. "Cait!"

Nothing. No one. Silently he repeated the curse word

Eric had used minutes ago. As he set out again, he sent up a prayer that his efforts to rescue Cait weren't too little. And too late.

She came to slowly. Someone was jostling her. A bright light was in her eyes. The sun? Had she overslept? Cait opened her eyes a crack. Not in her bedroom. In a grassy field. Why— She sat up quickly, and her head gave a sharp throb.

"Good. You're awake. Now you can walk for yourself."

She jerked her gaze toward the man who'd spoken and immediately regretted it. Pressing a hand to her aching temple, she eyed Peter's brother. Memory came back in a rush. Her pulse spiked. "David…"

He rolled a shoulder and squeezed his upper arm muscle with his opposite hand. "You could stand to lose a few pounds, girl. Carrying you was like toting a sack of concrete. Geez."

She narrowed a glare and told him with a terse expression what she thought of his opinion. Moving her fingers to a stinging spot on her neck, she found slick moisture, drew her hand away and saw blood. "You cut me!"

David still held the blade as he stumbled closer. "Your own fault. If you hadn't been thrashing around like a trout on land, you wouldn't have got nicked." He waved the knife at her. "But I swear I'll give you worse than that if you don't start cooperating. We can do this easy, or we can do it hard."

She wiped her hand on the knee of her slacks. "What do you want with me?"

"Told ya. I want my money," he said through clenched teeth.

She sighed. "And I told you I don't have it. I gave it to the cops. So why not let me go?"

"Well, that'd be a mistake. 'Cause one way or another, I'm getting that money back, and you're gonna help." He waggled his fingers, motioning for her to stand. "On your feet. Let's go."

"No." She folded her arms over her chest, seeing an opportunity to gather information. They were safely away from the kids. David was talking. At the moment, he was not acting overly hostile. And she was still on Cameron Glen property, as best she could tell. If she stalled, maybe the cops would arrive before he got her to a new, remote location.

David screwed up his face and sputtered, "What?"

"I said no. I'm not going anywhere until you tell me what the hell is going on. You say you and Peter didn't *steal* the money from Jake? Why do you think Jake owes you anything?"

"'Cause I done work for him this spring."

"And he didn't pay you? I find that hard to believe."

David scoffed and shook his head. "He paid some. But when I told him I needed an advance on the next job, that I had bills, debt I had to pay off, he refused to advance me what I needed."

"What kind of debt?" She eyed the knife, which he tapped against his jeans in agitation. Could she get it from him without getting cut?

"Never you mind that."

She lifted a hand. Remembering what Jake had said earlier about firing David for cause, she tested how forthcoming David might be. "Okay. Why did you think Jake should have advanced the money to you? He's a business owner, not a bank."

With a derisive snort, David sneered at her. "Peter's worked for him for five years! What about a little gratitude for that?"

She didn't bother correcting his timeline, focusing instead on the more pertinent detail. "Peter has. Not you."

"But Peter's my brother. Family. Jake talks big about being all about family. But help a guy out when his family is in need?" He wrinkled his nose as if something smelled bad. "The son of a bitch turned around and fired me. Bam! How's that for gratitude?"

"David, if Jake let you go, I'm sure he had cause—"

"Cait!" a male voice shouted from a distance.

She and David whipped their gazes up the slope of the hill behind them. Two football fields' length away, Matt appeared at the top of the ridge.

Hope sprang in her chest. "Matt!"

As she scrambled to her feet, David seized her arm again, near her hurt shoulder, and yanked her close. "Oh no you don't!"

"Stop it! Let go!" Cait wiggled and pushed against him, all too aware of the knife he still carried.

With a powerful jerk, he hauled her closer and pinned her against him, trapping her right arm. When he rammed the knife under her chin, the tip poking her skin, she gasped and stilled. One slip of the blade, intentional or not, would slice her jugular. "Stop fighting, or I'll flay you open like a catfish."

He dragged her, tripping and stumbling, into a thicket of small hardwoods and scrub bush. She could guess their destination. The highway lay a short distance through those trees. He could easily have parked a getaway car there. If he got her in a car, he could take her anywhere.

And then how would Matt find her?

* * *

Before they disappeared into the shadows of the trees, Matt caught a flash of sunlight on metal. The knife. At Cait's throat.

His pulse thundered as he charged down the grassy hill in pursuit of Cait and the man dragging her along. The guy had to have a car waiting on the highway, Matt reasoned. And if he got her to that car, got her *in* that car, he'd lose her. Forget the simple truth that he couldn't chase down a car on foot. Thanks to his crime writing research, Matt was all too aware of what statistics said about a kidnapping victim's chances of survival. Once trapped inside a car, moved to a new location...the odds of being murdered skyrocketed.

He gritted his teeth and pushed his legs to move faster. He couldn't let that happen to Cait. He'd sworn to keep her safe.

When he reached the line of trees, the going got tougher. Brambles, undergrowth and deadfall choked his path. Low branches smacked his face, and thorns snagged on his jeans as he waded through the tangle. He could still see Cait and the man ahead of him. They seemed to have stopped for some reason. Hope soared in his chest that he might reach her before—

He heard a shriek and angled his head for a better view. "Cait! I'm coming!"

Through a gap in the trees, he watched the man hoist Cait up and shove her over...hell! A fence. The man swung a leg up and vaulted the chest-high chain-link fence, catching Cait before she could scramble away.

"Matt!" she shouted, as the man dragged her out of his line of vision.

He reached the fence that marked the edge of the property along the highway and cursed under his breath. How was he supposed to negotiate this thing? Okay, just because he hadn't yet attempted such a task with his prosthesis didn't mean he couldn't do it. *Can't never could,* his father used to say.

Gritting his teeth, Matt planted the toe of his whole leg as high up as he could, then dragged himself up, swung his prosthesis over, bracing his arms to keep from scraping the top wires as much as he could. The sound of Cait's cries rang in his ears as he struggled, maneuvered, his heart thundering. After working to free his toe from the fence and wiggling over the barrier, he dropped clumsily to the ground on the other side.

Down the highway, an engine roared. He raised his head as he clambered to his feet. The rear backup lights flashed on then off as the kidnapper shifted into Drive.

Panic swelled in Matt's chest as he set off at a run. "No! Cait!"

With a squeal of tires, the kidnapper peeled out onto the road.

Matt gave chase for a short distance, even though he knew logically he couldn't possibly run down the truck.

A sick, sinking feeling, thick with a sense of how he'd failed Cait, flowed through Matt like hot tar.

Stumbling to a stop, he bent at the waist, sucking in air as he watched the black truck speed away. He tried to make out even one letter on the license plate. Was that a B? An 8?

"Damn!" he shouted to the wind. Then because it was all he had, he shouted again. Raw terror and frustration clawed at him. All he could do was go back to Cameron Glen and wait for the police. He straightened and scrubbed both hands in his hair as he growled and started back along the shoulder of the road. He'd reach Cait's house faster via the highway than traipsing back through the weeds and climbing that fence again.

He looked up when he heard another engine approaching from the opposite direction—then blinked, recognizing his own Jeep. "What the…"

Eric was behind the wheel, and he pulled onto the shoulder just in front of Matt. Striding over to the driver's window, Matt frowned at his son. "I told you to stay at the cabin. To lock the door! What are you—"

"And I chose to help instead of obeying you blindly," Eric returned without an iota of remorse. "I knew if Cait's kidnapper was headed for the highway, you'd need wheels. I was right, wasn't I?"

Matt pressed his mouth in a taut line. Bobbed a nod. "Any chance you brought me my phone from by my laptop?"

Eric grimaced, all the answer Matt needed.

With a wave toward the passenger door, Eric said, "So get in! Which way did they go?"

"Hell no!" Matt retorted. "You are not driving. Get out." He opened the driver's door and tugged his son's arm.

"Dad!"

"I don't have time to argue! Get out and go back to the cabin!"

Eric growled in protest but obeyed. "I'm not a little kid, Dad. I can help!"

Matt wedged past him onto the driver's seat. "Now's not the time for this!"

Slapping his hand against the side of the Jeep, Eric stepped back, frowning.

His gut tightened, regretting the tone he'd used, but

Matt shifted gears and punched the gas pedal. When he glanced in his rearview mirror, he saw his son's shoulders slump and felt his heart sinking. Matt jammed his foot on the brake.

Seeing the Jeep stop, Eric jogged to the side window, his expression hopeful.

"You're right. You're not a little kid," he said in a rush. "And you *can* help. By taking care of Fenn. Protect her. And second, when the cops arrive, tell them what's happened, everything you saw and heard. Tell them I've followed the kidnapper and Cait. Black Ford truck, last number of the plate is B or 8. And let the Cameron family know I've gone after Cait."

Eric's face said he was disappointed not to be joining his father on his mission, but took his responsibilities to heart. "I will."

Before speeding off, Matt added, "Eric, thank you. Bringing me the Jeep was smart and helpful." He aimed a finger at his teen. "I love you, son."

Eric's chin lifted, and his eyes brightened. "You too, Dad. Be careful."

With a nod to Eric, he pulled out on the highway and raced after Cait and her abductor. They had a head start, but he would find her, rescue her, if it was the last thing he did.

Cait clung to the truck door handle as David sped around the curves of the mountain road. Matt had seen both David and the truck. He would alert the police, give a description of both. That was something. Not much, but she'd hold to any hope she could. "Slow down or you'll kill us both!"

"Don't bitch at me, Cait. I'm not your man."

"Thank God for that," she mumbled under her breath.

"What was that?" he snapped back.

"Nothing. Forget it. But you won't get any money from me if you crash the truck and kill us both. Slow down!"

He took the next turn more carefully, but she still felt the tires slide.

"Where are we going?" Not for the first time, she thought of her cell phone back in the office, in her purse. Without any way for someone to track her location, without any way to call for help, she felt adrift at sea, lost, helpless.

Hearing the whine of a siren, she sat taller in the seat and craned her head to look for the source. David clearly heard it, too, and slowed to a sedate pace. He cast a nervous glance in his rearview mirror, but the police car appeared from the opposite direction, speeding past them. Headed for Cameron Glen, no doubt, in response to the teenagers' 911 call.

"Don't even think about it," David said, lifting the knife he'd laid on the seat on the far side from her and waggling it menacingly.

"Where are we going?" she repeated more sternly, fighting to keep the quaver of fear from her voice. She backed up her tone with an impatient and displeased glare.

"You'll see. Now shut up and don't nag me! I gotta think."

"You gotta think? You mean you don't know where we're going?"

"I said, don't bitch at me, Cait!" The car swerved as he sent her an angry scowl.

She gripped the door handle again, and a new idea came to her. If she could distract him, get him to run off the road, crash the car at the right moment...could she make a run for it? She weighed the chances that she could be injured in a minor wreck versus the odds of him hurting her if he didn't get his way, didn't get the money he was after—which he wouldn't.

Was any part of the David she'd known still somewhere under this man's unreasonable and angry veneer? She wanted to bank on the tenuous connection they'd had via Peter, but could she really? He was obviously drinking again, probably using drugs. That made people erratic on the best of days, and considering David's history...

"That cop was probably headed to Cameron Glen, you know." She sent him a side glance, then scanned the road ahead for a spot that had a shallow ditch or a fence that would stop them without causing too much damage. "I was with my niece and another boy. They saw you. I told them to call the police. It's just a matter of time before—"

She gasped when she saw the knife coming toward her. A flash of motion as his arm arced toward her chest. She squeezed her eyes shut. Heard the thud as the blade hit.

And she waited for the pain...

Chapter 21

Matt raced down the mountain highway, fighting to calm his ragged breathing and thundering pulse. The Army had taught him that panic and high emotion were the enemy of rational thinking and action in an emergency.

But the woman he loved had never been kidnapped by a knife-wielding thug when he was in the Army. Calming his speeding heart and thinking clearly weren't easy, not when Cait was in danger. Not when the thought of losing her caused a physical ache in his chest.

He banged his fist against the steering wheel, fearing Cait and the kidnapper were too far ahead of him to be caught. Although the highway didn't have many side roads or driveways, each one he passed splintered his search options and cut his chances of finding her. He slowed each time a side road intersected the main one, looking for clues the black truck had been there. Dust in the air, kicked up by the tires. A glimpse of black or flash of sunlight on a distant windshield.

Nothing. Nothing. Nothing. Except a farmer on a tractor cutting summer hay.

Damn! He hurried on, taking the curves in the road too fast. Scanning the switchbacks in the road ahead, until...

Was that a black truck or just his wishful thinking? He narrowed his gaze, and his heart jumped. Definitely a black truck! But still too far ahead. Matt pushed his Jeep to go faster.

Adrenaline made Cait's ears ring, and it took a beat for her to realize he'd missed her with the knife. The truck swerved as David freed the blade from the cushions of the passenger seat, an inch from her ribs.

"Good God, David! You could have killed me!" she gasped, her voice thick with fear.

"That's kinda the point. I warned you!" He plucked the knife free, finally, and flailed it under her nose. "Now shut up, or I won't pull the punch next time."

She sucked oxygen into tight lungs. "You don't want to do this. It's not worth it for a few thousand measly dollars. You don't want kidnapping or murder on your conscience. Or your criminal record!"

"A few thousand?" David gave her a sneering side glance. "I'm out a whole lot more than a few thousand. With interest, I owe Gibbs close to a hundred grand. You know what he'll do to me if I don't start paying something back?"

"Gibbs?" The name made her pulse jump. She had little time to process the revelation before the truck fishtailed around another sharp curve. She squeezed the seat and armrest as they skidded. She wanted any information David would give up, but she also hated to distract him from his driving.

Stop the truck, she thought again and resumed looking for a "safe" spot to cause the truck to crash. They were getting closer to town, heavier traffic. She didn't want anyone else involved or hurt if she did make the truck run off the road. She needed to act soon if…

There. Just ahead. The road had doubled back on a hairpin turn. While the driver's side had a steep drop off and no shoulder, an uphill slope of dirt and rock rose on the passenger side. Risky, but maybe her only chance. She just had to be sure he didn't overcorrect and send them plunging…

She gathered her courage, took a deep breath and grabbed the steering wheel.

Matt watched in horror as the black truck swerved sharply to the right, the left, then hard right again. The road had no shoulder here. Just rough mountain terrain. A tree-and-rock-filled embankment straight to the bottom of the mountain.

He muttered a curse under his breath as the truck plowed into the hillside and the tailgate slewed sideways. He lost sight of the truck then, as his Jeep moved down the road, away from his vantage point and into a denser section of woods. After negotiating the hairpin turn, he proceeded up the highway with caution, keeping an eye out for the wreckage…and for Cait.

Cait's head snapped forward and back as the truck came to an abrupt stop. Both front-seat airbags had deployed, and she coughed, choking on the powder that filled the cab. Her face stung from where the airbag had smacked her, but she was otherwise unhurt. Alive. *Now get out!*

Scrambling to get her bearings, she shouldered open the passenger door.

"Hey!" David grabbed for her, catching the hem of her shirt.

She slid the shirt up, wanting only to be free of his grip. With a wiggle, she worked the blouse over her head, but as she pulled it off, David's yanking twisted the material around her arm, wrenching her right shoulder again. A sharp pain speared through her muscles, and she cried out. He shifted his grip, trying to grab her, and she tumbled free. Stumbled. Then ran.

She cradled her injured arm, the shirt still dangling from her shoulder, but didn't stop moving. This was her chance to escape, and she refused to blow it. Her feet slipped in loose scree and dead leaves that littered the hill and the damp moss that covered the rocks. She clambered up the embankment, using one hand and her feet to climb. She made it a few feet then slid back down, bumping the back fender of the truck.

David had made it out the driver's door and circled the bed, cursing as he charged toward her.

"No!" Turning, she scrambled for purchase on the steep ground, at least until she could climb around the dented hood of the truck and reach the flat road. She could hear David's heavy breathing right behind her as he, too, grappled with the slick earth. Each jostling step sent a fresh wave of pain ricocheting through her shoulder. *Don't quit!* She cradled the sore arm with her good one, stumbling as she ran. Reached the paved road…

With a growl, David tackled her. Brought her down

hard. The asphalt bit her hands and knees as she landed, and an even sharper ache seared her shoulder. She'd have howled her pain and frustration, but the fall knocked the breath from her. She gasped shallowly for air.

David shoved a hand at the center of her spine and wrenched her injured arm behind her. Fire roared from her shoulder to her fingers and spots swam at the edges of her vision. Tears stung her eyes as agony, frustration and fear coalesced in her core. She was injured, trapped and alone.

A doubt devil whispered she was defeated.

But a louder, stronger voice reminded her she was a Cameron. *Camerons don't give up.* She might be down, but she was far from out...

The Jeep's brakes locked, and Matt skidded to a stop behind the wrecked truck. Ahead of him, the kidnapper chased Cait, flung himself at her, took her down.

Matt's blood boiled. He was out of the front seat and jogging down the edge of the highway in seconds. "Get away from her, asshole!"

The man craned his head to see who'd shouted. While holding her pinned to the ground with one hand and his knee, the kidnapper waved a hunting knife toward Matt, snarling, "Stay back. This doesn't concern you."

Matt held up both hands in a sign of surrender, even though he continued to creep closer. "It absolutely concerns me, man. Put the knife down, and let the lady go!"

"Matt!" The mix of relief and anxiety in Cait's voice broke his heart. She shouldn't be in this position. He'd known her life was in danger, and he'd promised to keep her safe. And let his guard down. For work. The way he'd let Jessica down. And Eric.

Not again. *Never* again. The people he loved would be his first and foremost priority over anything else from here on. Especially over work.

"I said *stay back!*"

Keep him calm. Defuse the threat. Maintain the upper hand. His MP training kicked in, and Matt halted for a moment to ease the tension a fraction. "Put the blade down, and we'll talk."

The dark-haired kidnapper snorted. "Talk? Screw that! You get back in your car and get—"

Matt knew the instant the situation changed. Knew what the man was planning. But even with a split second of forewarning, he was one step too slow. The kidnapper launched himself off Cait and beat him to the open Jeep door. With a gloating laugh, the man grabbed the key from the ignition.

"Not so fast," Matt barked, shoving his opponent with his hands and trapping him against the side of the Wrangler.

The man swung the knife up from his side in an arc, and the blade slashed across Matt's forearm. Not a deep wound, but enough of a surprise pain to give the kidnapper time to twist and duck free of Matt's grip.

"David, stop!" Cait cried, staggering up to the men with her hands raised. "Please, both of you, stop now before someone really gets hurt!"

Matt flicked a brief glance toward Cait to survey her injuries. "David? You know this monster?"

"He's Peter's brother." She paused to catch her breath. "They worked together to steal the money from Jake."

"Shut up!" David lunged toward her, grabbing for her arm.

She dodged the move but winced, holding one hand over her opposite shoulder.

Worry roared through him. "Cait?"

As Matt stepped toward her, David stuck the knife out in front of him, sidling between Matt and Cait.

"Uh-uh. I'm not done with her. Get back!"

Taking a slow breath, Matt estimated his distance from David and the blade. He hadn't tried the moves he was considering since losing his leg. Would he have the balance he needed?

Only one way to find out...

Matt assumed a fighting stance and swung a round-house kick toward David's knife with his left leg. His prosthesis knocked David's hand aside, but he clung to the blade.

Matt lost his balance as he completed the kick. He stumbled but stayed on his feet...

Until David charged, shoulder-first, like a linebacker. The tackle knocked Matt onto the road, and his head hit the pavement with a skull-rattling whack.

"Matt!" Cait shouted.

As she rushed forward to help him, David snagged her around the waist and poked the knife under her chin. "Get in the car!"

"No!" Cait braced her legs, but with the knife at her throat, she had little leeway to struggle.

Matt sat up, tried to get on his feet. Both his head and the highway under him spun. Damn!

He blinked, trying to focus, as David hustled into the Jeep. The engine roared to life, and taillights flashing, his Jeep sped off. With Cait inside.

Chapter 22

Matt gritted his teeth while every foul word he'd ever learned swam in his brain. He stabbed his fingers into his hair and encountered the sore spot where he'd hit his head. A knot had swelled where he'd bounced his head on the road. But an external knot was better than swelling under his skull. He needed all his faculties if he was going to rescue Cait.

He barked a sardonic laugh. He, who'd just provided Cait's kidnapper with a backup getaway car, leaving himself stranded, was going to rescue Cait?

The sting from his forearm drew his attention. His arm was bleeding a little, but the cut didn't look like it'd need stitches. He pressed the hem of his shirt to it to stem the flow. He wandered stiffly over to the wrecked truck. Was there any chance…

The front fender was bent into the passenger side tire,

so no chance he'd be following in David's discarded vehicle. Matt shouted one of the choicer foul words as he kicked the tire of the abandoned truck.

David. Peter's brother...

He might not have a way to chase down Cait and her kidnapper, but he at least had a clue where they might be headed.

Cait's spirits lifted when she realized where David was taking her. Any hope she'd had of bailing from Matt's Jeep at a stoplight or other traffic stoppage fizzled as David, clearly knowing her intent, ran two red lights and circumvented a line of stopped vehicles at another intersection by driving down the turn lane.

And where was a cop for a traffic stop when you needed one?

When he turned from the main thoroughfare onto the street where Peter lived, she was certain. And she clung to the shred of hope that Peter would do right by her.

As soon as David jerked to a stop in the driveway of the home she'd once shared with his brother, he seized her arm in a bruising grip. "This way. I don't need you trying to make a break for it again."

She had no choice but to clamber over the center console and gearshift to the driver's seat as he yanked her injured arm. White-hot pain shot from her shoulder with each of his tugs, and she gasped in agony. "Stop! I'm coming. Just don't...pull on...my arm again. I think you've sprained it or something."

"Hurt it, did you? Serves you right. You wrecked my truck, bitch! I'll be adding that to what you owe me." He aimed his knife at her nose to emphasize his point.

Peter appeared at the front door, scowling. His frown

morphed to surprise when he saw Cait emerge from the Jeep, then to fury. "What the hell? David!"

David only glowered at his brother, shoving her toward the door. "Shut up and help me get her inside before the neighbors see anything."

Cait perked. Neighbors... "Fire! Hel—"

David clapped a hand over her mouth and yanked on her bad shoulder, snarling, "Stop it!"

Cait yelped as lightning blazed down her arm and sent Peter a silent plea for help with her eyes.

Instead, Peter cleared a path and helped his brother hustle her inside.

"Find something to tie her with," David said. "She's been nothing but trouble since I got her." Steering her to the dining room table, he shoved her down in a chair and held the knife aimed at her.

"*Tie her?* Damn it, David! What the hell are—"

"Just get something! I'll explain once she's secure!"

After huffing with irritation, Peter stepped into the kitchen and came back with a box of plastic wrap. "*Why* do you have her? What's going on?"

David snatched the plastic wrap from him and pulled a disgruntled face. "What the— I asked for something to tie her with! What are you thinking?"

Peter took the box back, unrolled a long sheet of plastic and tore it off. "I'm thinking—" He twisted the plastic until it stuck to itself, forming a rope. He demonstrated the strength of the twisted plastic with two hands tugging opposite directions. "She's not getting out of this."

Cait's jaw dropped. "Peter! You can't seriously be thinking of helping him. He kidnapped me! Assaulted me! You really want to aid and abet him? Be an accessory?"

David grabbed the plastic from his brother. She yelped

in pain as he wrenched her arms behind the chair back and wrapped her wrists together.

Peter divided a glare between Cait and David, then growled, "I'm not happy about it. I didn't ask for it. But he's my brother, and here you two are." He leaned close, sticking his nose in Cait's face. "And I know where *your* loyalties lie. Or should I say, where they *don't* lie?"

"What does that mean?" she sputtered, then grunted in pain as David's vigorous efforts to bind her jolted her shoulder again. She clenched her jaw and took slow breaths to battle through the fiery ache in her muscles. "So because we broke up, you won't—"

Peter snorted. "We didn't break up. You left. You bailed on me." The muscles in his jaw flexed, and he hiked up one dark eyebrow. "I owe you nothing."

"Peter—" she started, but David talked over her.

"But you—" David moved around in front of her and poked a finger in her sternum. "You owe *me* quite a lot." He looked over at his brother and amended. "Us. You owe us. We'll call it forty grand, adding my truck to the total."

Peter folded his arms over his chest and stepped back to give David room to tie her shins to the front legs of the chair.

"Are you really going to stand there and let him do this? *Help* him do this?" she asked Peter.

Peter gave a negligent shrug.

"You'll go to jail!" she said, desperate to make him see reason. Peter had never been unreasonable before. She prayed he could still be relied on for that much. "Don't you care about *that*?"

Peter shifted his weight from one foot to another, and a restlessness flickered in his gaze. So he wasn't immune to the repercussions of his actions then.

"Shut up," David said, glaring up at her as he wound the ropey plastic around her ankles.

"This isn't you, Peter. Don't be fool—"

David landed a harsh slap across her cheek. "I said shut up! Don't talk to him!" Then to Peter, David growled, "Get a gag. Your girlfriend's too chatty."

Eyes still watering from the stinging slap, Cait cut her glance back to Peter. Her ex had narrowed a feral-looking glower on his brother. "That was uncalled for!"

"Was it?" David snatched a cloth napkin from the table and shoved it in her mouth. His expression was smug as he faced Peter. "I warned her."

Peter squared his shoulders and stepped closer to David. "And now I'm warning you, Dave. Don't hit her again."

David raised a finger, poking it near Peter's face. "Don't go soft on me, bro. We got—"

Grabbing David's threatening finger, then his arm, Peter dragged his brother through the living room and out onto the back porch. Cait strained to hear, trying to make out the angry words the brothers exchanged. Maybe Peter hadn't lost all common sense, but if he couldn't manage his brother, she was still in danger. She didn't miss the irony that her ex was her best hope of getting out of this mess. Especially since David had stranded Matt on the mountain. Was he injured? An additional pang stung her with that possibility.

With a deep breath she tried to refocus her thoughts on her own predicament, quelling the niggle of guilt concerning Matt. He was smart. Capable. Resourceful. He'd be fine.

Please, God, let Matt be fine.

* * *

Matt sent up a prayer that Cait would be all right until he got to her.

He'd flagged down the first car to come down the highway and given the driver a cursory explanation of the situation.

The driver, a college student on his way back to school from a hiking trip, was more than happy to drive Matt into town. "Should I take you to the police station?"

"No. I'll call them." Then he remembered his phone was at the cabin. "But I don't have my phone. Can I use yours?"

The guy nodded. "If you can get a signal. This road is a dead spot."

Sure enough, the cell showed no signal. Damn!

"Look, let me out at the corner of North Cumberland Street. I should walk from there. I don't want them to see me arrive."

"Stealth attack. Got it." The guy grinned and nodded, obviously enjoying his fringe role in Cait's rescue.

"When you get a signal, call the police for me."

His driver, Scott, nodded and made the trip down the curving mountain highway to the town in the valley with haste, and Matt directed him to the road where Cait's ex lived. He was proceeding on a hunch. If Cait and David weren't there, Matt figured Peter was his best chance to find them.

"Want me to wait? You know, in case she's not there?" Scott asked as he pulled into a parking lot at the corner where Matt had directed him.

"No." Matt used a firm tone. "Your part is done. Thank you for your help, but you don't want to get involved. Or get in the way. Just call the cops. Okay?"

His driver looked disappointed to be cut out of the excitement. "Yeah, all right."

Matt wrote down the college kid's PayPal address on a scrap of paper and jammed it in his pocket with a promise to send him some money for his efforts and assistance. With a rueful smile and a wave, Scott drove away, and Matt turned to hurry up the street toward Peter's house. He spotted his Wrangler in the driveway of the one-story house and breathed a sigh of relief. He'd guessed correctly where Peter's brother was headed.

As he approached the small brick home, he mentally replayed what he could of the interior layout. The living room had a door out to the back patio, didn't it? His memory was vague, but he was certain enough to make the back entrance his target. His first stop, however, was his Jeep. He quietly opened the passenger door, then, taking the spare key he kept stashed under the floor mat, he unlocked the glove box. Removing the handgun and magazine he kept there, Matt loaded the weapon, made sure a round was chambered and headed to the backyard as stealthily as he could.

Pressing his back against the brick wall, he eased closer to the porch, making certain he stayed out of sight of windows. Voices drifted out from inside, helping him pinpoint the location of his targets. With a careful peek through a window, one that proved to be in the dining area adjoining the living room, Matt assessed the situation. Peter was there, and he stood near a chair where David appeared to be securing Cait to a chair with some kind of clear tape or…plastic wrap?

Matt arched an eyebrow. Resourceful. And also an indication this kidnapping wasn't preplanned, if no supplies for holding Cait hostage—zip ties or duct tape or rope—had been arranged.

More important to Matt, as he surveyed the scene inside, was the apparent hostile mood between the brothers. Peter's posture was tense, his expression disgruntled.

Cait appeared to be unharmed, though she'd been trussed like a Thanksgiving turkey. His ragged nerves settled a bit, knowing she was safe—for the moment.

Matt leaned away from the window, pressing close to the house again. He looked down at the gun in his hand and made a calculated decision. Adding his weapon to this uneasy situation might make David panic. He was already acting rashly, seemed desperate, like a cornered animal.

Peter was an unknown. He could be swayed to help resolve the standoff, or he could take unkindly to Matt's presence and choose to defend his brother, his property. With a reluctant sigh, knowing his best move was to defuse the situation as best he could until the police arrived, he hid the handgun in the thick foliage of a lushly blooming pot of marigolds.

Okay, Harkney, so no weapon. What is your plan then?

Busting through the door to confront the men didn't seem like the best way to keep the situation low-key either. But he wasn't going to stand out here like a Peeping Tom while they threatened Cait either, so what—

His pulse spiked as the back door opened. He moved quickly behind a tall hydrangea bush and watched Peter stalk out, followed by his brother. Peter closed the back door then got in his brother's face. "Are you nuts?"

"I didn't have a choice!" David shouted, still holding

the knife and waving it as he ranted. "She walked in on me and woulda called the cops!"

Peter said something in return that Matt couldn't make out, and David shouted, "Because I want my money! And you're gonna help me get it!"

Peter jammed his fingers through his hair and barked a curse word. Aimed a finger at his brother and shouted back, "You shouldn't have come here! It's bad enough you grabbed her, but these demands of yours—"

"What about 'em?" David snapped back. "Don't you want our money? After everything we've done to get it, are you gonna let her get away with ruining everything? Gibbs isn't goin' away, you know. Every day I don't pay him back what I borrowed, he adds more interest. I'm out of time, man! He's made it clear he's coming for blood next."

Matt gritted his teeth. So there was the crux of it. David borrowed money from Gibbs—Jake had warned them Gibbs was dangerous—and needed to pay it back. So what did he do with that truth?

"I warned you not to get mixed up with Gibbs, didn't I?" Peter said, echoing Matt's train of thought. "You brought all this down on yourself. I've helped you all I can, bro."

"Peter! You gotta help. You know he's dangerous! He could even come after *you*. You know what he did to Thompson. Do you want him to bust me up that way, too?"

"Of course not! But this isn't the answer!" Peter growled.

Amen to that. Maybe Peter was the key to talking his brother down and resolving this standoff without anyone getting hurt.

"Oh, yeah? She took the money out of the cabin. She gave it to the cops. It's her fault we don't have it. So why shouldn't she be the one to pay us back?"

"Dave, you kidnapped her from her family's retreat and stole that writer guy's car! Don't you think the cops are going to be here any second? You have to let her go and disappear!"

"You're right. So we don't have time to be out here arguing. But I'm not leaving without my money! If I have to cut her to make her cooperate then I will!" David snarled.

Matt's gut swooped. David was panicked, impatient, irrational. Matt didn't have time to wait for the cops either.

Stepping out from his hiding place, he raised both hands to show he was unarmed. "What if I get you the money? Will you let Cait go unhurt?"

Both men whirled to face him, speaking at the same time.

"How the hell—"

"What are you doing here?"

"Never mind how I got here. The question is can we negotiate? Will you make a deal in exchange for Cait's safe release?"

Chapter 23

Cait's breath caught when the men came back inside—and Matt was with them. The sharp inhale around the napkin David had stuffed in her mouth made her cough. Gag. She had to fight her body's reflexes to calm her throat and still the choking sensation. No amount of self-control would calm the runaway beat of her heart as it thrashed against her ribs. Questions poured through her brain in rapid-fire: How had Matt gotten here? Had he brought the police? What was his plan?

Unable to verbalize any of the queries, she could only trust him, pray he didn't get himself hurt on her account. He was here because she'd been foolish enough to think she could reason with David. Now she had to do whatever she could to right the situation.

David had a grip on Matt's arm that was tight enough that she could see her captor's fingers digging into

Matt's skin. He still clutched the damn knife in his other hand.

Peter trailed after them, his face florid and his jaw and fists tight. "Don't trust him, Dave! It's a trap. A stall tactic!"

"If he wants to keep his girlfriend safe, he better not pull a fast one." David shook Matt's arm. "Got that, buddy?"

Peter seized David's arm to stop him. "If he's here, don't you think he's already called the cops? You have to get out of here!"

David shook off his brother's hand but lost his grip on the knife in the process. "No, you have to shut up and stop nagging me! I said I'm not leaving without my money!"

"Are you high or just stupid as hell?" Peter shouted.

David paused in the process of bending to pick up the knife. His reaction was lightning fast. Spinning toward his brother, he lobbed a punch that almost certainly broke Peter's nose.

Cait heard the crunch of bone, and her gut rolled. As Peter reeled back and tumbled to the floor, his head cracked with a sickening thud against the corner of the hearth. He didn't move.

Matt took a step toward Peter, and David grabbed him again. "Where do you think you're going? We still gotta talk business."

"Your brother—"

David cut him off with a strike aimed at Matt's cheek.

Matt ducked the blow and came up swinging.

Matt's first punch hit David's chin and sent shudders up his arm. He hadn't fought hand-to-hand in a while, but the skills had been ingrained. Balance would be an issue, but he still had strength and a quick mind. Judging by the glassy look of David's eyes, his opponent's reaction speed might be dulled. But he couldn't count on that.

David recovered from the chin strike and launched at Matt again like an angry rattlesnake. When Matt again dodged a swing of his fist, David lowered his shoulder and charged. The two went down on the couch, each wrestling and grappling to land a blow that would slow the other. As they scuffled, Matt's foot hit the knife, and he kicked it out of David's reach.

Another twist and a couple moments of struggling later, David got Matt on the floor, pinning him, straddling him. When David reared back with his arm to deliver a blow straight into Matt's face, Matt caught his opponent's fist with both hands, blocking the strike as he shouted, "Do you want that money or not?"

David stiffened, pulling his fist back and, breathing hard, he glared down at Matt.

"You were serious? You got my forty grand?"

Matt turned both palms toward David in a conciliatory gesture. "I have money that can be yours. But only if you stop this nonsense and let me up so we can talk."

David hesitated another moment before moving away and letting Matt rise from the floor. David retrieved his knife and held it in front of him as a reminder to Matt.

As Matt climbed up to sit on the couch and catch his breath, he cast a glance toward Peter. "Your brother needs an ambulance. Let me call—"

"Hell no!" David waved the blade toward the sofa, silently warning Matt to stay put. "You don't call nobody in here until I get my money. So talk fast."

Now Matt glanced to Cait. Her eyes were tearing,

and her brow furrowed with consternation. She shook her head.

He gave her a subtle nod as if to say, *Trust me.*

Wiping a drip of blood from his aching nose, Matt met David's gaze squarely. "Forty thousand? Is that what you said you needed?"

"Let's make it a nice round fifty grand, so I can get outta town and go somewhere Gibbs ain't looking for me."

He heard Cait groan.

"Fifty K then. I have investments I can cash in and scrape that much together in a few hours. But if I do this, Cait walks out of here, right now, unharmed, and you do not come near me, Cait, Cameron Glen or either of our families ever again."

David snorted his derision.

Matt narrowed a lethal gaze at his opponent. "Did I say something funny? 'Cause I'm dead serious, pal. I'll give you the money, but you stay the hell away from my family and the Camerons forever and ever, amen."

"And you can get the money now? Today?" David rubbed his reddened jaw and dropped into a stuffed chair.

Acid bit Matt's gut as he bobbed a nod. "If I can borrow your phone, I'll call my broker right now and have him cash out my more liquid investments. He can have money wired to a local bank in an hour or so."

Cait made a muffled squawking noise and shook her head more determinedly. Her eyes were dark with concern and disagreement.

Trust me, he hoped his own expression relayed.

A lower-pitched groan came from the floor by the fireplace where Peter stirred and raised a hand to his head.

David wiggled his offended jaw and scowled. "What's the catch? If this is a trick—"

"No trick. But you better hurry. Your brother was right about the cops being on their way, looking for you after you took Cait from Cameron Glen."

David bounced his leg in agitation, clearly growing flustered. "Then do it. Cash in your stocks or whatever, and get the money sent." He shoved to his feet and rubbed his hands on the legs of his pants. "But not sent to a bank. Have your guy use a courier to bring it here. Fast. Like yesterday!"

Matt held out his hand. "Then we have a deal? I can cut Cait free? Let her leave?"

Peter groaned and rolled on the floor, holding his head. "Don't be an idiot, Dave. He ain't really giving you money."

Matt spread his hands wider. "I really am. Cait means that much to me. I'd gladly give you all I have, if you'll just let her go, safe and sound."

Another weighty moment passed while David deliberated, his leg jiggling. Finally he shoved his phone toward Matt, growling, "I swear if this is a trick to call the cops, I'll slit both of your throats. Right here and now!"

Matt took the phone, adrenaline thrumming so loudly, he'd have bet David could hear it. With a forced smile and all eyes on him, he dialed the phone. Prayed Eric was near his cell and would answer the unfamiliar number.

"Hello?" his son's uncertain voice said.

"Jim! Hi there, Matt Harkney here." Matt boomed in a robust and cheerful tone, "So glad I caught you before you left the office!"

"Dad?"

"I'm fine, thanks," he said quickly. "Listen, I need a

favor, Jim. I'm out of town this summer and need some cash wired to me ASAP."

"Huh? Dad, what's—"

"In fact, if you could have the money sent by courier to 435 North Cumberland Street in Valley Haven, that'd be even better. I have a small emergency, nothing to concern yourself over, but the cash would be helpful."

Silence answered him, and Matt held his breath. *Please, Eric. Play along. Read between the lines, buddy.*

David's expression darkened further, and he snatched the phone back. "Hello? Who's there?"

Matt's gut flip-flopped, but he buried his reaction, remaining as outwardly cool as he could. He glanced quickly to Cait, whose blue eyes were moist and held his gaze.

"Jim who? Where do you work?" David yelled into the phone. "Can you really courier money here today?" The tension in his face eased, and he seemed pleased with whatever answer Eric gave him. The surprise flashed over his countenance. "Me? I'm…uh, his business partner. Never mind who I am! Just…send the money!"

David shoved the phone back at Matt. "Wrap it up."

Matt couldn't help the small, satisfied grin that tugged the corner of his mouth. *Well played, son.* When he pressed the phone to his ear he heard Eric, in a deeper timbre saying, "…do our best to accommodate your request…"

"Thank you, Jim. And you have that address for the courier?"

"435 North Cumberland. Got it, Dad."

Matt's heart lifted with relief and pride. Eric was no dummy.

Disconnecting the call, he set the phone aside. "There. The money is on its way. Now release Cait."

David shook his head. "Nuh-uh. Not until I get my cash."

Matt gritted his back teeth. "Then at least let me cut her loose. Take the gag out." When David hesitated, Matt spread his hands. "Come on, man. In the spirit of good-will and gratitude for what I'm doing for you, let me untie her. You gotta give me something, or I'm back on the phone canceling that money."

David twitched at the threat of losing his expected windfall.

From the floor, Peter groaned again. Tending to Cait's ex's injuries was his next bit of business.

With a huff, David jerked his chin toward Cait, giving grudging permission to release her.

His body aching from his round of fisticuffs, Matt hurried to Cait. He removed the gag and tossed it aside as she coughed and cleared her throat. Seeing the dense layers of plastic wrap binding her hands, he glanced back to David. "Let me have the knife to cut her free."

David's refusal was terse and profane.

Moving stiffly, Matt crouched to work at unwinding or ripping through the thick twists of plastic wrap while David paced and scowled. The process was tedious, but he finally loosened the ropey plastic enough for Cait to free her hands.

"Thank you," she whispered to him as she rubbed her wrists, then, wincing, she raised her left hand to massage her right shoulder.

He shifted in front of her, his back to the room where David prowled and Peter languished, to work at the wrap around her ankles. Catching her gaze, he signaled toward the back porch with a quick glance, then mouthed, "Marigolds."

Her brow dipped in puzzlement for a split second before her mouth tightened and she gave an almost imperceptible nod.

Now he just needed to buy her a little time.

Chapter 24

Marigolds? What in the world was Matt telling her with his cryptic message? She might not know, but she trusted Matt enough to follow his lead without knowing specifics. She gave her throbbing shoulder another deep rub and watched Matt shove to his feet with slow, pained movements.

"There," he said, raising both hands in a gesture of surrender. "All good."

David stalked toward Matt, his face a granite mask, the knife held in a menacing, raised grip. "I'm warning you, man. If—"

Matt cut him off, dropping a shoulder and driving it into David's chest. The move was so sudden, so decisive, David went down like a toppled domino.

Cait, too, was startled by the move, and stared, stunned for a couple heartbeats, as Matt used the last fraction of his advantage to pin David's knife hand to the ground.

David's angry roar shook her from her daze, and she sprang to her feet.

Marigolds. Darting out the back door, she spotted a pot of the orange flowers at the edge of the patio and rushed to it, not knowing what she was looking for. Instantly, she found the gun Matt had obviously planted there and rushed back inside.

Peter was still curled on his side by the fireplace, clutching his head. Matt and David were still grappling, the hunting blade still dangerously close to cutting Matt.

"David, stop! Drop the knife!" she shouted, aiming the gun at the wrestling men. She was ignored. "David!" Though she infused her tone with as much authority and volume as she could, David was clearly too preoccupied with the altercation with Matt to realize she held a weapon of her own.

Angling the gun away from the men and toward the couch, she fired once.

David, who'd managed to wrangle his way on top of Matt, stopped tussling with a jerk and whipped his head toward her.

Heart thrashing, she motioned with the gun and grated, "Drop. The. Knife."

David glowered at her. "You don't have the guts to kill someone in cold blood."

A shudder raced through her. He was right. She didn't. But she had to make him comply. Had to exert enough influence over the situation to buy time until the police arrived. Because she had no doubt now, if she'd had any before, that Matt's call to his broker was actually a call for help to…someone. *"Drop the knife!"*

"Cait…don't." With a quick glance, she saw that Peter

had managed to sit up. Still holding his bleeding head, he pleaded with his gaze.

She caught a movement from the edge of her vision and, swinging her attention back to David, aimed low and fired a round at his feet.

With a scream of pain, David dropped the knife and crumpled to clutch at his foot. "You bitch!"

Cait exhaled a trembling breath. "Maybe I don't have the guts to kill you, but to protect the man I love, I have no problem with nonlethal force."

While she held the weapon, still pointed at David, Matt rolled awkwardly to his feet and staggered over to assist Peter. The ringing echoes of the gunshot faded in her ears, and a new distant sound reached her. Sirens.

When Matt finished giving his statement to the police, he shook the officer's hand and waved off the EMT who approached him, offering to treat his split lip and other minor injuries. He was more concerned with Cait, who sat at the end of the open bay of the ambulance, wrapping up her conversation with a different cop and having the scrapes and cuts and wrenched shoulder she'd accumulated during her kidnapping treated by another medic.

The first ambulance to arrive on the scene had already departed with Peter and David aboard, the brothers under arrest and police guard. His body hurt from top to bottom, but he'd suffered far worse in the past. His priority was Cait.

Cait—who'd showed so much courage and gumption. Who'd kept David at gunpoint until the police arrived to take control of the situation.

Pride and affection swelled in his chest for her…along

with relief that the men responsible for threatening Cait and her family, trespassing at Cameron Glen and stealing from Jake's business had been revealed and taken into custody.

He knew Peter's part in the crimes was a hard pill for Cait to swallow, but he intended to do everything in his power to help her put that betrayal in the past and make a fresh start.

To protect the man I love, she'd said. A grin tugged his cheek, and his heart pattered.

Matt hung back, not wanting to intrude on her interview with the cop, until he saw the officer flip his notepad closed and say something to the EMT before walking over to confer with his partner.

"Where'd you learn to shoot like that?" he asked, and she met his gaze with a smug grin.

"My dad and Brody both hunt. Dad decided when we were little that if he was going to keep guns in the house, all of his kids would learn gun safety and how to shoot. Just in case." She pulled a face. "I haven't been to the range in a while to practice. I'm actually surprised I hit his foot."

Matt grunted and cast a glance toward the police officers. "You in trouble?"

She shook her head then winced and grabbed her shoulder. "Don't think so. He seemed to think that, given David was armed and a threat to you, no charges will be pressed."

"Good."

The EMT divided a look between them and asked, "You ready to go?" Then to Matt, "You can ride with her. You really should get checked out at the ER, too, ya know?"

"Maybe, but I want to stay with her at the hospital." He started to climb in the ambulance when the thud of a car door and a panicked-sounding shout of "Dad!" reached him.

He turned to find Eric racing across the street, his expression full of fear and anxiety. Behind Eric, Emma and Fenn climbed out of a tan SUV and headed toward them, as well.

"Eric? What are you doing here?" He embraced his son, who returned the hug willingly and mightily—another indication of his son's distress.

"Nothing would do but that we come check on you both," Emma said as she approached. "We've all been worried sick! And when you gave Eric this address? Well…" Cait's sister exhaled heavily, "I swear he'd have walked here if I hadn't brought him."

Fenn rushed to Cait and threw herself against her aunt for a hug, and Cait grimaced. "Ow. Watch the shoulder, kid. I'm injured."

Eric backed up from their hug and gave Matt an appraising scrutiny. "Oh my God, Dad! You look horrible! What happened? Are you all right?"

Matt flashed a lopsided smile to ease his son's worry. "Gee, thanks. You know how to wound a guy's ego."

"No lie, Matt. You look rough," Emma said, her face creased with concern.

"It looks worse than it is, I'm sure. I got in a scrap with David, but I'll be fine." He returned a steady gaze to Eric, squeezing his son's shoulders as he said, "I'm okay. I promise."

"And you?" Emma turned her full attention to her sister. "Did you say you're injured?"

"Nothing serious." Cait gave her sister a reassuring

smile. "Maybe a sprained shoulder. The rest of these scrapes are just surface wounds. Nothing serious."

Emma's scowl said she wasn't convinced.

"We're headed to the ER now for X-rays," Cait added. "You can meet us there. Matt?"

When Cait glanced at him as if to say, "Let's go," Matt balked. He looked into Eric's eyes, saw the doubts and anxiety that still clouded his son's expression. Eric needed him. Needed the reassurance only his father could give him. Needed the proof that only Matt could give that everything would be all right, that his dad wasn't seriously hurt, that his world was safe again. "Umm…"

"Matt?" Cait repeated. "Aren't you coming?"

His heart ached as he faced Cait. If this frightening episode had taught him anything it was how deeply he cared for Cait. That he loved her. He desperately wanted to go with Cait to support her, to confirm for himself that she wasn't more gravely injured. "I, uh… I'm going to stay here. With Eric."

Cait's expression shifted subtly. Understanding of his dilemma, a flicker of hurt and disappointment before she schooled her face and looked away. "Okay."

"Cait, I'm sorry. I'll catch up with you—"

"No, it's fine. I get it." She sent him an unconvincing smile then turned to climb, with the EMT's assistance, into the ambulance.

"Here," Emma said, shoving a wad of keys at him. "I'll ride with her. You take the kids home. Okay?"

He wrapped his bruised hand around the key chain, a war still waging inside him over the decision he'd made. He knew it was the right choice, but the flash of pain he'd seen cross Cait's face gouged a deep furrow in his soul. The last thing he wanted was to hurt her. Ever.

He wrapped an arm around each of the teenagers and backed them up as the ambulance doors were closed. He stood stiffly in the driveway, knowing at his core that something had changed between him and Cait in that moment, and his heart broke as he watched the ambulance drive away.

Cait tried to keep a stiff upper lip as the ambulance carried her to the hospital to be checked, but a lone tear slipped free. Though she quickly dashed moisture away, Emma saw it.

Emma reached over to rub her uninjured arm. "Caitie? What's wrong? Are you hurting? Do you need a pain-killer?"

Cait shook her head. "I mean, yes. I'll get something for my shoulder at the ER, but, no, that's not why I'm…" She flapped her hand in front of her face as emotion clogged her throat, choking her words. And then, damn it, she started crying in earnest. *So much for being Cameron strong.*

"Cait! Oh, honey, what?" Emma scooted closer on the bench seat and grasped her sister's hand with a fierce grip. "What's wrong?"

"It's just…" She had to pause to take a couple restorative breaths before she could continue. "I guess I just realized how much I actually love Matt."

Emma sat taller. "Oh. So, then these are good tears? Happy tears?"

Cait shook her head. "No. Because in the same moment I also realized that, with Matt, I would always be number two. Second to his son and first family."

"But that's how it is for all parents." She hesitated before qualifying, "Or, at least, how it *should* be. For most parents, their kids are their priority. My kids are everything to me. So…I think it's a good thing that Eric's his priority. It shows he's a good father."

"I never doubted that."

"But that doesn't mean he loves you any less." Emma patted her hand, her expression passionate and fiery. "A man can put his children first and still love his wife unconditionally and make her an equally high priority."

The intensity in Emma's eyes made Cait wonder if perhaps she was getting a glimpse of the trouble her sister was having with Jake. Before she could ask, however, Emma asked, "Has Matt ever said he loves you? Does he share the same feelings for you that you have for him?"

"I thought so. But I'm not even sure that matters now. I've seen the future." She waved a hand toward the doors to indicate the scene that had just unfolded. "And because of the troubled relationship he's had with Eric, the work he has to do to heal that relationship, I'm always going to be an afterthought. The lower priority. The one who has to wait or get pushed aside." Her voice cracked, and she shook her head as she gave Emma a forlorn look. "I left Peter because I knew I just didn't matter to him the way I should if we were going to build a future together. I want someone who can love me wholly and completely, without any reservation or distraction." A sharp ache of longing pierced her soul. "Am I selfish? Am I being unrealistic?"

Nudging Cait's head down to her shoulder in a maternal embrace, Emma whispered, "No, you're not."

They rode in silence for another moment until the ambulance bumped over the curb as it pulled into the hospital parking lot and slowed at the ER door.

As Cait moved to exit the ambulance, Emma framed

Cait's face with her hands. "Don't lose the hope that you mean exactly that to Matt—even as he negotiates his relationship with Eric. He did risk his life to save you, after all."

Over the next several hours, as she was X-rayed and her cuts treated, Cait tried to hold on to the hope Emma encouraged. She waited expectantly for Matt, having soothed Eric's concerns and seen the need to get his own injuries checked out, to arrive at the ER. But he never came. Once Cait was discharged with a diagnosis of a torn rotator cuff and given orders for physical therapy, Emma hailed Jake to drive them back to Cameron Glen.

"I had a call from the police just now as I was parking the truck," Jake told them as they left the hospital. "Seems Peter is telling all about embezzling from the company."

"He's cooperating? Good." Cait sighed sadly. "Jake, I'm so sorry for—"

"Stop." Jake raised a hand to cut her off. "None of this is your fault, so don't go there."

"And Peter's brother? The one who kidnapped Cait? What did they say about him?" Emma asked.

Jake grunted. "David was being less forthcoming about his crimes before they took him into surgery to repair his foot, but given your statement and Matt's, Officer Martinez said they have enough to hold him after he leaves the hospital. When verbally cornered, he admitted to breaking into the Hemlock cabin, using information he got from Peter, to hide the money. He confessed to knocking poor Mr. Gilbreath out when the old guy came to investigate noises from the kitchen, and he was also present when Mary had her heart attack and didn't render aid."

"What a scum!" Emma growled.

"Agreed," Cait said.

"So this mess is over?" Emma's expectant gaze broke Cait's heart. "We know what happened to the stolen construction money and who has been breaking in here at the Glen. Can life go back to normal now? Please?"

Jake returned a pained look to his wife. "God, I hope so."

When they reached Cameron Glen, Cait had Jake let her out at her house, despite Emma's assertion her sister needed pampering.

"I'll put Isla to that task as soon as she lands tomorrow. I promise," Cait said with a half grin. "Really, I'm fine." But when Jake and Emma drove away, instead of going inside, Cait felt pulled toward the Fraser cabin to check on Matt. Thanks to the painkiller she'd been given at the hospital, her shoulder wasn't throbbing quite as badly as before, and she took the opportunity to see where things stood with the Harkneys.

Just normal concern for her guests' well-being, she told herself. She wasn't going to confront Matt about the status of their relationship. She wasn't—though questions still nagged.

Matt, looking even more bruised and battered now that his injuries had had more time to color and swell, answered her knock quickly and stepped out on the porch to wrap her in a gentle hug. "Are you okay? What did the doctors say?"

She gave him a recap of her ER visit, what Jake had said about the call from the police, then tipped her head in inquiry. "Is Eric feeling better? Have *you* seen a doctor?"

He bobbed a nod. "Yes and yes. I stopped in at an urgent care center, and I don't have a concussion. I waited too long to get stitches for this—" he pointed to the cut on his arm "—so I'll have another scar to add to my collection, but they cleaned it and gave me an antibiotic just in case. The rest of this will just take time to heal."

"Good. I mean, I'm glad it's not worse. I—"

Matt's gaze left her and shifted to the driveway as a red sedan pulled in to park. He sighed. "What the—"

A woman with long black hair, olive skin and exquisite bone structure climbed from the driver's seat and jogged up the walk. "Matt!"

A prick of something cold and uneasy burrowed deep into Cait's core.

Matt embraced the woman, and when he backed out of the hug, he asked, "Why are you here?"

"Really? You think I wouldn't come when our son calls and says you're off chasing criminals, and he's scared to death you'll be killed?" the woman, gorgeous even without makeup, replied.

"Eric called you?"

"Of course, he did!" She gave Matt an up-and-down look. "And from the looks of you, I'd say he had cause! What the hell, Matt?"

Matt stabbed a hand through his hair, then motioned for the woman to follow him. He paused when he reached Cait and introduced her. "Cait, this is my ex, Jessica. Jessica, the property manager here, Cait Cameron."

The property manager.

Not my girlfriend or the woman I love. His use of the overtly platonic and formal title stabbed Cait anew. But she pasted on a smile and offered her hand to shake. "Nice to meet you."

The front door burst open, and Eric plowed outside. "Mom?"

Jessica grabbed him into a tight embrace. "Oh, honey!"

"Um." Matt rubbed a hand on his chin. "Cait, can I catch up with you later?"

And the blade twisted.

"Sure. Right." She swallowed hard to keep the hurt from her voice. "You have…family things to do." With a pitiful, awkward wave, she turned and scuttled down the driveway, not daring to look back lest Matt see the moisture stinging her eyes.

If she needed any clarification on her standing with Matt, she'd gotten it. Dismissed. Set aside when his family required his attention. Not that she could begrudge him his loyalty to his family. She loved her clan with her whole heart, would do anything for them.

But knowing she didn't rank with Matt's highest priorities stung. She wanted more from a relationship, and the truth was Matt would always be Eric's father, Jessica's ex and co-parent. If she were in Matt's life, she feared she'd always be second.

It was tempting to proceed on those terms. She cared that much for Matt. But her experience with Peter cast long shadows of doubt. She wanted more.

Even though it jolted her shoulder, she jogged back to her house. She only wanted to get home, pull a blanket around her and forget that she'd ever fallen in love with a man who couldn't love her back the same way.

Chapter 25

The next night, as Matt was closing the living room window blinds, preparing to watch a movie with Eric and Jessica, he noticed movement across the fishing pond. One of the many forms of wildlife that populated Cameron Glen? Another guest enjoying the evening? A prowler?

His pulse bumped at the last possibility before he told himself his assumption was just residual tension from the last few harrowing weeks. And maybe his conversation that afternoon with Neil Cameron.

He cupped his hands around his eyes to make out the dark figure that moved to the end of the fishing pier and sat down. Human. And based on the body size and shape, female. Then the woman checked her cell phone, and the light from the screen gave enough illumination for him to recognize the beautiful face. Cait.

His heart thumped for a different reason now. He was

overdue to have an important conversation with her, but he'd been distracted by equally important discussions with Jessica, who'd spent the day at Cameron Glen and would be leaving in the morning. Today he, Jessica and Eric had held a family meeting about what the future might look like for the Harkneys. When that conversation had been wrapped up, Cait's father had arrived at the cabin with an interesting proposal that seemed like a sign confirming his recent decisions.

The only thing worrying Matt at this point was the weird feeling he'd gotten when he stopped by the rental office to talk to Cait at the end of the workday. She'd been polite, but far too formal and reserved. She'd put him off, saying she had a pile of work to catch up on and didn't feel there was anything left for them to discuss.

"I'm not talking about the business with David and the police," Matt had said. "I thought we could—"

But the phone had rung, and she'd answered it, pausing only long enough to say, "Can we do this later?"

So he'd given her space, let her work. But not without a nagging pit in his gut that something was off. What "this" did she think they needed to "do"? The memory of the odd look in Cait's eyes bit him again, reviving his edginess.

He turned to the living room, where Eric was settling on the couch with a large bowl of Mayfield Dairy Rocky Road, and said, "I'm going out for a minute. If I'm not back in ten, y'all start the movie without me. Okay?"

"Oh." Jessica waggled the second bowl she was carrying in from the kitchen. "Should I put your ice cream back in the freezer then?"

"Probably so. Thanks."

Eric grunted around a mouthful. "Wait. I'll eat his. You snooze, you lose."

With a humored snort for his son with the bottomless stomach, he hurried outside and down to the wooden dock.

Cait turned when his steps on the pier shook the wood planks and thudded hollowly, announcing his arrival. Was it his imagination or did she tense when she recognized him?

"Hey," he said, motioning to the spot beside her. "Can I join you?" When she hesitated, he added, "Please?"

"Yeah. Okay." Cait waved a hand to the empty spot, and Matt sat down, his stiff joints and bruised muscles protesting.

"How's your shoulder?"

"Still sore, but the anti-inflammatory med the doctor gave me helps."

"Good," he said, and they lapsed into an awkward silence.

Then, "Pretty night," he said at the same time she said, "What's on your mind?"

He laughed drily. "Okay, so no small talk first, huh?"

"I'd rather not." She looked back out over the calm pond where water bugs skimmed along and the flash of fireflies reflected on the glassy surface like twinkling Christmas lights.

"Right, so…straight to business." But where to begin? "Well, Jess, Eric and I had a long talk today, and among other topics related to Eric and his issues, we've hammered out a plan so that I can move here and not disrupt our custody arrangement."

Cait's head snapped around. "Move here? As in Valley Haven?"

He didn't like the note of horror and dismay in her tone. Not one bit. "Meaning Cameron Glen, actually." Cait only stared at him, so he forged on with his explanation. "I had been thinking I'd take an apartment in Valley Haven until your dad stopped by today and offered me a great rental rate that would let me stay in the Fraser cabin indefinitely."

"What?"

Again her stunned tone sat on his chest with a weighty dread.

"He understands I already have a job, writing my books, but he asked me to be sort of a security officer of sorts here at Cameron Glen."

Cait's mouth dropped open, and her eyes widened. "He did, did he?" She chuffed a flat laugh. "He didn't mention anything about it to me, and I am the property manager."

"Oh, well. I'm sure he will. Tomorrow." Matt shifted his body to face her more fully and bent his right leg to prop his arm on his knee. This wasn't going at all as he'd envisioned, and sweat beaded on his top lip. "He was thinking I could patrol the grounds, help you monitor the security cameras, advise the family on further security measures you can take to make Cameron Glen safer."

"And you told him you would?"

Matt nodded. "Yeah. Why not? I think the incidents of the last few weeks just have him rattled, and if I can help him—"

"I wish you wouldn't," she said, so softly he almost missed it.

Matt frowned, his gut tightening. "Wouldn't…help your dad?"

She raised her chin, and in the glow of the half moon, he saw moisture sparkle in her eyes. "Wouldn't move here."

Her words were a boot kick in his chest. His breath left him, and his ears buzzed. "Oh. I—"

She exhaled, wiped her nose and continued, "Seeing you here around the property every day, knowing you were just down the driveway…" She blew out a harsh breath. "Can't you see how hard that would be for me? How am I supposed to get over you and move on if you're always—"

"Whoa, whoa, whoa!" He sat taller and waved both hands. "Back up! Why are you thinking you have to get over me and move on? What did I miss? I thought we had something special. Something that was going somewhere."

"We did." She glanced away, sucking her bottom lip between her teeth.

"Then what's wrong? What's changed?"

She sniffed heavily and swiped a finger under her lashes. When she spoke again, her voice cracked. "Matt, I can't… It wouldn't have worked for me."

Nausea swirled in his belly. Had he blown another relationship without even knowing why or how? "I don't get it. Why do you think it won't work?"

A fish jumped nearby with a little *kersplish* that drew Cait's gaze. "Matt, you have a family already. A son who needs his father. I can't compete with that."

He shook his head, thoroughly confused. "It's not a competition, Cait. I can love both of you without—"

"But Eric would always come first. I get that," she said tearfully.

And his heart wrenched. Because *he* got it. She'd told him how Peter's indifference had made her feel, how she refused to settle for a relationship where she felt she was just biding her time.

"That's how it should be," she was saying as he grappled for the right words to say to correct her misinterpretation of his feelings, his intentions, his love for her. "He's your son, but I—"

"Will you marry me?"

She canted back slightly as if he'd physically knocked her with his words. "I… Matt, you're not listening. I can't—"

"I am listening. And I hear you. I understand what you're saying. And I understand *why*." He took both of her hands in his and pressed them against his chest. "Now you listen to me. Hear me. Understand what I'm telling you."

Her gaze locked on his, and the poignant, expectant look she wore wrapped around his heart.

"Cait Cameron, I love you. I want to spend the rest of my life getting to know everything about you. I want you to be center of my world, the embodiment of my love, the breath of my future. And I want to be the same for you."

Her fingers curled as if to cling to him. "But Eric…"

When she let her voice drop, as if reluctant to speak her fear, he finished her sentence with, "Will always be my son. And I will always love him and be there for him. But love isn't finite, darling. I can give you one hundred percent of my heart without taking any away from him. Families do it all the time. Your family is a perfect example. Does your father's love for you mean he loves your mom any less?"

Her chin dimpled, and her brow creased as a sob tore from her throat. "No," she squeaked.

"Oh, sweetheart," he crooned, pulling her into his arms. "Then why do you doubt that I can love you completely and unconditionally?"

She buried her face in his shirt and shook her head. "I was scared. Hurt. Con-f-fused."

He stroked a hand over her back, savoring the feeling of having her in his arms as he reflected on the events of the last couple of days.

"And I compounded your fear when I put you off in favor of Eric at the ambulance. And when Jessica arrived." He groaned as his realization sank in.

A small nod. She lifted her head and gave him an odd look. "You do get it. You…see me."

He sighed. "I'm trying. I want to. I may not always get it right. I have a poor track record, I'm afraid, but… I want to do better. For you."

She exhaled a trembling sigh. "I'm sorry. I should have trusted you. I let my past get tangled up in—"

He pressed his lips to hers in a deep resounding kiss, silencing her unneeded apology. "Done. Forgiven. Over." He framed her face with his hands and smiled down at her. "Now about that question I asked you earlier…"

Her cheek twitched as she shot him a playful grin. "Something about moving here and being on staff as a security officer?"

He laughed. "Yeah, that's the one I mean."

Her smile brightened. "I want a few months to plan the wedding. I want it to be here at Cameron Glen. This fall. When the hardwoods are all red and gold, and the air smells like pine, fir and fallen leaves."

Matt's spirit leaped, and warmth glowed in his soul like the sun rising over a Smoky Mountain ridge. "Anything you want, my love. Anything at all, for you."

* * * * *

#2179 STALKING COLTON'S FAMILY
The Coltons of Colorado • by Geri Krotow

Thinking he was engaged, Rachel never told James about their baby. Now he's back in her life, along with his stalker—a woman who wants Rachel and baby Iris out of James's life, no matter the cost.

#2180 CAVANAUGH JUSTICE: SERIAL AFFAIR
Cavanaugh Justice • by Marie Ferrarella

When a serial killer surfaces in Aurora, California, Arizona-based detective Liberty Lawrence takes vacation time to see if the detective, Campbell Cavanaugh, has any leads. And so begins an unlikely partnership: the playboy and the loner.

#2181 HER SEAL BODYGUARD
Runaway Ranch • by Cindy Dees

Gia Rykhof is a woman in hiding, afraid of everyone, with a mysterious killer hunting her. And then a soldier, newly arrived in small-town Montana, starts to show interest in her. Is he the protector he says he is, or is he really the enemy?

#2182 GUARDIAN K-9 ON CALL
Shelter of Secrets • by Linda O. Johnston

K-9 cop Maisie Murran believes a veterinarian who works for the highly secretive Chance Animal Shelter is being framed for murder. But is her attraction clouding her judgment? Or is someone else in Chance, California, a threat to Maisie's future?

She lunged forward, slamming him against the brick wall at his back, her forearm against his throat. "Who are you?" she snarled.

Stunned, he didn't resist her. Clearly, Rachel had some serious self-defense training, which only furthered his certainty that this was a woman who believed herself to be in mortal danger.

"I told you," he rasped past her forearm. "I'm Marcus Tate."

"That's your name. Who are you?"

"I don't understand—"

"How did you follow me without me spotting you? How do you know I look in shop windows to check my six? For that matter, why are you here? Why did you think you could take down some bad guy who might be following me?"

Ah. He didn't usually talk about his job, and certainly not with civilians. But this situation was not usual in any way. "I'm a soldier," he gasped.

All of a sudden, the pressure from her arm was so heavy he couldn't breathe, and he abruptly feared she might actually crush his larynx. Urgently needing to breathe, he reached up in reflex and pinched the pressure point in her hand between her thumb and fingers.

She yelped and jumped back from him, settling into a fighting stance with her hands in front of her and her weight lightly balanced on the balls of her feet.

"I mean you no harm, I swear," he said desperately. "You were just cutting off all my air."

"Who. Are. You," she bit out.

"Lieutenant Marcus Tate, US navy SEAL."

She hissed in sharply at that. Welp, she knew who the SEALs were. More to the point, she wasn't thrilled he was one. Which was weird as heck. Most people would be jumping up and down for joy that a SEAL had their back.

He continued doggedly. "I messed up my shoulder a couple of months ago. Had surgery on it a few weeks ago, and I'm here in Sunny Creek to rehab it. I'm staying with my old teammate, Brett Morgan, at Runaway Ranch. He'll vouch for me and everything I've just told you."

Speaking of which, his shoulder was screaming in protest at all the exertion he'd just put it through.

"If you don't mind," he said carefully, "I'd like to walk back to my truck and get some ice for my shoulder. It hurts like a sonofa—" He broke off. "It hurts a lot."

"You can walk in front of me. I'll follow behind you," she said grimly.

Don't miss
Her SEAL Bodyguard *by Cindy Dees,*
available May 2022 wherever
Harlequin Romantic Suspense books and ebooks are sold.

Harlequin.com

Love Harlequin romance?

DISCOVER.

Be the first to find out about promotions,
news and exclusive content!

Facebook.com/HarlequinBooks

Twitter.com/HarlequinBooks

Instagram.com/HarlequinBooks

Pinterest.com/HarlequinBooks

YouTube.com/HarlequinBooks

ReaderService.com

EXPLORE.

Sign up for the Harlequin e-newsletter and
download a free book from any series at
TryHarlequin.com

CONNECT.

Join our Harlequin community to
share your thoughts and connect
with other romance readers!
Facebook.com/groups/HarlequinConnection

HARLEQUIN

Heartfelt or thrilling, passionate or uplifting—Harlequin is more than just happily-ever-after.

With twelve different series to choose from and new books available every month, you are sure to find stories that will move you, uplift you, inspire and delight you.